A MANHUNT ESPIONAGE THRILLER

GW00630520

THE
FILE

ASH GREENSLADE

ISBN: 979-8353190165

In honour of Lt. W— B—, M.C.

War hero, writer, spy

BY THE AUTHOR

STATION HELIX SERIES

Station Helix
The Elzevir Collective
Torus
Short Fuse

RYAN KERREK SERIES

Sinister Betrayal
Deadly Acquisition
Black Scarab
Hunting Caracal

EDWIN CRAUGH SERIES

The Fate of Edwin Craugh
Beneath Dead Oaks

FOR MORE ONLINE

Website: www.ashgreenslade.net
Twitter: @AshThrillers

THE
FILE

1

YASMIN BOUZIDI stepped out from her apartment block in Tehran's Narmak district into suffocating thirty-degree afternoon heat. Glad of the shadows cast by familiar three-storey residential buildings, she strode past the neighbourhood's fruit-and-vegetable stands, detecting a tingling aroma which told her the hawkers' produce was past its best.

The blet of shrivelled tomatoes and aubergines capitulated to the gritty taste of car fumes as Yasmin left the back road and headed for Sany Boulevard. It could have been worse. A cool wind from the stunning Alborz Mountains north of the city had mercifully broken up the recent summer smog that had weighed upon Tehran. The reprieve from the pollution was welcome; Yasmin nursed too many patients with respiratory tract infections at the hospital.

White cars – they were seldom any colour but white in Iran – rolled along the main road without attention to the crossings and red lights. Yasmin used the local technique of judging time and distance with a practised eye and simply stepped out, hurrying past the bumper of one car and then waiting for another to go by before advancing further. Within seconds she'd navigated a precarious route across all four lanes and reached the safety of the tree-lined pavement on the far side. Leaving the noisy main road behind her, Yasmin took another quiet street between more housing blocks, glancing up occasionally at the pitted sandy paintwork and wooden balconies.

Ignoring the reproving glare from an old woman in a black chador robe, Yasmin loosened her headscarf to allow a little air to reach her neck and face. Most Iranians were indifferent to the dress and behaviour codes but adhered to them to avoid trouble in public places. She'd been hassled by the authorities, like most of her friends, but these days her fellow citizens were more likely to rebuke officials for bullying a woman than disregard the admonishment. It was one of innumerable paradoxes in her country – most Iranians had hearts of gold and would defend strangers from harm, but they lived under a regime that made the Stasi look like amateurs.

The thirty-four-year-old, along with everyone else in this city of ten million people, compartmentalised the fear and forbade it to encroach on daily life. In truth she loved Tehran – a city founded on ancient civilisations that preserved its history while evolving into a chaotic but oddly beautiful metropolis. The state-of-the-art subway could whisk her to the labyrinthine alleyways of the Grand Bazaar or the ornate majesty of the Golestan Palace. Even her own district was famed for having a recreational park at the heart of every city block; on a map the Narmak neighbourhood looked like a pattern of exquisite tiles which might adorn the finest mosque.

Yasmin's mobile vibrated and beeped with an incoming text message. She interrupted her walk and reached for the phone in her jacket pocket, stepping under a pharmacy sign to read the SMS. Deftly keying in her unlock code with her thumb, Yasmin saw the message was from her friend Leila, asking if she was on her way.

Yasmin tapped a quick response. *You're early. I'll be there in five minutes. Coffee first? Xxx*

Leila's reply arrived in seconds. *Sure. Quick one though. I need to go shopping. Xxx*

Yasmin grinned as she put her phone away.

And frowned when she saw the minibus halfway down the street behind her, driving at a crawl. Sunlight reflected on the windscreen, preventing her from observing the driver, but Yasmin's radar for trouble caused a bead of sweat to run down her spine. Trusting her instinct, Yasmin carried on up the street, slightly increasing her pace. She risked a glance over her shoulder and saw the van accelerate just enough to keep up with her.

A memory flashed into her thoughts of when the police had knocked on the apartment door and questioned her about Farzad. They'd left unsatisfied with her answers but had not bothered her again. The same wary unease enveloped her now, clinching her chest and making her breathing rapid and shallow, as if the city smog were causing an asthmatic reaction. She turned right at the next junction and sprinted past a couple of weatherworn residential blocks. She took a left and hoped she'd been quick enough for the driver to lose sight of her.

Engine noise told her that her evasion attempt had been futile. Cursing her mediocre fitness, Yasmin sucked in warm air as she tried to get her breath back. Glancing down the street she'd just run up, she saw the minibus again, still moving unhurriedly after her. The sunlight was at a different angle now, allowing her to get a better look through the glass. She realised there were two men in the vehicle, possibly wearing some sort of uniform.

Fucking morality police.

Yasmin steeled herself to get to the coffee shop. She'd overstated her arrival time to Leila, and with the dash through the back streets she was only thirty seconds away. If the authorities wanted to reprimand her for not wearing her headscarf properly, they could damn well do it in front of a crowd where she'd make a scene and hopefully get support from irate locals. Shaking the scarf's blue fabric to waft air against her face, Yasmin continued along the pavement.

The minibus stopped next to her twenty metres from the coffee shop. Yasmin kept walking. Both men got out and strode after her.

"You!"

Yasmin turned and raised her arms. "What do you want? I've done nothing wrong!"

The taller of the two stepped forward. Dark hair, short beard,

9

muscular in a way that Yasmin would have found attractive in different circumstances. He made a gesture. "Your hair. It should be covered."

Yasmin glowered at him but wrapped the headscarf tighter. "Better?"

He shook his head. "Your scarf is unsuitable."

"It is not. Leave me alone. I am meeting a friend. A *female* friend."

The man grabbed her arm. His fingers felt like a vice around her triceps. "We're taking you in."

Yasmin tried vainly to shake him off. "You are not!" Turning her head, she saw Leila emerge from the coffee shop.

Her friend rushed over and started screaming in the face of the second officer. He shoved her back, causing her to stumble over the kerbstone and fall onto the pavement. The man yelled a warning to stay down while the other tugged Yasmin to the van and slid open the side door.

She resisted at first, bracing her feet against the sill of the compartment while the policeman tried to manhandle her inside, but his patience grew thin rapidly and he kicked the tendon of her right ankle with a well-aimed but restrained strike. Her legs buckled and the officer grabbed her with both hands and threw her into the van. She tried once more to fight, but the man followed her inside, forced her into a seat and held her there while his colleague slammed the door shut. Seconds later the other man was at the wheel, beeping the horn and forcing his way in front of a yellow taxi.

Compressed into the seat, Yasmin could only moan wordlessly as her heart raced, feeling her captor's warm exhalations on her cheek. There was a surprising sweetness to his breath, as if he'd recently drunk some pomegranate juice or hibiscus tea.

"I'll let you up if you sit still," the man said calmly after holding her down for what seemed like a minute or two.

His Farsi was accented. Yasmin wondered if he was from Tabriz or the border region with Azerbaijan.

Yasmin nodded. "Why did you not just give me a warning on the street?" she inquired as he allowed her to twist round in the seat.

"You ran from us. A warning would be insufficient."

"You followed me. I thought I was being harassed. It's happened to me before."

"Your mistake."

Yasmin glanced at the driver then back at her captor. "Your colleague hurt my friend."

"Hardly. She will be fine."

"Will you let me call her?"

The man shook his head.

Undesirous to attempt further conversation, Yasmin turned her head and watched through the side window as the minibus traversed a maze of city streets. It occurred to her that the journey was irregular, favouring shaded residential roads over the principal boulevards. Familiar territory became districts she barely recognised. They continued northward, passing under a large road bridge beneath the Zeyn od-Din Highway. In moments they were on the outskirts of the city, ascending a narrower road into forested hills.

Yasmin snapped her head around. "This is not the way to the police station."

The driver looked at her in the rear-view mirror. "We are not taking you to the station."

The comment struck her like a blow to the stomach. She fought to hold back tears. "Please, take me there. You can call my father. He will reprimand me and assure you of my future attire. That's what you want, isn't it?"

The man next to her made eye contact. "We do not actually care about your attire, Yasmin Bouzidi. And your father is dead. He passed from a stroke while giving a lecture at the university." He paused. "Before his time. My condolences."

Yasmin froze. She stared at him, her mouth tasting like sawdust. "Where..." she choked. "Where are you taking me?"

"Away from the city," he replied.

"Please, no!" Yasmin's fear boiled into anger. She lunged at the man in the seat beside her, aiming blows at his chest and face. But he caught her arms with little effort and pressed her against the window glass.

"Calm down," he ordered. "I don't want to hurt you."

"Let me go," Yasmin sobbed. She'd heard the stories – women and girls who'd been picked up on the streets by fake officials, only for their violated bodies to be discovered days or weeks later – but she'd never truly believed the rumours. Recalling how they had followed her through the Narmak streets and bundled her into the minibus, Yasmin feared she'd fallen victim to criminals posing as morality police. Or perhaps they were genuine officers gone rogue.

But they know my name! Is this because of Farzad?

Staring through tears smeared on the window, Yasmin saw the snaking trails of the Lavizan Forest Park, far from the streets of the metropolis. Soon they joined another highway and headed east for two kilometres before turning onto a rural road. The driver dropped a gear as the route took them away from the city into rugged foothills, gradually ascending to eighteen hundred metres above sea level.

Images flashed through Yasmin's mind. Yes, there were two of them, but she would fight, even as they held her down to rape her. Then she remembered how easily they had overpowered her outside the coffee shop, and her resolve instantly cracked. There was nothing out here but remote towns, touristic beauty spots and the villas of the rich. No one would find her until it was too late.

The man beside her placed his hand on her shoulder as she cried. "Do not be upset," he mumbled, trying to make the words sound sincere.

"Go to Hell," Yasmin replied as she hunched her body in a foetal position against the door panel.

"Lashgarak first," the man countered. "We'll soon be there." He glanced through the glass as the minibus engine whined on the ascent of steep hairpin bends. "I bet this road is treacherous when it snows," he commented innocuously as if trying to make conversation. Yasmin kept her mouth shut.

The road straightened and a collection of industrial units came into view, partly concealed by trees. A muezzin's call to prayer sounded from a mosque, briefly distracting Yasmin from her predicament. But then the droning voice was gone and Yasmin's dread returned with a vengeance. The minibus slowed for a turn and bounced up a dirt track. The driver applied the brakes a little too hard, killed the ignition and got out. He walked around the van and tugged open the rear compartment's sliding door.

"Bring her inside," he said.

The taller man took hold of Yasmin's arm once again, gentler this time, and encouraged her to get out of the vehicle.

If I'm outside I can run and scream for help, Yasmin told herself, but cramp burned her muscles as she stepped down from the van. The clear air smelled fresh in contrast to the city haze. Scanning her environment she saw they were among a handful of warehouses near a riverbank. She couldn't see another living soul. The stream drifted lazily along a twelve-metre-wide channel in a much broader riverbed. Yasmin guessed it was the Jajrood River, meandering down from the Alborz Mountains, quiet and languid prior to the tumult of the spring melt.

"We'll rest here a short while," the taller man said.

Yasmin wondered what he meant and realised he'd let go of her arm. She locked eyes with him. "Are you going to hurt me?"

A dusty pickup truck manoeuvred from behind a shed and headed for the track; a young fellow with tousled hair at the wheel and a hefty Sarabi mastiff with a sable coat chained in the back. Yasmin's minder put his arm around her shoulders and turned her away, facing the river to avoid attention. She thought about yelling but couldn't find her voice. Her abductor tilted his head at the nearest industrial unit. "I need you to go inside the warehouse."

Yasmin tried to back away.

The man grabbed her wrist and marched her to the building.

2

THE VICTORIA LINE carried me to Highbury & Islington Underground Station and, once I'd induced the barriers to slam open with a well-aimed swipe of my Oyster card, I emerged onto a broad pavement by a junction bastardized in fealty to another of London's infuriating cycle lanes.

The directions I'd received proved adequate once I'd scanned my surroundings, and I waited briefly at the crossing with a small crowd of fellow travellers until the lights changed in our favour. On the other side I walked along a short stretch of road that was blocked to all traffic except bicycles – naturally – and entered Highbury Place.

A sculpted bronze statue on a stone pedestal caught my eye. I stopped momentarily to read the plaque, now tarnished blue with age, and discovered it commemorated local men who'd fallen in the Boer War. A pair of replica cannon stood at its base. I paused for a moment, gave a brief nod in salute to the lost warriors, and continued my walk.

London plane trees and elegant streetlamps of vintage ironwork stood in a neat row along the pavement. Soon I saw the sprawling lawns of Highbury Fields on my left, but I crossed the road to examine the door numbers on the long terrace of Victorian and Georgian townhouses which overlooked the parkland.

I found the one I had been summoned to. A broad navy door with a brass letterbox stood before me, three steps up from the pavement, guarded by black metal railings which partly hid the basement level. The building was adorned with brown brick and had some quiet dignity to it, even though it wasn't the finest example of the era's architecture.

I pressed the buzzer and gave my name when prompted. A lady of sixty-something years with reading-glasses on a cord around her neck opened the door shortly thereafter and gestured for me to come inside. The skirt, jumper and white hair in a bun made me think I'd been greeted by a school mistress transported from the 1950s.

She offered no formal greeting but glanced at the stairwell. "She's ready for you. First floor."

I nodded and made my way upstairs. The psychologist's door was the only one open, and she'd positioned herself so that I could see her from the landing.

"Come in," she said in a neutral voice that was just welcoming enough without being enthusiastic. I was grateful for that. These assessments aren't meant to be enjoyable and there's no room for pretence. I don't respond well to false platitudes.

I eased the door shut behind me and heard the brass latch click solidly in place. I appreciate fine craftsmanship and attention to detail. I assumed the shrink already knew that.

"Take a seat," she said as she returned to her own.

I nodded, holding eye contact as I sat down. The woman before me wore a pale grey trouser suit over a plain white blouse. I reckoned she was in her early thirties. Hazel eyes looked back at me, enhanced by almost imperceptible makeup, and a single hair-band held her dark brown hair in a ponytail. Attractive as she was with her Eastern Mediterranean complexion, she didn't flaunt her looks at all, and I respected her for it. We're all masters of manipulation in this line of work, so we're good at noticing the trickery when it's attempted on us.

"These things come around fast, don't they?" she offered, inviting my first response.

"The evaluations? I guess you're right." I stroked the fabric-covered arms of the chair. "At least it's more comfortable here than some places I've been debriefed."

"I can imagine." She stood, turned her back to me and walked to the window. "I find these meetings quite a challenge."

The words took me by surprise. "How do you mean?"

She glanced over, gave me a sly smile and placed her hands on her hips. "You're trained to lie with utter conviction. Your safety – even your *life* – can depend upon it. You've been taught how to identify and suppress all those little tells that catch out most people." She paused. "As you've survived this long, I reckon you must be pretty good at it."

"I'd like to think so."

"Whereas I am trained to detect when I'm being lied to. I couldn't do my job otherwise. It makes interviewing men and women with your skills rather thought-provoking."

"When you put it like that," I replied, "I suppose it presents a curious predicament."

"Fun, though," she added. "In a professionally rewarding way, of course."

"Of course."

"Is it hard work? Maintaining the pretence?"

"It takes effort," I answered. "But there are ways of coping. The best lies are wrapped up in the truth. We use aliases with our actual initials. We adopt cover stories that are grounded in our real lives." I offered a smile. "But I'm not telling you anything you don't already know."

The psychologist returned to her seat and crossed her legs. "Yeah, but I'm interested to hear it from your perspective."

I leaned forward. "That's not why I'm here though."

"True enough. Why *are* you here?"

"It's a requirement."

She shook her head. "Forget that. I'm talking about *you*, not the rules."

I held her gaze for a moment. "You're the one who has to sign me off before my next mission."

"Go on."

"They're worried if I'm ready after what happened in France."

"That was over a year ago," she commented.

"Apparently there's no time limit on stress reactions or trauma."

"That's true. Do you think you're ready for another deployment?"

I nodded. "I'm an operator. I need to get my hands dirty. Besides, London bores me."

"No trauma?"

"None."

"You're not waking up in a sweat? Seeing things that aren't there? Shouting at invisible threats?"

I grinned at the list of stereotypical symptoms and shook my head once more. "None of that."

"Good. Promise me you're not fibbing."

"I promise."

She peered at me. "You would say that."

I felt myself raising an eyebrow before I could stop it. One of those involuntary tells she'd mentioned. But I wasn't lying about my readiness for work.

She gave it half a minute before speaking again. "The operation was a fuck-up."

I winced at her choice of words, not because they offended me but because she wasn't wrong. "Missions rarely go like clockwork," I replied noncommitally.

"You were the team leader."

"And?"

"Your colleague snapped her lower spine in the explosion."

I frowned with irritation. "I know. I was there."

"Tell me about it."

"You've read the file."

"Tell me about it."

I glowered at her for a moment then forced myself to soften my posture. Honestly, I begrudgingly admired the woman for cornering me like this. "How long have you got?"

She made an openhanded gesture. "Here all day."

I shifted position in the chair. "I'll try to be concise. I'm the leader of a kill squad…"

The psychologist raised her left hand to stop me. "Apologies for interrupting just as you were getting started, but it's unusual for someone to use that terminology. I don't think I've ever heard it during a session."

"Kill squad? It's an apt description," I replied. "Or would you prefer something more nuanced? Hit team, perhaps?"

"Kill squad is fine. I don't want to put words in your mouth. We subconsciously link the language we use to our experiences and thought processes. I appreciate your honesty."

"And yet you've already conceded that you don't expect a straight answer from a spy."

A smile lit up her face. "Intriguing, isn't it?" She paused. "You were telling me about the mission in France."

"I presume you know the context. Assadollah Assadi, a spymaster of the Iranian Ministry of Intelligence and Security, had established an extensive network of agents throughout Europe. He was eventually arrested in Germany for his part in a thwarted bomb attack at a rally in Paris. A Belgian court sentenced him to twenty years in prison in 2021."

"A good result."

I shrugged. "Not the outcome I would've chosen." I took a moment to gather my thoughts. "He worked for Department 312. They specialise in assassinations outside Iran. Even with Assadi captured, that still left several dangerous MOIS cells operating under his authority in France, Austria and Germany. We had good intelligence about his commanders. We were sent to neutralize them."

"You nearly achieved your objective."

"Almost. We killed two cell members and had the rest on the run. But we ran into a problem."

Her dark eyes held mine. "What happened?"

"It was meant to be a joint operation. Our support was withdrawn. Instead of forcing the Iranians into a bottleneck where the second team would take them out, my squad had to improvise. We ended up chasing them. The bombers had a contingency – they'd rigged a car with triacetone triperoxide. Sarah and I were caught in the blast. She was flung against a bollard in the street. The impact crushed her lower vertebrae."

"What about you?"

"Snapped clavicle, dislocated shoulder and lacerations from the glass. Oh, and the hearing in my right ear is about thirty percent of normal." I paused. "I got off lightly."

The psychologist tapped her lips with a forefinger. "Do you blame yourself?"

"No. I blame the person who abandoned us."

"Did you find out the reason?"

I offered a mirthless smile. "As I mentioned, you can't get a straight answer from a spy."

She gave me a thoughtful look. "You've been candid."

"That's for you to judge," I replied with a blank stare.

"You want my professional opinion?"

"Do I have a choice?"

"You're not suffering from trauma," she replied. "As an individual you're resilient and objective. Most of the time, anyway. I can see no reason to block you from operational work."

"Thank you. Does that mean we're done?"

A raised hand dissuaded me from leaving my chair. I was getting used to the gesture. "Not yet. I told you I'm good at detecting lies."

"I remember."

"You *do* blame yourself for your colleague's injury."

I held her gaze. "I suppose this is the moment you tell me it wasn't my fault."

The psychologist shook her head. "It *was* your fault. You were the squad leader. Live with it."

My jaw clenched. "Is that evaluation based on operational experience?"

She ignored the remark. "Don't like the provocation? That rather proves my point."

"Fine. I should have looked at other options. But time wasn't exactly on my side."

"What happened to the Iranians?"

I hesitated, detecting dryness in my mouth. "I lost them."

She rose to her feet and offered her hand. "Now we're done. Find your own way out?"

"I can manage." I shook her hand, turned away and left the office.

3

BY THE RAILINGS outside the Highbury Place office I turned left, ostensibly to make it look as though I was on my way back to the Tube station but really to determine whether I was being followed. The caution was probably unwarranted. I was confident that no one had tracked me on my outward journey; it thus seemed unlikely that my reciprocal one would draw attention. Since the inquiry into the Paris incident and my enforced discontinuation from covert missions, I'd become a fairly uninteresting person in shadowing terms. That, naturally, was always the goal, but in my case it was true, not feigned. I was nevertheless determined not to let my anti-surveillance skills fade, and London provided ample opportunity for practice.

Of course, I wasn't planning on retracing my steps. The brief walk south allowed me to check the line of vehicles parked along the pavement. Seeing nothing untoward, I spun on my heels and walked back up the road, past the location I'd just come from. I gave it another thirty seconds and then crossed over to the park. I had a pretty good map of the area in my mind, and I knew that the Emirates Stadium was nearby.

The summer had brought the crowds to Highbury Fields. Men and women in their twenties and thirties sat on the grass in small social groups, enjoying the weather and each other's company. It was the territory of the ubiquitous picnic hamper and its antisocial cousin, the portable barbecue grill. I'd never understood how so many Londoners could skip work when the sun came out. I followed the footpath across the lawns away from the indolent horde to the junction of Highbury Crescent and Ronalds Road, then took the latter because it was a quiet one-way street.

I paused at the junction with Battledean Road, pretending to check my bearings. If anyone was keeping tabs on my movements, they were doing a fine job of it, for I saw no one around. I carried on down a gentle incline, passing a handful of gated low-rise residential blocks. The road curved to the left, mirroring a neighbouring bend. A line of bollards prevented vehicle access from one road to the other. I walked through the gap and headed northward, passing red-brick townhouses with large bay windows and gabled roofs. A train rumbled along a track somewhere on my right, concealed by a fence and a patchwork of allotments. I reached Drayton Park Railway Station but did not stop there, opting instead to stroll for another half-mile past the football ground, up to Arsenal Underground Station on Gillespie Road.

Once through the barriers, I moved to the side and waited for five minutes in the entrance hall, observing everyone who entered, concentrating mostly on the people who wore plain unbranded clothes and shoes. I'd come at a fairly quiet time and the travellers were relatively few. No one gave me cause for concern, so I waited until I heard the next westbound train leave and then made my way down to the platform. None of the individuals who'd passed me in the ticket office were lingering there.

The next train arrived eight minutes later. I boarded only when I heard the rapid beeping that announced the doors were about to slide shut. The carriage was less than a third full. I picked a seat at one end and sat down, using my vantage point to scan the occupants. I remained alert until the train reached Leicester Square where I disembarked.

Tube stations with more than one entrance tend to muddle me briefly; I'm seldom sure which direction I'm facing when I reach the street. I found my bearings without making it obvious and then took a circuitous route around the landmarks of London's Theatreland. The only habit I stuck to was walking along pavements facing the oncoming vehicles. Even yobs on scooters intent on snatching phones or handbags follow the traffic flow before veering onto the pavement, so it's better to see them coming than risk an attack from behind. That said, my strategy was aimed primarily at spotting covert surveillance officers driving toward me.

Still rattled by the psychologist, I thought again of Sarah. If I'd been circumspect with my answers, it was only through wariness of the evaluation process, not because I was trying to deny my hasty actions in France had led us into a trap. The formal chat hadn't been purely for the benefit of my mental wellbeing; my competence as a team leader was under scrutiny. I presumed the psychologist – who, I realised, I rather liked even though she'd tested me – had a not insignificant influence on my superiors. Or perhaps the decision had already been made, in my favour or against, and the assessment was nothing more than a training scenario.

The pressure I could handle, but I felt I ought to call Sarah. Somewhere quieter was needed, so I zigzagged through Covent Garden for ten minutes and emerged on the Strand opposite the Savoy Hotel. From there I cut through Victoria Embankment Gardens and crossed the road to Cleopatra's Needle and its accompanying bronze sphinxes on the waterside. I took a moment to look at the shrapnel damage on the plinths, caused by a German bomb in the First World War, then stepped onto the waterside terrace behind the obelisk.

I retrieved my phone and unlocked it from the fingerprint sensor. I found Sarah's number in my contact list, dabbed the dial icon and waited, watching tourist riverboats motor back and forth beneath the hideous concrete spans of Waterloo Bridge.

Twenty seconds later, Sarah answered. "Hey."

"Hey. Thought I owed you a call."

She laughed. "Right. You've just had your psych evaluation, haven't you?"

I chuckled. "Yeah. She wound me up. Needed someone normal to talk to."

"Glad to be of service. How was it?"

"She made me talk about you."

"Ah. That's the real reason for the call. They should know when to drop it."

"It's not that straightforward, Sarah. They're deciding whether to give me a new team. I made the wrong call in Paris. You were injured."

"Forget them. You know how I feel about it."

"Yeah, but..."

"Do me a favour, would you? Put the phone to your other ear. The one that works properly. I was your second-in-command and I supported your decision. We almost had the fuckers. It was the right call." She paused for a couple of seconds. "Listen – what would you have done if I'd objected?"

"I would've called it off," I replied. "Found another way."

"Exactly. You always took my advice. I thought you were right then and I still do."

"I appreciate that, but it was my responsibility. That's what they're dissecting."

Sarah huffed. "They're taking a bloody long time over it." She paused. "At least they didn't boot you out. They'd have done that already if you were in trouble. I don't think you have anything to worry about. You're still working."

"Not fieldwork."

"It's all important."

I sighed. "True enough. Talking of work, how are preparations for the conference?"

"Going well. It's good to get out of London for a while. Fresh air, marvellous views and all that. You'd love the hotel. Acres of grounds. It even has a deer park, apparently."

"Sounds luxurious."

"Nothing but the best for the delegates. Thank God it's on expenses. I'd never get to stay here on my salary. And it's not perfect – the main lift was broken for the first two days. I had to

25

use the service one from the kitchen, and that really wasn't designed for wheelchairs. It was all rather undignified."

"That's out of order," I said.

"Funny. Well, the food more than makes up for it. And I have the general manager wrapped around my little finger. His apologies were getting nauseous."

The remark made me smile. "Glad you're making friends. I should let you get back to work. There must be some pens to line up or something."

"Keep that up, sunshine, and I'll recommend you get sent back to the psychologist."

"She was quite attractive."

"You won't be saying that when she's lobotomizing you. Hey, this'll cheer you up – guess who's in charge of security for the DGSE delegation."

"No idea," I replied.

"Laure Béraud."

A chill ran down my spine. "You're okay with that?"

"Doesn't bother me. I'm a professional, remember? The sodding lift was more annoying."

"Have you spoken to her?" I asked.

"Briefly, in the corridor. There hasn't been time for a friendly catch-up. We're all too busy making sure the pens are straight." Sarah paused for a moment. "Sure you're okay?"

"I'll be fine. I'll see you when you get back."

"Will do. Be good." And that was the end of the conversation.

I put my phone away, wondering what to do with myself for the rest of the afternoon. The chat with Sarah had raised my mood above grumbling irritation, but not quite to the level of peace and goodwill to all. The news from the conference venue nagged at me but I let it go, and Sarah sounded like she was enjoying herself, at least as much as befitted a security expert with VIPs under her watchful eye. I decided that an hour in the gym would help me work out the knots in my shoulders that had inexplicably formed in the psychologist's office.

I stepped past Cleopatra's Needle, crossed Victoria Embankment and headed for Charing Cross.

4

THE ELDERLY CUSTOMER pulled some notes from his wallet and handed them to Harry Beech. "Keep the change, Harry," he said to the thickset Bristolian as he retrieved his anorak from the coat stand in the corner of the barber's shop.

"Very generous," Harry replied in a strong West Country accent. "Thanks, Eddie." He held up his client's jacket as the man slid his arms into the sleeves.

"I'll see you in a few weeks," Eddie said, zipping up the coat as Harry held the door open for him. He glanced back at Harry's co-worker. "Take care, Ismail."

"You too, Mr Holtham. Thanks for coming in." The younger man gave him a quick wave and returned to his task of wiping the surfaces of his workstation with disinfectant.

Harry flipped the sign over inside the door to indicate the shop was closed for the day. He grabbed a soft-bristled broom and started sweeping hair trimmings into a pile. "Good work today, Ismail."

The Middle Eastern man smiled at the praise. "Thanks. We were busy."

The shop owner nodded and looked out the window, leaning on the plastic broom handle. "Shame it's drizzly. Thought it might be a nice evening. Finish clearing up, son, and I'll treat you to a Coke at the pub over the road. You don't mind if I have a beer, do you?"

Ismail laughed. "Course not." He picked up a dustpan and brush, scooped up the pile of hair and deposited it into a black bin liner. "I'm almost done." He shook the bag and tied a knot.

Harry repositioned an assortment of clipper attachments and

lotions on his counter as Ismail took the bag out the back door to the wheelie bins. He rinsed his hands under the tap and towelled them dry. The bell pinged as someone pushed open the front door.

The barber looked round and saw two scrawny men enter the shop. "Sorry, lads, we're closed," he said. "Come back tomorrow."

The first grinned, exposing a mouth of rotten teeth. "Think I can't read, old man? I saw your fucking sign in the window."

Harry shifted his stance and balled a fist. "Then I'd ask you to kindly pay attention to it." He watched them closely. The sallow skin and reeking clothes told him they were both drug addicts. He noticed splodgy tattoos on the first one's knuckles that were as indeterminable as his age.

The user glanced round at his mate. "Hear that? 'Kindly pay attention'." Dilated pupils stared back at Harry. "You're a polite wanker, aren't you?"

The other one gave a weird high-pitched giggle that made Harry think he was still off his head from his last hit. He seemed jittery, or maybe it was just the effect of whatever poison he'd injected. The second man scratched his pocked cheek. "Give us the money," he demanded, spitting saliva as he talked.

Harry shook his head. "You're not getting any money."

The addict who'd spoken first pulled a Stanley knife from his jeans pocket and thumbed the blade forward. "You ain't got a choice," he threatened, waving the weapon in Harry's direction. "Everything from the till. Do it or I'll fuck you up."

Harry heard Ismail come back through the office door into the shop.

"Everything alright, boss?" Ismail asked cautiously, eyeing the scene.

"It will be when these gents leave," Harry replied, keeping his tone as calm as he could.

"The cash!" screamed the one brandishing the weapon, stepping closer.

Harry smacked him hard in the mouth, breaking teeth. The

man reeled, but he was so high that the pain didn't properly register, and he didn't fall. He swung the Stanley knife in a wild strike that barely missed Harry's face. The barber stumbled backwards, slipping on the smooth floor and hitting his hip against the nearest sink. As Harry went down, he caught sight of Ismail grabbing a pair of scissors from his workstation.

Ismail lunged at Harry's attacker and thrust the scissors into the addict's left side, just below the ribs. The smackhead stared for a moment in astonishment at the wound and involuntarily dropped the knife. He looked at his mate with horror. "He fucking stabbed me!" he screamed before slumping to the ground.

The jittery man trembled for a moment, his heroin-riddled brain struggling to decide, and then fled from the shop. Harry got to his feet and stamped on the injured man's hand as he groped for the Stanley knife. He kicked the weapon and it skittered toward the office door.

The wounded man groaned, clutching his side and gasping for breath. "The Paki done me!" he choked.

"You're not going to die," Harry replied, grabbing a towel and tossing it at the addict. "Press that against the wound. I'm not touching you – I'd probably catch hepatitis. And he's Persian, you racist cunt." Harry turned round and saw that Ismail was still clutching the scissors and staring at the wounded man. "Put those down, Ismail, and take a seat."

Ismail's pallor indicated shock. He didn't move. Harry touched his arm gently and made him drop the scissors into the sink. Harry led him to the customers' bench and told him again to sit down. Ismail responded this time, obeying the instruction.

"He'll be fine," Harry told him, reaching for his phone. He dialled 999 and waited for an answer. "Police, please. Thanks." He paused as the operator connected him. "My name's Harry Beech. A couple of druggies just tried to rob my barber's shop on Church Lane, Redcliffe. One ran off but the other one's still here. He had a knife. You'd better call an ambulance. No, *I'm* not injured. Yes.

He's bleeding from his side. Would you just send someone quickly, please? I want the tosser nicked." Harry ended the call, evidently bored with the questions.

"I didn't mean to do it," Ismail murmured. Harry looked at him, wondering if his assistant was about to throw up all over the floor.

Harry sat next to him. "Wasn't your fault, son. You defended me. Trust me, I'm grateful."

Ismail shook his head. "You don't understand."

"What do you mean?"

The Persian shook his head. "Trouble."

Harry frowned. "I know it looks bad, but he had a knife and attacked me with it. In English law, that's self-defence all day long. You did the right thing."

After a minute, sirens sounded outside and Harry got to his feet. The blue strobe lights of the patrol car flashed through the glass for a few seconds as the vehicle came to a halt.

Two uniformed police officers entered the shop moments later. "Mr Beech?" one asked.

Harry nodded at the policewoman. "That's me."

"Are you okay?"

"I will be when you get that criminal out of my shop."

A smile crossed her face. "Just need to get the details straight first." She glanced at Ismail and noticed blood on his right hand. "Who are you?"

He glanced at her. "Ismail. I work for Harry. I..."

She interrupted him. "Hold that thought, Ismail. Let me talk to Mr Beech first, okay?" She turned to her colleague. "You got this?"

The policeman nodded, pulled on some Latex gloves and bent down to look at the injured man. "Hello, Dwayne!" the male officer remarked with barely restrained glee. "You screwed that up, didn't you?"

"I'm fucking dying!" the drug addict wailed.

31

"Hardly. Barely a scratch from what I can see. The paramedics will be here in a minute. Oh, Dwayne. One more thing."

"What?"

"You're nicked for robbery and possession of a bladed article."

"Whatever."

While her colleague cautioned the drug addict, the female officer took Harry into the back room and made him go through his account, leaving Ismail on the bench seat.

An ambulance pulled up in the alley next to the shop. The policeman got up to make space for the paramedics when they entered the premises, briefly describing the injury. He made a call on his radio, asking for some evidence tubes and another unit to escort the prisoner to the hospital. Ismail heard him talk about cross-contamination but didn't understand what it meant.

Harry and the policewoman returned from the office five minutes later, still in conversation.

"I'll need to come back and get a statement from you, Mr Beech," the officer said as they walked back into the shop. "And if you can get a copy of your CCTV footage ready for me, that'd be a great help."

"Fine, but do you have to...?" Harry started to say.

"Let's finish that conversation in a minute, shall we?" she interjected. She approached the paramedics. "Is he fit to go?"

One of the crew gave a nod. "Whenever you're ready."

"Thanks."

A second patrol car arrived after a couple of minutes. Harry finally got his wish when the drug addict was escorted from the shop to be conveyed to the hospital for treatment. The officers placed the Stanley blade and the scissors in plastic tubes with exhibit labels. The policewoman returned her attention to Ismail. She sat down next to him on the bench.

"Ismail," she prompted.

He turned to make eye contact.

"I've spoken to Mr Beech about what happened. Listen to me

carefully. It seems pretty straightforward, okay?" There was a message in her tone but it didn't register with him. "However, because of the injury that the suspect received, I'm required to investigate this from all angles. For that reason, I have to take you in to interview you under caution. We'll sort this out at the station."

"But..."

"Ismail Khadem, I'm arresting you on suspicion of causing grievous bodily harm. You do not have to say anything, but it may harm your defence if you do not mention, when questioned, something which you later rely on in court. Anything you do say may be given in evidence. Do you understand?"

Ismail stared at her. "But you don't understand. The man attacked Harry."

"We'll talk about it later, okay?"

He shook his head. "I *can't* be arrested."

Responding to his tone, the policewoman got to her feet and unclipped her rigid handcuffs from her body armour. "It's not up for negotiation, Ismail. Put your hands out for me."

Accepting defeat, the Persian did as she instructed. The cuffs ratcheted around his wrists and the officer used her handcuff key to double lock the restraints.

"Don't worry, son," Harry called out as Ismail was led from the shop. "We'll sort it."

He glanced back, a forlorn expression of defeat plain on his face. "It's too late for that."

5

Nᴇᴡs ᴛʜᴀᴛ ᴛʜᴇ ᴘᴀᴄᴋᴀɢᴇ had arrived at the safe-house was welcome, but it meant I was compelled to bear another journey across London in those disagreeable hours of the evening migration. I considered taking a car but decided otherwise. I had to collect an untraceable phone from a contact in Drury Lane, so it made sense to walk from there to Holborn Underground Station and pick up the Central Line.

The platform was so crowded that I couldn't get on the first train, and I barely squeezed onto the next. I embarked at the end of a carriage, not just for the security rationale but also because the ventilation was marginally better. I found a few spare inches of handrail to grab onto with one hand, remembering the mountain climber's rule about three points of contact. The train nevertheless did its cruel best to throw me and the other passengers off-balance as it hurtled along the subterranean bends.

My limpet grip only relaxed when the train reached Stratford and numerous passengers departed. I could finally claim a seat and did so, even though I wasn't all that far from my destination. I arrived at Wanstead seven minutes later. Outside, I took a moment to glance back at the concrete carbuncle of the station building, and wondered why modernist architects were not reviled with the same vigour as paedophiles and terrorists.

I navigated the junction opposite The George pub and headed southwest alongside the stretch of the A12 known as Cambridge Park. I walked past a parade of houses whose ground floors were occupied by small businesses. If I ever found myself in need of an estate agent, an Indian restaurant and a dentist on the same day, I'd know where to visit. Despite the rose and crimson hues of the evening sky, this suburban corner of Greater London was drab.

I turned right onto Addison Road. Most of the small front gardens had been paved over, but a few privet hedges and flowerpots remained. The houses were satisfyingly uniform. Net curtains or blinds shielded the interiors from the street. I was confident that few of the residents cared to know each other; I sensed that neighbourliness was all but extinct hereabouts. The road was perfect for a safe-house.

I thumbed the doorbell switch and looked up at the discreet miniature camera hidden behind the arch of the narrow porch. Someone unfastened a bolt and opened the door for me. I recognised the man as I stepped into the hallway. I gave a quick nod but didn't bother with pleasantries.

"She here?" I asked.

The minder pushed the door shut and locked it again. "Back bedroom. She's expecting you."

"Thanks." I headed up the narrow stairs. They were carpeted, but the old wooden treads underneath the worn fabric creaked in places, adding a touch of bleak character to the home.

The landing light was on, shining with a clean white glow. We'd swapped out the aged filament bulbs for daylight-balanced LEDs to reduce eye strain. Someone from the weapons training department had come up with the idea, having reasoned that an operative who'd sat for hours under the jaundiced wash of old-fashioned bulbs was less likely to shoot straight if the premises were attacked. I'm not sure how significant a factor that would actually be in such a scenario, but I appreciated the off-the-wall logic.

At the top of the staircase I had a quick look around. A female colleague was sitting in the upstairs office at the front of the house, typing something on a laptop. She flashed me a quick smile and pointed.

"Thanks," I said, before tapping on the open door of the small bedroom opposite.

Yasmin Bouzidi was sitting up on the single bed, flicking

through the pages of *Grazia*. She looked at me and tossed the magazine aside. I didn't get the impression she'd been reading it with focus.

"Salam, hal-e chetore?" I said in Persian. *Hello, how are you?*

She flapped her hand to invite me in but didn't reply. I entered and sat down on a padded chair with beige upholstery, guessing we'd bought it and the rest of the furniture from a charity shop specialising in house clearances. The Iranian woman looked exhausted, but that wasn't a surprise considering what she'd been through in the last few days.

I held her gaze and waited for her to speak.

"Aya shoma farsi sohbat mikonid?" she finally asked. *Do you speak Persian?*

I shrugged. "Yek kami." *A little.* Which wasn't strictly true.

"English then," she countered. "Your pronunciation is terrible."

"Very well." I eased back in the chair, hoping the forty-year-old springs wouldn't pick that moment to snap. "Have you rested?"

Yasmin frowned at me. "Perhaps you could tell me what's going on."

"You were not safe in Iran," I replied.

"I was fine until your agents snatched me from the street in Narmak. My best friend will think I've been raped and killed." She stared at me with forlorn hope as she asked her next question. "Can I call Leila? To tell her I'm safe?"

I shook my head. "I am sorry. You cannot contact your friend under any circumstances. That would put her in grave danger. They will monitor her telephone number and e-mail address." I considered my next words for a moment. "It would've been only a matter of time before the authorities imprisoned you."

"I did nothing wrong."

"Since when did that prevent the regime from detaining its citizens? Besides, it was never about *you*. They would have

36

punished you because Farzad fled the country." I paused. "Yasmin, they lock up women for twenty years for not wearing the hijab. What would they do to the sister of a traitor?"

"My brother's actions are not my responsibility," Yasmin answered.

"*I* know that. But it wouldn't be *me* you'd have to convince in Iran."

"I don't even know where he is. I haven't heard from him since he disappeared. That was months ago. For all I know, Farzad is already dead."

I hesitated for a few seconds before speaking again. "He's not dead, Yasmin."

The tiredness vanished from her face as she stared at me. "How...?"

I retrieved the phone I'd acquired earlier from my jacket, stood up and handed it to her. "There's only one number saved in the contacts. It's Farzad's. I need you to call him right now. Tell him where you are."

She handled the mobile as if it were delicate glass. "Farzad is in England?"

I nodded. "He made it out."

She put the phone down on the duvet. Her eyes burned into mine with open hostility. The change of mood caught me off-guard. "What are you not telling me?" She got off the bed and stood, glancing around the room and raising her hands in a questioning gesture. "Why this? Why the secrecy? If Farzad is here, why have you not taken me to him?"

I wasn't prepared to respond in detail, so I deflected. "It was the only way to extract you from Iran. You really think they'd allow you to board a plane on your own?"

She put her hands on her hips and glowered. "That's not what I meant. Why can't I see my brother?"

"I need you to calm down," I replied, endeavouring to hide my irritation at her impertinence. "There are protocols. It will take a

37

little time. We must be careful."

"But you'll let me see him?"

"Of course." I picked the phone up from the bed and placed it in her hand, gently curling her fingers over it. "Why else would I give you this? Please, call him."

"Now?"

I nodded.

"Alright." Yasmin found the number and dialled. She listened for a few seconds and then frowned again. "It's switched off." The suspicion returned to her visage.

"You're sure?" I asked.

She slapped the phone into my hand. "You try it."

I dialled Farzad's number and, as Yasmin had declared, it didn't connect. I gave the phone back to her. "I told him to keep it turned on," I said, annoyed. "Try again later."

"I will." She set the mobile down on the cabinet next to the bed.

"Thank you." I walked to the door. "Is there anything you need?"

"Some books – if I'm going to be here a few days."

I discerned her choice of words but didn't confirm or reject the timescale. "I can arrange that. What sort?"

"I quite like English romance novels."

I grinned in genuine surprise. "You could get hold of those in Iran?"

"Not easily."

"I'm not familiar with the genre but I'll see what I can do."

She smiled for the first time; it brought an attractive lightness to her face. "Thanks."

"Khodahafez." *Goodbye.*

"Khodahafez." Yasmin slumped down on the bed and picked up the magazine.

I stepped across the landing and leaned into the study. "Make sure she calls her brother," I said with a soft voice to avoid being overheard. "The idiot switched it off for some reason. Get her to keep trying until he answers. It's important."

The female operative gave me a half-smile. "No problem. I'll give you a bell when it's done."

"Thanks, I appreciate it. See you later."

"Will do."

I headed back downstairs and saw the other minder in the kitchen with a kettle and three mugs on the counter. "I'll be on my way if you can let me out," I remarked.

"Oh, I was just going to offer you a drink," he said.

"No thanks – I've got to endure the Central Line back to town. Should be better in that direction, at least."

"Well, if you can hang on for half an hour, the night crew will be here to take over babysitting duties. I can give you a lift then."

I grinned. "In that case, I'll take you up on your offer. Dash of milk, no sugar."

6

SIXTEEN HOURS after his arrest, Farzad Bouzidi was told he could leave the police station. His pseudonym hadn't been challenged, and the piece of paper addressed to Ismail Khadem said he was 'released under investigation'. Farzad had tried to listen when the custody sergeant explained what that meant, but the sleepless night in the noisy cell block and the subsequent interview about his role in the incident at Harry's had left him exhausted and confused.

But one emotion surpassed all the rest: fear. Until the events of the previous afternoon, Farzad had kept a low profile and avoided contact with the authorities, just as his handler had requested. He'd never formally sought asylum in the UK, but his contact had arranged a genuine national insurance number in his false name. It hadn't mattered that the police never doubted his identity; he was now on their databases, and that meant others could find him.

As he walked away from the police station's front office in Bristol's Old Market district, Farzad wondered if telling the custody sergeant he was Iranian had been the right decision. His handler had insisted he did so if he ever spoke to the police – for two reasons. First, due to the tense animosity between the British and Iranian governments, the UK police had no protocol to contact the embassy about detained Iranian citizens. Second, it was the truth, so he wouldn't be caught out by someone testing him in a dialect or language he didn't understand.

The instruction had made sense then, but it now felt as though it had more holes than a sieve. It made no difference that Avon and Somerset Police would probably drop the grievous bodily harm case. They'd hinted more than once that his defence of Harry

Beech amounted to reasonable force. The CID officer who'd interviewed him had asked him uncomplicated questions and wrapped up the interview after thirty minutes. None of that mattered. Farzad's photograph was now stored on a police computer system, and that terrified him.

He stood outside the police station and blinked in the sunlight, allowing his eyes to adjust after his confinement. The drizzle from the previous evening was long gone, and the afternoon was warm with a touch of humidity. Farzad inhaled slowly, trying to settle his tattered nerves and convince himself that, since no one knew his real name, the situation couldn't be as bad as he imagined. He realised he was hungry; they'd given him microwaved vegetarian sludge in a foam box during the night and a single-serve cup of cereal for breakfast. He had some cash in his wallet and decided to buy a sandwich somewhere. Farzad started walking to the junction at West Street.

And saw a Middle Eastern man watching him from the grounds of the church across the road.

In that moment Farzad knew he'd been found out. The man was younger than him, maybe thirty or late twenties, and wore a bright red Bristol City Football Club shirt and black jeans. Farzad's first thought was to go back into the police station to ask for help, but he instantly dismissed the idea. He turned and walked down a narrow road behind the police building, then took a quick right past a four-storey residential block toward a small green space.

Farzad chanced a look over his shoulder and saw the man ambling after him, glancing at his mobile phone. He made no effort to catch up. Farzad didn't know what to make of the man's unhurried pursuit or why he'd been standing there in plain sight. The expression on the guy's face revealed boredom, as though he'd been given a task without being told why.

Was the overt surveillance meant to intimidate him? Farzad doubted the red-shirted man was acting alone, but where were the others? Farzad's chest tightened as he guessed he'd been unwittingly funnelled into the park, but a quick scan of the small area revealed no one else. Something didn't feel right but he wasn't inclined to analyse it. Putting distance between him and the man in the football shirt was all that mattered.

Farzad took a few seconds to oxygenate his lungs and then veered behind the apartment block. He reached the corner and turned left, skirted around some iron railings, and then ran for a hundred metres down a cobbled lane which brought him onto West Street. He paused at the junction and looked back. He watched with disbelief as the man in the red shirt slowed to a jog and then a walk, puffing hard, half the length of the lane away.

Perhaps, Farzad guessed, the sprint had caught him by surprise, but it seemed unfathomable for an operative to give up that easily. Farzad wasn't done yet though. He started running again, back in the church's direction, hoping the move would be unexpected. Instead of going all the way to the junction, he ran across the road and darted down another side street, passing some modern-looking offices and small industrial units. He found a footpath and jogged along it into a housing estate.

Now short of breath, Farzad slowed to a walk, forcing himself to inhale slowly and deeply. He looked around several times but knew he didn't really need to; the man in the Bristol City top was nowhere to be seen. Farzad, however, wasn't inclined to draw attention to himself in the housing estate, so he found a route through it and leapt over an iron fence at the end of a cul-de-sac.

The residential streets were unknown to him, but a pair of ugly tower blocks reset his bearings. He worked his way around them and emerged near a large roundabout. He realised he was taking a chance walking along the main road, but his energy had diminished and his need for food meant he couldn't concentrate on another zig-zagging route through unfamiliar estates. Back on the main road, he remembered a Lidl store and several small cafés stood nearby.

Needing to sit down, Farzad decided against going into the

supermarket, opting instead for a small kebab house. He ordered a lamb kebab, a tray of chips and a can of 7Up. The seats were of the rigid plastic type, bolted to the frame of the table, but the discomfort never crossed his mind. He remembered he hadn't switched on his mobile after they returned it to him in the custody suite, so he turned it on and put it back in his pocket. He forked the food into his mouth and tried to assess what had happened.

The puzzle about the man outside the police station made no sense. If the Iranian authorities had discovered his location, they would have acted with greater precision and skill to capture him, for he was a target of significant value. Farzad concluded that trying to second-guess their operational tactics was a distraction; he needed to work out how to evade them until he could seek help. He was close to Lawrence Hill Railway Station but needed a better strategy than just embarking a train.

Having given his correct address at the cell block, Farzad feared returning to the rented flat. He couldn't contact Harry either – the barber's shop was as likely to be under observation as his own place. Farzad didn't know anyone else in Bristol well enough to ask for help; without Harry Beech he was alone. That meant he had only one option: to call his handler to request an urgent relocation. Farzad's mood soured as he realised he'd never see his employer again. The jovial but no-nonsense Bristolian had become a friend; he'd miss him.

Farzad finished the food, swallowed the last drops of his fizzy drink and made his way outside. He thought again about going to the railway station but told himself *no*, it was better to avoid it until he had a plan. He carried on walking east, crossed the railway line and continued for half a mile until he saw the entrance to the St George Park recreation ground. He followed the path past the tennis courts, looking for somewhere uncrowded where he could make the call. He ended up near the man-made lake and sat down on a bench overlooking the water.

His phone rang with an unknown number while he was still

trying to figure out how to explain the arrest and his concern about the man who'd followed him. Farzad hesitated, reluctant to answer. The mobile buzzed and chirruped in his hand as he thought about his options. He could, he supposed, remove the SIM card and discard the phone if the caller was someone he didn't know. Answering the call wasn't without risk, he speculated, but he would have to use the thing before long anyway.

He swiped the screen and held the phone to his ear. "Yes?"

"Farzad?" A woman's voice said. "Farzad, it's Yasmin."

Relief flooded through him and he felt tears in his eyes. "Yasmin? Is it really you?"

"It's me. How are you, Brother?"

Farzad deflected. "Where are you?"

"I'm in England. Somewhere in London. They asked me to call you. They said I could see you soon."

Farzad sighed. "That might not be possible just yet."

"Explain." Yasmin paused, waiting for an answer. When her brother didn't reply, she followed with, "You sound agitated. What's wrong?"

Farzad choked through a dry throat. "I'm in trouble, Yasmin. I can't stay here. I think they've found me."

"Shit. Where are you?"

"I can't say. I need to speak to the man who helped me before." Farzad hesitated. "How can I be certain that you are safe?"

"What do you mean?"

"How do I know you're not under duress?" Farzad asked, his voice faltering.

"Brother, I'm fine. I'm in a house in some quiet London street with a nice cherry tree outside. There are people looking after me." She thought for a moment. "The man who gave me this phone had scars on his cheek and jaw. He said you were told to never switch it off. Is that true? I've been trying to call you since last night. Why was the phone dead?"

Yasmin's words finally convinced Farzad that she was speaking freely. "He's my handler. Is he with you now?"

"No. He left after we spoke yesterday. Why was your phone off, Farzad?" Yasmin pressed.

"I was arrested last night," he replied. "I did nothing wrong. Someone followed me from the police station when I was released. That's how I know I'm in trouble."

"Then you must call him at once," Yasmin stated firmly.

"I will, Sister. I promise. But first there is something I must tell you."

"Can it not wait?"

Farzad shook his head as he answered. "No. Listen carefully, Yasmin."

7

MURAD ZAM, clandestine operative for Department 312 of Iran's Ministry of Intelligence and Security, reclined in a plastic garden chair and watched eight goldfinches compete for space on the bird feeder. An avid ornithologist, Zam enjoyed observing the colourful birds as they competed for the two available perches. He noticed different tactics at play. The more boisterous finches bickered noisily, hovering just centimetres apart to dislodge each other from the pegs. Others waited nearby, on the feeder's brackets or in the branches of the shrubs, slyly picking the moments when their duelling companions became distracted and left the feeder unoccupied.

Wherever in the world he was assigned a mission, birds kept him company and relieved the stress that a covert operation always induced. From black-winged kites in the Atlas Mountains to demoiselle cranes on the southern shores of the Black Sea, avifauna enthralled the former Quds Force soldier. The garden in the Wiltshire town of Swindon was hardly a comparable scene to some of the more exotic locations he'd worked in, but it was the birds, not the setting, that held the enthusiast's attention.

Zam's mobile phone rang in his shirt pocket. He fished it out and cupped his hand over the screen against the afternoon sun's glare. Recognising the fictitious business name, he touched the incoming-call graphic. He held the device to his ear. "Yes?" he said in English.

The male caller used Farsi. "This is Control."

"I know," Zam replied in his native language, irritated. "What do you want? You were not meant to contact me until the day after tomorrow."

"I will call you whenever I see fit," the speaker replied. A pause, then, "Are you ready?"

"You put me in charge of this operation for a reason."

"Then I take it everything is on schedule?"

"It is," Zam replied, returning his attention to the goldfinches.

"And your team?"

"They know what they have to do. They await my orders."

"Good. Is Haydar with you?"

"No, he's at the other house, of course."

"Fine. I need you to call him once we have spoken. I have another task for you."

Zam frowned. "You want to interrupt the timetable?"

"Not at all. You've just told me everything is in order and the squad is ready. Something's come up that needs to be dealt with. Haydar is your second-in-command and is competent to manage in your absence."

"I have no doubt about Haydar's ability," Zam retorted, "but it's unwise to break the schedule."

"That's not your decision."

"Fine. What do you want?"

"Jerboa has been located in Bristol. I need you to deal with him."

The cryptonym instantly had Zam's full attention. "You're sure?" he questioned.

"He's been using the name Ismail Khadem to avoid detection. But it's definitely the scientist."

"Tell me what you know."

"Our contact in Avon and Somerset Police has a search filter on his computer system. He discovered an Iranian national was arrested yesterday afternoon, around nineteen hundred hours. He checked the photograph on the custody record. It's definitely him."

"Is Bouzidi still with the police?" Zam asked.

"No. They had to let him go." Control paused. "There is a

47

problem."

"Go on."

"Our contact endeavoured to have Jerboa followed, but his options were limited. The man given the task was not a professional, and he lost him."

"Jerboa knew he was being followed?"

"He saw the man and ran off."

"That's fucking helpful. How am I supposed to find him?"

"There is a lead. They arrested him at his place of work – a barber's shop. He hasn't been back there either." Control paused. "Take Rasul and Samir to Bristol with you. Leave at once. If you use the motorway, you'll be there in forty minutes. Find the traitor and silence him."

"Do you know how big Bristol is?" Zam snapped.

"Are you telling me you are not capable?"

"I'm telling you the odds."

"You're the nearest MOIS unit. I will arrange for a second team if necessary, but they would come from London. If you do not find Jerboa, you will return to Swindon for your primary objective, and the others will take over. But I want boots on the ground there now."

"Fine. Text me everything you have."

"I will," Control replied, "and I will send you any updates from our man in the police force. He will have to be discreet, naturally, so do not rely on him. This is your area of expertise, Murad."

The compliment sounded more like a warning. "Anything else?" Zam asked.

"No. Keep me informed."

"I'll phone Haydar and then get on the road." Zam ended the call. He stood up and the goldfinches flew away.

8

My hopes for a more enlivening day than the previous one with the psychologist were dashed when I was told to read the overnight reports from our assets on the Poland-Belarus border. The information was important, but it scolded me that I ought to be in the field, working alongside the Polish special forces – or anywhere else on a covert mission – not sitting in a discreet office in Camden Town. Although I made it my business to keep abreast of global tensions, I was the wrong person to be analysing signals intelligence.

By mid-afternoon I'd had enough. Needing a decent workout, I decided that a few quick miles running up and down Regent's Park would blow the cobwebs away. I had some kit with me, so I changed, filled up a water bottle and left the office.

I entered the park opposite Gloucester Gate and jogged to warm up. I reached Broad Walk and increased my speed, following the tree-lined avenue southward. There were hundreds of people in the park but I had plenty of room.

I'd completed three lengths and started on my fourth when I felt my phone buzz in the sports pouch around my waist with an incoming text. I ignored it until I returned to the north end of the park near London Zoo. The message told me Yasmin Bouzidi had spoken to her brother. It was good news because I now had some leverage. As I started another length of the path, I thought about how I could put a bit of pressure on Farzad. It was about time he delivered.

The phone rang a few minutes later, and it surprised me to see the Iranian's name on the screen. I stopped my run and strolled toward an ornamental fountain before answering. "You're calling me unprompted, Farzad." I took a sip from my water bottle and swallowed. "That's a first."

"I... I need your help," the Iranian stammered.

I detected the anxiety in his voice. "What's the problem?" I asked.

"There are people after me. I can't stay in Bristol."

Frowning, I said, "How do you know?"

"Someone chased me from the police station. I ran and got away, but I'm not safe here."

"Hang on. What's this about the police?" This revelation gave me cause for alarm.

"I was arrested yesterday. Two men tried to steal from Harry. I... I hurt one of them."

"Never mind that," I replied. "Someone followed you? When was this?"

"About an hour ago. He was waiting across the road from the police station."

During my interactions with Farzad, I had never considered him to be prone to flights of fancy, but I had to know whether he'd misjudged what he'd seen. "How do you know he followed you?"

"I made a few turns and sprinted. He ran after me but couldn't keep up."

"What did he look like?"

"Younger than me, a little overweight. Arab or Persian. He wore a red football shirt."

The description was pretty good but it hardly sounded like a threat. "Probably some kid who thought he'd hassle you for money, Farzad."

The line went silent. "That could be true," Farzad conceded. He didn't sound convinced.

And experience had taught me not to make assumptions about anything. I took a second to gather my thoughts. "You reckon he was Iranian?"

"I don't know. Maybe."

"Alright." I paused. "What name did you give to the police?"

"Ismail Khadem."

"Good."

"No, no! It's not good!" Farzad retorted, his voice increasing in volume. "I'm on their computer now. They have my photograph. Someone will recognise me."

"Okay, calm down. I'll help you." But it was time to lean on him. "I need the file."

"What? You must get me out of Bristol."

"Listen to me, Farzad," I intoned. "When you contacted us, you promised you'd deliver certain information."

"I've given you information," he replied, the desperation returning to his voice.

"Yes, and it's been helpful. But I want the rest. All of it."

"I told you..."

I didn't let him finish the sentence. I knew I was manipulating a terrified man, but that's the best time to do it. "Shut up, Farzad. Any help I give you now is conditional. You spoke to your sister?"

"Yes, just before I called you."

"Then you know she's safe?"

"I do."

"We got her out of Iran, just like I said we would. That was *your* condition, wasn't it? We extracted your sister in exchange for the file. So now it's time for you to fulfil your end of the bargain. Or were you bullshitting me all along?"

"No, I have it all. The names, the blueprints, the firewall codes... Everything. It's yours. Just get me out."

"If you're lying to me, Farzad, I swear I'll hand you over to the regime myself. Your sister too. I'll tell them she arranged your escape from Iran." I realised I was probably laying it on a bit heavy at this stage, but the missing data was, frankly, a lot more valuable than Farzad's wretched life.

"I'll keep my word," he said in response.

I waited a few seconds before speaking again, just to make him fear I was on the verge of abandoning him. "Alright. How much cash do you have?"

"About seventy pounds."

"Good. I don't want you catching a train, and definitely not a taxi. Do you understand?"

"Yes," he replied.

"How far away from the bus station are you?"

"I'm not sure. An hour's walk. Maybe more."

"Fine. Give me a minute or two to look something up, alright?"

"Okay."

I opened my mapping application, zoomed out from Regent's Park and swiped until I had a view of Somerset and the neighbouring counties. Getting Farzad away from Bristol was essential, but I needed a coherent plan that he could follow while under stress. The town of Bath was reasonably close but too obvious if someone really were after him. Gloucester was too far away. I also had to be able to find him without complications, so a large town was impractical. I scanned the map and came up with an idea. I switched to my browser and tapped in a search inquiry about bus routes.

"Have you heard of Glastonbury?" I asked when I was done.

"Yes," Farzad replied at once. "Church tower on a hill. The famous music festival."

"Good. There's a regular bus service from Bristol Bus Station. The number 376. You got that?"

"376. Yes."

"Okay, I want you to go there and catch the 376. Ask for a ticket to Glastonbury Town Hall. You won't miss it – it's next to the abbey ruins. Once you're there, find a bed-and-breakfast hotel for the night. It doesn't matter which one."

"You want me to stay there overnight?" Farzad asked, concerned.

"Yes. It's safer that way. No one will know you're there. I'll drive down from London early tomorrow."

"I'd prefer you to come tonight."

"I'm sure you would, but that means you'd have to wait outside on the street, and I'd have to spot you in the dark," I told him. "You need to stay out of sight for a few hours to let the trail go cold."

"Alright," he said, reluctantly accepting the logic of my plan. "Where will I meet you in the morning?"

"Let me check my phone," I said, looking once more at the map. After a minute I spoke to him again. "Okay, this is what we'll do. I'm going to give you a schedule. You'll have to remember a few details but they won't be difficult."

"Go on," he replied.

"Plan A is simple. Go to the Lazy Gecko Café at eight o'clock. It's opposite the abbey, so you'll see it easily. Buy a cup of tea. If anyone asks, say you're meeting a friend for breakfast. If I'm not there by eight-twenty, switch to Plan B. Leave the café and walk up the High Street. Take a footpath up to the Tor – that's the name of the hill with the church tower. Walk to the top and wait for me. I'll find you easily enough. Are you still with me?"

"Yes, I think so."

"Summarise what I just told you."

"Lazy Gecko Café at eight. Leave if you're not there by eight-twenty. Walk to the Tor as a backup plan. Go to the top and wait."

"Good. I'll give you one more contingency plan. If I don't find you by ten o'clock on the Tor, go back into the town and wait in the abbey grounds. It won't come to that, but you need to know what to do if I'm delayed."

"Can't you call me if there's a problem, instead of making me wander around like a tourist?" Farzad asked.

"No. I want you to destroy your phone. Take the SIM card out and get rid of it."

"I will."

"Good. Get to the bus station as soon as you can," I told him. "And remember, Farzad, I expect you to keep your word."

"Understood," he replied.

I ended the call, zipped up my phone and resumed my run.

9

ZAM SPOTTED A SIDE ROAD opposite the Northfield House tower block that led to a rundown collection of garages and reserved parking bays. He didn't bother driving to the end; he just reversed up the kerb near the junction and parked on the double-yellow lines. Zam wasn't planning on a lengthy stop.

It had taken an hour and a quarter for Zam and his men to reach Bristol. Rush-hour traffic had meant unexceptional progress on the motorway from Swindon; the city roads had slowed them further. Once through the centre, they'd crossed the River Avon into a district that was almost entirely residential. The car's sat-nav had guided them the rest of the way.

Rasul Heyat and Samir Davari climbed out of the black Renault Captur and joined the cell leader on the pavement. Zam aimed the key card at the vehicle, locking it. The three operatives took a few seconds to glance at the eighteen-storey tower and saw its name on a sign above the entrance door. They crossed the street and entered the sheltered area.

Breaking in through the security door wouldn't have been possible without the help of the fire brigade or an oxyacetylene cutting torch, but such measures weren't required. Zam punched the number of the flat adjacent to Bouzidi's into the keypad on the wall. The panel trilled with an electronic ringtone. The connection timed out after a few seconds, unanswered. Zam keyed in another door number.

"Yeah?" a distorted male voice questioned through the speaker.

"Amazon delivery for your neighbour," Zam stated. "I tried the flat number but got no reply. Buzz me in, please, fella."

"Alright, mate." The speaker clicked off and the door mechanism droned loudly as it unlocked.

Zam grabbed the handle and tugged it open, leading the way into the foyer. It smelled like someone had vomited on the floor. He and the others went to the lift, hit the call button and waited for the doors to slide open. The lift's interior smelled even worse. They exited a few seconds later onto a dimly lit landing. Zam checked the door numbers.

Shielded from view by the others, Davari picked the lock in seconds and gave the door a shove. The men entered the small flat, quickly finding out that it had two bedrooms, a bathroom and a sitting-room which adjoined a narrow kitchenette. A brief scan of the place told them their target lived frugally. There was a rickety wardrobe in the corner of the larger bedroom with a few garments on hangers. More clothes were folded in the drawers.

"Rasul, check his clothes," Zam ordered. "Samir, look in the second bedroom. I'll see if there's anything in the kitchen. Put your gloves on."

Zam found a step stool tucked next to the washing machine. He rolled it across the kitchen floor and stood on it to check the cabinet tops. Seeing nothing of interest, he got down and moved the stool back to its spot. He found a few pieces of crockery and some drinking glasses but ignored them, checking the packets of food instead. He pulled a bag of corn flakes from its box to see if anything was hidden inside, found nothing and repeated the process for the remaining containers.

He had a look in the drawers next, lifting out the cutlery trays and other items. After a while he found Bouzidi's paperwork. A couple of utility bills confirmed the occupant had been using the name Ismail Khadem. Zam flicked through the sheets of paper, eventually finding a recent payslip from the barber's shop, but it didn't tell him anything new.

He walked out of the kitchen. "Rasul?"

"Nothing of use," Heyat replied.

"How about you, Samir?"

"The same. The place is empty."

"Let's not waste any more time here," Zam said. He tossed the Renault's key card to Davari. "You drive."

"Where to, Murad?"

"Head for the barber's shop. I'll check the opening times on-line."

The men left Bouzidi's flat and called the lift. Minutes later they were back in the Renault. Rain had begun to fall hard, making the late afternoon feel more like autumn than summer. Davari entered their next destination into the sat-nav, flicked on the wipers and drove out onto the side road.

"How long?" Zam asked.

"Ten minutes if the traffic's moderate. It's not far."

"Good. We should make it before he closes for the day."

The journey was straightforward but slothful as vehicles crawled between traffic lights. They passed a huge Asda super-market and crossed the Avon into the Redcliffe district, then navigated a few smaller streets before finding the parade of shops where Harry Beech's business stood. The clock in the Captur's dash told them they were a few minutes late, and it looked like the barber's was already shut.

Zam cursed. "We might have to find his home address."

"Hold on. I saw movement through the blinds," Rasul commented. "I reckon he's still there."

"Good." Zam directed the driver to park in the lane behind the church. "There's a back door," Zam said. "I guess one of those cars belongs to him." He turned round in his seat. "Jump out, Rasul, and watch the front."

Rasul grinned. "Thanks. I get to stand in the pissing rain."

"You've just proved you have the best eyesight. Stand under a tree."

Heyat grabbed the door lever and let himself out. In moments he'd disappeared around the front of the building. Zam and Davari approached the back door but waited as a woman and two children hurried through the churchyard, keeping their heads down against the weather.

Satisfied that no one else was nearby, Zam knocked on the door. "Mr Beech?" he called out.

The door opened a few seconds later. The large Bristolian frowned at the two Iranians. "Can I help you?"

"I really hope so," Zam replied courteously in clear English. "Sorry to trouble you just as you're going home. Is Ismail here? I'm his cousin."

Beech eyed him with suspicion. "He didn't come to work today."

"I don't suppose you have any idea where he could be, do you? He's not at the flat."

Beech rested his arm against the edge of the door. "You're Ismail's cousin?"

The operative held his gaze and knew in that moment that the encounter would not end well for the big man. Wariness was etched all over his face. Somehow, in the short sentences of their conversation, Zam had made a mistake. He gave the Bristolian a second chance. "That's right. I'm Mohammed. I know they arrested Ismail last night. He hasn't answered the phone. My aunt is worried sick."

"The thing is, Mohammed," Beech said slowly, "Ismail told me he didn't have any family in England. So, even if I knew where he was, I wouldn't tell you."

Zam's face hardened. "A pity." He slammed a punch into the barber's stomach then shoved him back into the office, pinning Beech over the desk. Heyat followed him inside and kicked the door shut. The Bristolian wheezed but immediately pushed himself up. The man's determination to fight back impressed the MOIS spy, but the resistance was met with a jab to the throat.

Beech choked and clutched his throat, gasping for air as his eyes watered.

Zam hit him again. "Where the fuck is he?"

"Don't know," Beech coughed. "I told you."

The Iranian glanced around the tiny room and saw the barber's mobile phone next to a desk lamp. "Hold him, Samir."

The second operative grabbed the Bristolian's right arm and hammered a palm strike into the shoulder, dislocating the joint. Beech screamed and the disabled arm dropped to his side. Davari circled his victim and wrapped his arms around Beech's neck in a choke hold.

Zam picked up the phone and thumbed the on-switch. The message on the display told him to cover the fingerprint sensor. He grabbed Beech's right forefinger and pressed it against the scanner. Nothing happened. "The other hand?" Zam questioned. "You might as well tell me, or I'll break all your fingers until I find the right one."

Beech attempted to nod, conveying more with his eyes than through the physical movement. Zam took hold of his finger and tried again. The screen unlocked. Zam went to the messages first. There was nothing recent from Ismail Khadem, so Zam checked the call logs. He saw Beech had tried his employee's number several times during the day. He held the phone out. "He didn't answer?"

The barber shook his head.

"You were telling the truth," Zam commented. "I appreciate that." He fished his own mobile from his jacket and made a call. "I'm going to read out a phone number," he said when the call was answered. "Triangulate its position. Call me back as soon as you have the result." He read out the number listed under *Ismail Khadem* and then ended the call. Zam put his own phone away and wiped the other with a cloth before tossing it onto the desk. "Kill him," he said to Davari.

The agent increased the pressure around Harry Beech's neck, crushing his windpipe and shutting off the blood flow to his brain. The Englishman's eyes filled with blood and horror as the Iranian strangled him. Soon it was done, and Davari let the body slide to the floor.

Zam picked up Beech's keys, walked through to the shop and checked the front door. It was already locked. He returned to the office, ripped out the CCTV recorder and tucked it under his arm. He made eye contact with Davari. "Tell Rasul to meet us at the car."

Davari nodded and walked out the back door, reaching for his phone. Zam turned off the light switches, followed him out and secured the door once he'd identified the right key. Both men went to the car and waited a minute for the third member of the team to return. Moments later Davari put the SUV into gear and eased out of the lane. He glanced at Zam with a questioning look.

"Find a housing estate somewhere," Zam said. "A quiet road. We can do nothing more without the phone data."

"Understood."

Davari drove for a while, not worrying about the sat-nav, and soon found a road which went under a pair of railway bridges. They passed a large park on their right; on the left a terrace of three-storey houses stood on elevated ground. They continued a short way and then entered a grid of roads where the flat-roofed houses were painted in a range of pastel colours, giving the streets more character than the unimaginative architecture deserved. Davari found a gap in a line of cars and parallel-parked.

Zam's phone rang twenty minutes later, just as he was about to tell Davari to find another spot.

"The tech people have mapped the triangulation data," Control stated.

"About time," Zam said. "Give me something I can use."

"The phone was switched off over two hours ago. I'm afraid we have no idea where it is now."

Zam frowned. "Before that?"

"He was heading back into the city centre from the east side. The phone's identifier pinged to several masts. He was moving slowly, so he must've been on foot."

"Where did the signal drop out?"

"They couldn't give a precise location. Somewhere near a road called The Horsefair. There's a large shopping centre nearby."

"That doesn't help me," Zam retorted. "Give me a minute." He turned to Davari. "Put a road named The Horsefair into the sat-nav. Show me what's there." Davari did as he instructed. Zam studied the screen. "This is no good," he remarked into his mobile. "The three of us..." He paused. "Wait. The bus station."

Control spoke again. "What about it?"

"Jerboa is no longer in Bristol. That's how he got out." Zam took a few seconds to formulate a plan. "I need you to speak to your police contact. Tell him to send someone to the bus station to check the CCTV for matches to the custody photograph. He's probably still wearing the same clothes."

"That will take some time to organise," Control replied.

"Do you want me to deal with Bouzidi or not?" Zam snapped.

"Watch your tone, Murad. I will call you when it is done." The line went silent.

Zam gestured through the windscreen. "Let's move. This will take a while and I need something to eat."

10

I SET OUT FROM THE CENTRE OF LONDON at four-thirty in the
morning, behind the wheel of a three-year-old Vauxhall Astra
that looked like a standard model but wasn't. The grease monkeys
who maintained our surveillance vehicles had de-badged the car
and swapped the sports alloys for less conspicuous alternatives. Unsurprisingly, it had a grey paint job, although that made little
difference in the soft pre-dawn light.

I crossed the snaking River Thames at Chiswick Bridge and
again a mile later at Twickenham Bridge. The main road became
the M3 at Sunbury-on-Thames. I put my foot down, overtaking
scores of articulated lorries. I kept my speed to eighty-five, knowing it wasn't fast enough to draw the attention of traffic cops but
nevertheless allowed me to make progress.

The sun rose in my rear-view mirror as I headed southwest. I
didn't have much of a view – tree-lined embankments concealed
the suburbs from the motorway – but it felt good to be away from
the city. The scenery opened up a little as I left Surrey and entered
Hampshire. I'd decided beforehand against stopping at the motorway services, and I munched through a half-decent ham-and-egg
sandwich that I'd bought from a Tesco Express the previous night.

I left the M3 five miles after Basingstoke and joined the A303
as it headed west, following an ancient furrow toward Salisbury
Plain. The gently rolling landscape, now vivid in the summer light,
told me I had undoubtedly left claustrophobic London behind.

My speed on the single carriageway was now down to fifty-five;
traffic bound for the West Country had built up. But I saw Stone-
henge among ancient downs where the long grass was brittle and
wheat-coloured after weeks of hot weather. I lowered my side

window a few inches to enjoy the warm salubrious air; it was a revelation compared to London.

I was still among Wiltshire farmland when I found myself in a tailback. The smoothness of the journey thus far was instantly overturned, and I waited in the stationary line of traffic with exasperation. As time passed and progress could only be measured in feet and inches, I realised my breakfast-time meeting with Farzad Bouzidi was in jeopardy. I turned on the radio for a traffic report; some time later I learned that an accident had occurred a few miles ahead.

Reaching Glastonbury early had been my goal; I had intended to find a spot near the café and conduct counter-surveillance while Farzad drank his tea, just in case his paranoia contained a kernel of truth. As I mentally prepared to move to my contingency plan to meet him on the Tor, I noticed some vehicular movement ahead, even though the report said the road was shut in both directions while the police managed the scene. The Astra's radiator fan whirred, trying to cool the engine as I inched forward.

Eventually I discovered what was going on. Drivers further on in the queue were turning round and doubling back, looking for alternative routes. Those behind them were also edging toward those same country lanes. The three-point turns created delays of their own, but the improvisation was broadly effective. In a necessary abandonment of the rules of the road, drivers gave way and manoeuvred to allow their fellow citizens the chance to escape. It all felt very British.

It was unlikely now that I would recover the lost time, but when I reached a road on the left I took it, pausing only to allow a fellow driver turning right to proceed before me. It was a decent carriageway, and my sat-nav told me I was heading south on the A350 toward Shaftesbury. That was all well and good, but I needed to get back on the A303 on the other side of the accident.

I figured it out, but I had to abandon Plan A.

11

ZAM DROVE SLOWLY up the High Street in Glastonbury for the second time, locking features into his memory and confirming that the road was on one side of a square that surrounded the abbey grounds. At the top of the slope he turned right, then stopped seconds later in the entrance to Dod Lane, opposite an ancient stone archway that led to the ruins. A sign on the corner marked a walking route to the Tor.

Rasul Heyat got out of the Captur without a word, pushed the door shut and stepped onto the pavement in Dod Lane. Zam flicked on the indicator, checked over his shoulder and pulled away, continuing south along Chilwell Street.

"I'm convinced he's meeting someone," Zam muttered as he drove.

Samir Davari gave him an inquiring glance from the passenger seat.

Zam pursed his lips and lifted a hand off the wheel in a brief demonstrative gesture. "It's Glastonbury," he said. "Why else would Jerboa come here? To buy some crystals from one of those New Age shops?"

Davari shrugged. "He was in a hurry. Probably didn't have a lot of money. It's easy to get here from Bristol, and less obvious than jumping on a train."

"You're proving my point," Zam replied as he turned right at the mini-roundabout for Bere Lane. "Someone gave him directions. Think about it. Landmarks that even a blind man could find. Remote but reachable. A discreet town that everyone's heard of. It's a clever and subtle choice."

"Assuming the bus driver remembered correctly," Davari commented.

"Why wouldn't he? Jerboa might not stand out in Bristol, but in rural Somerset? No one comes here on the bus who isn't white British."

Davari nodded in agreement. Zam's point was a generalisation but likely to be true. "That raises an interesting question. If the scientist has a contact, what's he been saying? He must've offered information."

"Agreed, but that's not our concern. We'll search for a few hours as instructed. If we don't find him, we'll go back to Swindon and let Control worry about it."

"Do you reckon he's still here? He might've been picked up during the night."

"I have no idea," Zam replied with a dismissive shrug. "We've wasted enough time already." He turned right again and headed north, ignoring the road to the Travelodge where they'd managed a few brief hours' sleep. He slowed for the car park entrance next to the information centre, found a space in the shadow of the abbey's boundary wall, and reversed into it.

"What do you want me to do?" Davari asked.

Zam killed the engine. "Check the High Street and those side roads near the bend. I'll do Magdalene Street and the abbey grounds. There's no point looking anywhere else."

"I'll call you if I find him. If he's here, he should stand out."

"Don't spook him. The town centre is already busy. We'll need to surveil and develop a box," Zam replied. "And keep your eyes open for counter-surveillance. We might not be the only assets in town."

Davari grinned, patted the pistol hidden beneath his jacket, and headed for the High Street.

12

Somerset's gentle farmland and quaint hamlets were pleasing to the eye as I followed an improvised route away from the main road, but the scenery failed to distract me from a singular pressing thought: I'd missed the scheduled time for the rendezvous with Farzad Bouzidi. I now had to use my backup plan and meet the Iranian on Glastonbury Tor. The delay on the A303 had annoyed me, but I felt confident in the simplicity of the contingency scenario. All I had to do was walk him down the hill to the car and fly back to London.

The only obstacle was the shortage of parking on the south side of the famous landmark. My research the previous night had told me there was a small car park near an attraction called the Chalice Well and Gardens, but it accommodated fewer than a dozen vehicles and was likely to be full when I arrived. The country lanes were also out of the question; they were barely wide enough for bicycles. But there was a large middle-class housing estate within walking distance, so I decided to leave the Astra there.

Approaching Glastonbury from the south, I eventually reached the estate, soon discovering that the plots were set out in sinuous patterns rather than the straight rows I was used to in London. I estimated there were roughly two hundred detached houses and a handful of bungalows, probably built in the 1970s judging by their plain red-brick construction, and the uneven layout matched the contours of the ground upon which they stood. There were as many cul-de-sacs as cut-throughs, and I had to turn around a couple of times as I tried to find a spot that would shorten my walk.

I ended up going in what I thought was the wrong direction,

but the mistake turned out to be fortuitous when I saw a small layby on the corner of Chalice Way and Bretenoux Road, backing onto a field. I reversed and parked the car next to some trees, ensuring I didn't block access to the farm gate. A quick check on my phone's mapping software told me I was about a quarter of a mile from the main road. Not ideal, but if I walked along Chalice Way a short distance and then took the footpath into Cinnamon Lane, I'd emerge a stone's throw from the base of the Tor.

The morning was warming up gradually, portending a comfortably hot day, but my phone had indicated the possibility of summer showers. I wasn't planning on a long visit, but I kept my grey lightweight jacket on as I began my walk. It took me five minutes to reach the road which led into the town. Even though the Tor was nearby, I couldn't actually see it behind the trees and cottages which lined the road. I crossed over and found the start of the footpath in Wellhouse Lane.

The route followed a series of steps through a short corridor of trees. Within moments I'd passed the private gardens and arrived at the foot of the hill. I was disappointed to discover that the concrete steps continued all the way up the tussocky slope, but I could understand why they'd been installed at such a popular landmark. The ascent continued over rough grassland that was still quite lush, despite the season.

I'd climbed much more challenging hills than Glastonbury Tor. It was, I recalled, little more than one hundred and fifty metres above sea level at the summit. The light exercise was welcome, especially after sitting in the car for several hours. I paused about a third of the way up to allow myself a look at the view. Turning around, I saw a glorious eiderdown of fields to the south and west, isolated patches of woodland and remote villages.

The manmade path continued toward the church tower; a concrete scar along the ridge of the hill. Unsurprisingly, I didn't have the place to myself. Most of the people I encountered were coming down the slope. Almost everybody wished me good morning, which I reciprocated each time. Glastonbury certainly wasn't like London. The breeze picked up as I neared the summit, circulating the pleasant scent of the grass and making me glad I'd worn my coat.

There were dozens of tourists and walkers standing around the fourteenth-century tower, but Farzad Bouzidi was not among them. I wasn't concerned because, although I was late for Plan A, I was in ample time for Plan B. I didn't know how long it would take the Iranian to come up to the Tor from the town. I walked around the landmark twice, trying to stay out of the way of photographers as I studied the view. In different circumstances I might have wanted to linger there, for it really was a fine three-hundred-and-sixty-degree vista in the morning light.

Having told Farzad to head to the Tor from the High Street, I knew he'd end up approaching the hill from the north side. There were several routes open to him, but they all converged on Stone Down Lane where the gate for the Tor path stood. The track crossed a wildflower meadow and then wiggled back and forth across the bulbous end of the hill as it ascended. It then curled around and met the church tower on the south side, close to where the route I'd taken touched the summit.

Despite the snaking nature of the other path, the obvious place to observe people climbing the hill was from the north slope. I stepped away from the tower and descended about thirty metres down the far side, giving myself an unhindered view of the lower stretch of track coming up from the meadow – the perfect observation point. I still couldn't see the man I had come to meet. There was nothing I could do but wait, so I sat down on the dry grass and watched.

13

With a view of Glastonbury Tor over the hedgerows to his right, Rasul Heyat followed the incline of Wellhouse Lane as it rose gently through the rural landscape on the northern side of the landmark. The route from the town had been simple to follow, but the network of tiny country lanes told him the way he'd come was not the only approach to the famous hill. He paused where the narrow road met Stone Down Lane, waited for some fellow walkers to overtake him, and then retrieved his phone. A quick check of the map locked in his bearings. Instead of progressing to the Tor, he stepped off the road and sat on a bench, weighing up his options.

Heyat shared his team leader's opinion about the wild goose chase they'd been sent on. The Department 312 cell had far more pressing matters to attend to than running around the English countryside after an errant Iranian scientist. Murad Zam had deciphered a handful of clues in Bristol – he was a proficient manhunter when the situation called for it – but, with no more information in Glastonbury, the likelihood of finding Bouzidi was thin.

He looked over the hedgerow at the church tower on the top of the hill, wondering if the target had already trekked up there or had gone somewhere else entirely. The Tor was a good choice for a rendezvous because it was fairly difficult to approach without being seen. But if you needed to meet someone in Glastonbury and thought you might be followed, would you not avoid the obvious landmark? Heyat frowned. No, the scientist was pressed for time when he fled Bristol, and he probably didn't know Glastonbury that well. The plan had to be kept simple.

Heyat distracted himself for a moment, watching bees and

hoverflies as they collected pollen from the colourful wildflowers on the verge. He trusted Zam to end the operation before it dragged on too long; the commander loathed working without a strategy and he'd waste no more time than absolutely necessary. For all they knew, Farzad Bouzidi had climbed Glastonbury Tor at the crack of dawn and escaped hours ago. Even worse, the bus ride to the Somerset town might have been a ploy; he could have crossed the road and caught the next one back to Bristol the previous night.

The Iranian decided he'd give it twenty minutes on the bench and then climb the Tor. The wooden seat was set back on a grassy verge where the two lanes met. A hedgerow blocked the view back down Wellhouse Lane, but that worked to his advantage because it also obscured him. He leaned against the wooden backrest, listening to the birds chirping and whistling as they darted between the trees and shrubs. On the other side of the track, in a meadow behind a five-bar gate, sheep grazed under the heedful gaze of the church tower.

The lane he'd followed remained sporadically busy with walkers, usually hiking in pairs or small groups. Thankfully no one joined him on the bench, although he feared one red-faced elderly man might do just that until his wife spurred him on, announcing that they only had another two hundred yards to go. Pedestrians also approached the junction from behind Heyat along Stone Down Lane, but he could usually hear them from some distance away; a quick turn of the head was all he needed to establish if they were persons of interest. They weren't.

Heyat was about to get up when he heard more voices – children and adults. He waited as a family of five approached. He allowed himself a brief smile as he noticed how the kids seemed determined to out-pace their parents. The adults glanced his way and wished him good morning.

Heyat nodded. "Nice day for it."

The father glanced up at the Tor then back at the Iranian.

"Nicer on the way down."

Heyat chuckled. "You'll enjoy the view."

"Hope so. Have a good day."

"You too."

The children and their parents continued their hike. Heyat hoped they'd forget his face because the next person he saw, trailing the English family by thirty metres, was Farzad Bouzidi. Heyat pulled the zipper on his jacket halfway down, partly exposing the shoulder holster and its Glock. Bouzidi didn't notice him until the last moment, distracted by the effort of the ascent, and he froze to the spot as Heyat stood up and revealed the gun.

"Salam, Farzad."

"You've mistaken me for someone else," Bouzidi stammered, foolishly answering in Persian.

"I don't think so. Your reaction tells me otherwise. Oh, and I've seen your CCTV photo from the bus station. You're still in the same clothes."

Bouzidi backed away, snapping his head around in search of witnesses. The lane was empty.

Heyat pulled out the silenced gun. "Take another step and I'll put you down like a rabid dog."

"Let me go," Bouzidi said, struggling to talk.

The gunman made a gesture, indicating toward Stone Down Lane. "There. Keep walking."

"You'll kill me!"

"You're mistaken, Farzad. We just need to talk. Now move before my patience runs out."

Bouzidi obeyed, stepped past the bench and rounded the corner into the lane. Heyat walked next to him, concealing the weapon under the material of his jacket but keeping it aimed at his captive's side. The narrow road was almost straight, giving the operative a clear view for roughly one hundred and fifty metres, but they didn't walk that far.

Heyat spotted a farm gate and shoved Bouzidi toward it.

"Climb over. Go behind the hedge."

Bouzidi clambered awkwardly over the gate into the field, his palms sweating against the rough metal bars. Obeying the signal made by the man with the handgun, he stepped to the right behind the cover of the hedgerow. The leafy canopy of an oak shaded the lane.

The operator followed him. "Stand there," he said, pointing the gun again.

Bouzidi's face was ashen. "What do you want?"

"I want to know who you've been talking to, Farzad," Heyat replied.

"No one," Bouzidi insisted. "I've spoken to no one."

"That's not true. You're meeting someone."

Bouzidi shook his head but didn't speak.

"You're a traitor," Heyat stated.

"No. I left Iran because I was afraid of the regime. I haven't spoken to anyone, I promise. I found a job and kept quiet."

"Liar," Heyat said. He shot Bouzidi in the stomach, the gun's suppressor dulling the noise.

Bouzidi's legs gave way instantly. He collapsed next to the hedge, helplessly clasping the catastrophic wound as blood soaked his clothing.

"Who's your contact?" Heyat said.

The dying man looked up and stared with incomprehension, gasping for air.

Heyat shrugged. "I'll find out. This is what we do to traitors." He shot his victim again, twice in the chest and once through the forehead.

Bouzidi's body slumped over, his face falling onto the rose prickles in the hedge.

Heyat made a quick check of the lane to ensure he was still alone, secured his weapon and crouched down. He searched the scientist's pockets, doing his best to avoid the blood, finding only a set of keys and a leather wallet with cash but no cards or identity documents. He pocketed the wallet; not for the money but because he had no desire to leave fingerprints anywhere. He stuffed the keys into his jacket as well.

Heyat was about to stand and walk away but reminded himself that Farzad Bouzidi had betrayed his homeland. Death was not punishment enough. He slid a flick knife from his back pocket, opened the blade and sliced open Bouzidi's throat. Cleaning the blade on the dead man's trousers, he peered into the lane once more, noticing two walkers about a hundred metres away. Heyat scrambled over the fence and sprinted the short distance back to the bench, then turned left and jogged up the lane toward the start of the Tor path.

He halted, realising that following the track up the hill was exactly what any surveillant would want him to do. Jerboa had come here for a rendezvous – of that Heyat now had no doubt. It would have been time-critical too, so whoever was waiting for the Iranian was likely to be on the hill at that moment, but he wouldn't stay for long if Bouzidi failed to appear. Heyat needed to get up there but could not reveal himself. The concrete path was out of the question. Heyat moved away from the stile, walking further along the lane next to leafy hawthorn trees.

Remembering the terrain from the map on his phone, Heyat recalled there was another small junction around a bend just a hundred metres away; the adjoining lane headed directly south, near the eastern side of the landmark. There was an orchard or copse that sat between the road and the foot of the hill; it was his best chance of approaching his quarry while shielded from view.

Heyat ran. He reached the turning within seconds, veered right and carried on down the lane. The hedgerow on his right seemed impenetrable; he wondered if he'd actually be able to find a way onto the Tor. His concerns were allayed when he reached the orchard, for there was a break in the hedge with a wooden gate. He climbed over it and ran between the apple trees, soon reaching the far side. Mature trees, set out in a curve along the base of the

Tor, provided another barrier from observers. Heyat stayed behind them for a while and then decided he had no choice but to break cover.

He stepped out from the treeline and started making his way up the grassy terraces, realising he'd probably chosen the steepest side of Glastonbury Tor for his exertions.

14

M Y AVERSION to staying in one place for too long was lessened
because I was at a popular landmark, but the amount of time
it was taking Farzad to reach Glastonbury Tor nevertheless per-
turbed me. Tourists lingered near the church tower or sat upon the
grassy terraces, enjoying the glorious morning views across the
Somerset countryside. A few unwashed nutters with beads in their
hair appeared to be attuning themselves to ley lines or communing
with King Arthur's ghost, but they seemed harmless enough.

And yet that inexplicable doubt crept in, manifesting itself as
tension at the top of my neck, just beneath my occipital bone. I
wondered if I'd mocked the Glastonbury spiritualists unfairly
when my own instinct seemed less than scientific. There's a curious
irony that surveillance operators are trained to react not just to
visible threats but visceral ones as well. If it feels wrong, it probably
is. I'd learned to ignore that gut reaction at my peril.

The wail of a police siren cruelly shattered the solitude, re-
inforcing my uncertainty as it rose in volume. Almost a minute
passed before I caught sight of the patrol car. Even then I only
snatched glimpses as it made progress along a tree-lined lane north
of the Tor, the driver wary on the narrow bends to avoid bouncing
walkers off the grille. I repositioned on the hillside for a better look
to no avail; I couldn't see much beyond the hedgerows. But I
didn't need to; the ululating shriek from the police car told me all
I needed to know about Farzad Bouzidi's demise.

Annoyance flared inside me. If my Iranian asset had been
killed, my plan to acquire valuable information was just as stone-
cold dead, and I'd have to find some way of dealing with his irk-
some sister and her bad attitude. But that was a problem for

another time; my immediate task was to return to London to report my failed attempt to secure the file I'd been promised.

I consoled myself with one thought: Farzad hadn't been paranoid. My trip to the West Country hadn't been entirely wasted. I now knew that MOIS agents – for it could be no one else – had pursued the scientist. My superiors would be keen to learn about the Iranians' murderous incursion into the quiet English town. I concluded they must have had resources in Bristol as well. With luck I'd be tasked to do something about them; I needed to get my hands dirty again.

The siren died but rang in my ears for a moment longer. I couldn't see where the police car had stopped. There was no point in staying where I was, so I walked the short way back up the slope to the tower. I circled the building, taking a last look at the footpath from Stone Down Lane as it rose from the meadow to the north and snaked around the east and south sides of the hill.

And that's when I realised my mistake.

I'd kept my eye on the lower section of the path the whole time, assuming that anyone ascending the Tor would pass the stile and take the obvious route. But I'd missed the Persian man who was now halfway up the steep section, approaching the upper stretch of the track from the grassy hillside. And, I realised, he'd seen me first. He could hardly have missed me, standing as I was like a beacon in the morning sunlight. We locked eyes in a moment of recognition. I saw him instinctively reach toward his jacket, but he didn't withdraw the weapon which, almost certainly, had taken Farzad Bouzidi's life.

Had I been armed, there would've been a decent chance I could kill him from the high ground, but I'd seen no reason to sign out a weapon before driving to the West Country for a simple asset grab. Nor was I reassigned to field operations where such measures would be automatic. Rasul Heyat gave me a quick smile and continued his climb, nearing the path. He'd expended some effort and moved slowly, but I was wise enough not to underestimate this man. I only had one option.

Run.

I turned around and sprinted along the ridge I'd taken earlier, pounding my way down the concrete path past bemused tourists, detouring onto the grass occasionally when the way was blocked. Begrudgingly, I recognised what Heyat had done. He'd rightly calculated that Farzad Bouzidi had come to the Tor to meet someone. He'd decided to find out whom, and carefully approached the landmark from a place of concealment. I'd watched every person on the lower section of the path; Heyat had not been among them.

There was no chance the Iranian killer would reach me now; I had a decent head start and his legs would be more tired than mine after climbing the steep hill. But that wasn't the problem – he wouldn't be working alone. Department 312 cells comprised at least six members. Rasul Heyat didn't need to chase me up and down Glastonbury Tor; he just needed to call the others and arrange an ambush.

I had to hope that I had the time advantage. The Astra wasn't far away. I barrelled down the slope, doing my utmost not to twist an ankle, knowing Heyat would shoot me if he caught up. The sensation I'd felt at the base of my skull dropped several inches to the middle of my back and expanded to the size of a target. The motion and distance would make me hard to hit for even the most expert shooter, but I didn't want to put that theory to the test. I left the track again, using the terrain as a shield.

I spotted the gap in the trees near the foot of the hill and kept running.

15

Rasul heyat grabbed his mobile phone the moment the spy took off along the ridge. He found Murad Zam's number and dialled. The MOIS cell leader answered as Heyat completed his ascent and walked through the shadow of the church tower on Glastonbury Tor's summit.

"Yes?" Zam answered.

"Are you with Samir?" Heyat asked.

"We're in the car. Time to abort. Where are you?"

"Hold on. Jerboa was here to meet someone. Move to intercept on the south side of the hill."

"I'll tell Samir," Zam replied. Heyat heard him give instructions to the driver. "You're on speaker, Rasul," Zam continued. "We're heading that way now. Talk to me."

"I found the traitor," Heyat explained. "He's no longer a problem." He paused. "You were right, Murad. They arranged a rendezvous. I saw his contact on the Tor but could not reach him in time."

"Description?"

"You won't need one. It was the man who came after us in France."

Zam took a deep breath before speaking again. "You're certain?"

"I am."

"Good work. That would appear to validate our belief about Jerboa's treachery."

Heyat shrugged as he spoke. "Perhaps, although I searched the body and found only a wallet and keys. I think he panicked in Bristol and fled. He never made it to his meeting. I eliminated the problem."

"Let's not draw conclusions," Zam advised. "We know something of our adversary." He paused for a few seconds. "We're in Chilkwell Street now. Are we in time?"

"Hard to say," Heyat replied. "He was running flat out. You might have missed him."

"He can't be far. Make your way down and we'll pick you up later. You'd better tell me what he was wearing. We'll search the area."

"Fine," Heyat replied, and proceeded to describe the clothes of the man who'd killed Murad Zam's brother in Paris.

16

I DIDN'T KNOW what vehicles the Iranians were driving, so I didn't bother looking too hard as I hit the bottom of the footpath opposite the Chalice Well's boundary wall. I turned left out of Wellhouse Lane, crossed via a gap in the slow-moving traffic on the main street, and jogged the forty metres to the junction with Cinnamon Lane. Nothing followed me into the narrow road. If I suddenly heard a car speeding after me, I pondered, I could veer into the meadows on my left and run across country while my pursuers were forced to check the map.

I slowed to a walk as I headed south along the sheltered lane, giving myself a chance to lower my heart rate and settle my breathing, just in case I had to run again. My exertions had not taxed me thus far, and I had plenty more in the tank, but I had to deliberate strategically about the situation I'd found myself in. I could run for ten kilometres and more at a decent pace if I needed to – I'd done so in much warmer climes than southwest England – but I'd eventually dehydrate without water, and that would screw up my ability to think clearly.

Not that I was planning to flee across the English countryside, however charming it might be. I continued along the lane beneath the shelter of overhanging branches, knowing I would soon be back at the little cut-through to the housing estate. A conversation filtered through the hedge from one of the nearby gardens, but the voices spoke in West Country English, giving me no cause for concern. Once back at the car, I'd have to figure out a quick route home from Glastonbury, but I reckoned I'd be London bound on the A303 within half an hour.

Three minutes later I was almost at the bend on Cinnamon

Lane where it kissed Chalice Way, and I reached the shaded gap moments after a black SUV crawled down the road toward the spot where I'd left the Astra. I couldn't see the occupants because of the sunlight reflecting on the windows, but I stopped myself from zig-zagging through the metal barriers. I peered between leafy slender trees across someone's front lawn, watching the vehicle as it travelled the short distance to my parking place.

Willing the car to take the right-hand bend into Bretenoux Road, I was disgruntled – to put it mildly – when it stopped next to the Vauxhall. Someone got out of the passenger side and walked up to my car. I was fewer than a hundred metres from my means of escape; that avenue was now blocked to me. The distance was such that I couldn't make out a face, but it was a male with black hair and a solid build. I didn't need to get a better view to know he was an Iranian operator.

The Astra was not, of course, registered in my name, although when my adversary checked the numberplate he'd find it linked to a small London-based consultancy firm that had a glossy website but didn't actually exist. The cover would fool most people but not a determined intelligence asset. The clues would be deciphered, even if they led nowhere. The location of the car, the dead-end website, the proximity to Glastonbury Tor. I could try to wait it out, but there wouldn't be much point, and there was the distinct possibility that Rasul Heyat was behind me somewhere on Cinnamon Lane. Even if I could evade capture, they'd disable the car. I had to move.

One thing was certain: I couldn't stay in Glastonbury. Putting distance between me and the Iranian team was the priority. I needed to resolve my predicament one step at a time. If I could find cover I could call for an extraction team and nominate a secure rendezvous point. A sudden thought struck me: had Rasul Heyat found Farzad Bouzidi's mobile phone? I'd instructed him to ditch it, but what if he'd kept hold of it instead? A terrified man might hesitate to give up his only means of communication. If the

Iranians examined the call log, there would be a bloody good chance my number would appear at the top. And if they had my number, they could track it.

I grabbed my phone and held down the power button. I really needed to remove the SIM card as well, but I didn't have time for that, and my mobile was one of those awkward beasts without a removable cover. I had one of those little wire keys for unlocking the SIM holder in my wallet – it was a handy covert tool for implanting data grabbers in the second slot on targets' phones – but fiddling with it while on the run would be impossible. The phone shut down and I stuffed it into a zipped pocket. The finer technical details could wait. I ran.

Cinnamon Lane took a sharp turn to the left, leading roughly eastward and providing a decent hedgerow barrier between me and the housing estate. I had no other option, so I rounded the corner and passed a playing field on my left and a large cottage on my right. I encountered a handful of expensive-looking properties as I jogged, but most of the lane bordered fields and pastures; soon I was out in the middle of nowhere. My only companions were sheep and birds.

I'd resolved one problem by putting some ground between me and the Iranians, but I couldn't run through rural England forever. I remembered there was a town called Street just a short distance from Glastonbury; if I could make it there, I should be able to lose myself in a pub until help arrived. That presupposed I could contact my colleagues without compromising my location. I could rob someone's phone, but that wouldn't be conducive to my strategy of concealment.

But communication with the outside world wasn't the immediate difficulty. Street was about a mile southwest of Glastonbury, and yet I was headed southeast, adding to the distance from the town with every stride. I briefly considered trying to find another location, but my mental map of Somerset wasn't detailed enough to include remote hamlets and small towns further afield, nor was I prepared to wander without a proper bearing to follow. It had to be Street.

I reached a turning for a side road that was even narrower than the lane I'd just run down. I could see the church tower on Glastonbury Tor in the distance; its position confirmed that the lane I'd found headed due south. It was a start, and I guessed I'd soon find more roads or footpaths that would take me west to the next town. Before I continued, I dug out the wire key from my wallet and removed the SIM card from my phone. If the enemy agents wanted to find me, they'd have to do it the old-fashioned way. I set off once again.

I noticed a twelve-foot-wide drainage channel running alongside the lane, but didn't figure out its significance until I reached a ninety-degree bend in the road a quarter of a mile later. The ditch spilled into a slow-moving canal. My heart sank as I examined the topography. The lane had turned abruptly eastward because of the waterway; my route south was completely blocked and I saw no sign of a bridge. I resolved to cross the drainage ditch and then follow the course of the river to the west.

The ditch was too wide for me to jump over. I thought about removing my hiking shoes but dismissed the idea. The water was silty and I had no way to know if scrap metal had been discarded there. I brushed my way through grasses and wildflowers to the water's edge. With care I stepped into the murky stream, trying to work out its depth. I squelched into the mud as the water soaked my trousers past the knees. I waded across, reached the far bank and dragged myself up the other side. My shoes were soaked and ruined, but the sun was getting hotter. I reckoned they might get partly dry by the time I reached Street.

The canal was now on my left, providing a decent route to follow. I walked next to a riverbank that was flushed with spikes of purple-loosestrife and bulrush, trying to ignore the discomfort that my feet endured in the wet footwear. Insects buzzed around me and a kestrel hovered over the wheat field on my right, searching for prey.

I turned my thoughts back to the Iranians as I hiked alongside the river. Farzad's belief that they'd been alerted to his arrest seemed undeniable now. It wasn't difficult for any competent spy to hack into the computers used by the British police – unbelievably, their principal database still ran on DOS architecture – but an insider wouldn't even need to go to that trouble. Everyone from Pakistan's Intelligence Bureau to China's Ministry of State Security had infiltrated the UK's police forces. It wasn't hard, given their amateur vetting and recruitment methods.

Farzad's death was an irritation but not a surprise. I'd given him advice on how to keep a low profile, but he wasn't a trained operator, and the arrest would have spooked him. He was now dead and there was nothing I could do about that. The mechanics of how he'd been hunted down were a side issue. I was more concerned with the fact that a Ministry of Intelligence and Security hit squad was operating in the UK. I very much doubted they'd been looking for my asset beforehand. And I knew exactly what kind of monster Rasul Heyat was. Whatever the Department 312 operators were up to, it was a lot more serious than killing a former scientist.

17

ZAM DIDN'T BOTHER with even the merest of courtesies when Control answered his call. "I need a vehicle registration number checked at once. Are you ready to write it down?"

"Hold on," the man replied, the tone of the two words enough to express his irritation at Zam's unhidden contempt for MOIS hierarchy. "Go on."

Zam recited the details. "You have that?"

"Someone is looking it up now," Control replied, then paused. "Perhaps you'd deign to give me an update on the Glastonbury situation?"

"Rasul found Jerboa near the Tor and eliminated him."

"You got lucky."

"No, I considered various options and planned accordingly," Zam said, deliberately disagreeing even though Control's words weren't exactly wrong. He paced along the pavement and looked down Bretenoux Road as he spoke, glancing at the Astra forty yards away in the parking spot on the corner. "There's more. Jerboa had arranged to meet someone."

"He confessed that to Rasul?" Control asked.

"No, but his intention was obvious. Rasul scouted the area and spotted the contact on the hill."

"How could he be sure?"

"He recognised him. It was the operator who hunted us in Paris."

Control sucked in a breath through his teeth. "Interesting. We lost track of him after he was hospitalised."

Zam shrugged. "You didn't know where Farzad Bouzidi went either, and he was just a scientist."

"Did Rasul engage?"

"No, he was too far away. He was seen, though, and the man fled. We've been looking for him since then."

"The relevance of the numberplate?"

"The vehicle stood out. The result?"

"Hang on." Control's voice went quiet and muffled as he consulted with someone. Moments later he spoke again to Zam. "London-based company, questionable provenance. You could be right."

"I usually am." The Iranian paused. "He was on the run, but we found the car before he made it back there. He has to be close by."

"A backup vehicle?"

"Doubtful."

"But a possibility, nonetheless?"

"Of course," Zam conceded.

"If he spotted Rasul he'll have adapted. You're unlikely to find him now."

"There aren't many places he could go. I've damaged the tyre valves so he can't drive away, and I have the car in view as we speak."

"By the sound of it, he probably saw you standing there."

"I agree, but that's not a problem. He already knew about Rasul."

Control hesitated. "I don't follow."

"Put yourself in his position. His rendezvous went wrong and Rasul was on his heels. He can't use the car, and he'll rightly assume we're searching the local streets and tourist attractions. We know who he is, so he can't stay visible."

"Are you expecting me to decipher your thoughts, Murad, or will you just tell me what you mean?"

The unspoken admission of incomprehension made Zam smile. "His focus will be on putting distance between himself and us. He'll move away from the town and try to take cover in the countryside. He can't do that indefinitely though, so he'll have to surface before long."

A wordless exclamation told Zam what his superior thought of his tactical assessment. "Sounds like guesswork. You have no idea. Accept that you've lost him."

"Look at a map," Zam persisted. "We're on the south side of the town and have effectively blocked his egress. He can only go in one direction."

"Speculation," Control retorted. "It doesn't matter. You've dealt with Jerboa. Accept my praise for a successful operation. Go back to Swindon."

"Not yet."

"Perhaps you misheard me, Murad. I didn't present that as an option; it was an order."

"You don't have the authority to give me orders. He killed my brother. I have the right to go after him."

"No, you don't. Your duty is to obey commands and complete the task we brought you to England for. I regret what happened to Ahmad in Paris, but that is irrelevant. He died in service of the agency and now rests as an Unknown Soldier of Imam Zaman. I will not allow a vengeance mission which could put our primary goal in jeopardy."

Zam felt his anger rise, but instead of responding with a stinging retort, he took a breath and considered how he might object diplomatically. Even though he disliked the haughtiness of the unidentified voice on the telephone, he would obey orders if so pressed.

"With respect, I believe there is a tactical benefit in finding this man," Zam said quietly. "This is not just about revenge."

"Explain," Control replied.

"You rightly directed me to find Jerboa," Zam said, smoothly reminding Control who had sent him to locate Bouzidi. "That problem has been dealt with, but another has replaced it. The enemy now knows about our presence in England. We still have a chance to contain this before he makes contact. If we let him escape, our mission could be thwarted."

Control sighed. "You told me everything was in place."

"It is, but if the British authorities received intelligence about an active MOIS cell, they would work out our purpose and alter their plans. The months of preparation would be worthless."

"You make a reasonable case."

"That's not all," Zam continued, hoping to emphasise his point. "It is precisely because we are ready that we can afford a day or two to hunt the spy. And I don't need to tell you what a coup it would be to capture and interrogate him."

Control chuckled. "I thought you wanted him dead."

"I'd still kill him," Zam responded, "but only once I'd bled him dry for information."

"The clock is ticking, Murad. We cannot allow this to drag out."

Zam detected that he'd convinced his anonymous contact. "Of course. I'm acutely aware of the timescale. If I fail, I'll abort and head back to Swindon for final preparations. You have my word."

"You can do this with Samir and Rasul?"

The cell leader thought for a moment. "I'll need Orodes. That will give me a second car. We can operate as a pair of two-man teams."

"I damn well hope you have a plan in mind. The longer this takes, the greater the risk of exposure."

The agent gritted his teeth. It was exactly the point he'd raised. "Then let me get on with my job. Do I have your agreement?"

The line went silent for several seconds. "Don't let me down, Murad."

Zam ended the call without offering a reply.

18

My HIKE ALONG the wildflower-bedecked riverbank brought me to a flat road bridge. I stood in the lee of the stone ramparts and considered my options. The geography was easy to decipher. The road ran in a north-south orientation, and I was certain that I'd find a way into Street if I headed south. But it was a fast road through open countryside with few hedgerows for cover. If I went that way I'd be easy to spot. I had two alternatives. I could continue to follow the river along the bank I had travelled thus far, or I could try the opposite side. I dismissed the first option immediately because I had no way of knowing if I could cross the waterway when I needed to. The second option was better, but it meant a continued trespass on open ground with the possibility of needing to traverse more drainage ditches. In the end I decided to risk the road.

I made my way onto the carriageway and started to jog, occasionally stepping onto the verge as traffic sped toward me. My trousers were almost dry but the same could not be said for my shoes. I pushed the thought from my mind as I ran, concentrating on my next goal. Hedgerows and trees obscured my view, but I was fairly sure that Glastonbury's neighbour couldn't be too far away. For a moment I felt rather forlorn at having to turn my back on the Tor; the landmark seemed more impressive from a distance as it loomed over the flat countryside.

I noticed dryness in my mouth as I ran, and the sun was now hot on my back. The rumoured clouds had failed to arrive. Not wishing to discard my jacket, I tugged it almost completely open, keeping just an inch or two of the zip done up to prevent the garment flapping. I recalled that I'd only sipped through about half a small bottle of water on the drive down from London. The early signs of a dehydration headache throbbed behind my forehead.

I perked up a bit when, after about a third of a mile, I encountered a crossroads. I turned right and actually increased my speed a little as the road cut through fields and rough pasture. I was still exposed though, and hoped I wouldn't have to fling myself into a ditch to avoid capture. This route would, I was now convinced, take me to Street. I couldn't be at all sure where the road would connect with the town, but connect it would, and I'd be able to purchase some water and food. I considered abandoning the road and trekking across the fields, but I soon saw another stream which put me off the idea. The landscape featured many channels and rivulets, and I wasn't yet ready to wade through another one.

The lane remained straight for two-thirds of a mile, and I finally saw a collection of modern houses as I looked across meadows of sorrel and ragwort. I slowed to a walk when I reached a left-hand bend and took a few moments to fill my lungs. The lane snaked around a small housing estate and brought me to a roundabout opposite a church. A large car park for a college campus was on my left, and I could see the main building itself a little further away. The town was, of course, unfamiliar to me, but I guessed I was at its north end. I followed the road between the churchyard and the campus grounds, reckoning I'd find the town centre shortly.

I reached another roundabout and spotted a row of small shops occupying former houses constructed from local stone. Thankfully the first was a convenience store. It had a cash machine in the wall, so I withdrew two hundred and fifty pounds, knowing the amount – plus what I already had in my wallet – would cover taxi fares and train tickets should I need to purchase them. The risk of using the debit card was minimal if I refrained from doing so again. I stuffed the cash into my wallet.

While many of the buildings I'd seen so far in Street were in keeping with the historical architecture, I could not say the same for the hotel across the road from the grocery store. It was built to resemble an American motel, and a wing of plain rooms on concrete stilts overlooked a car park. It was cruel upon the eye but its simple utility appealed to me; I reckoned it might be a reasonable place in which to conceal myself to arrange an extraction with my colleagues in London. But first I needed some water, so I stepped into the tiny convenience store and looked around, giving my eyes a few seconds to adjust to the relative dimness of the interior.

One of the double doors opened as someone followed me inside. The elderly lady with her shopping bag wasn't a threat, but I instinctively turned as I heard the swooshing noise and glanced outside through the pane of glass in the door. A black SUV crawled slowly past the shop and turned left into the hotel's parking area. I couldn't be certain it was the same one that I'd seen parked next to my car in Glastonbury, but the coincidence rattled me. I stepped further into the shop, giving myself a moment to process what I'd just witnessed.

It made sense that the Iranians would figure out I would make my way to Street; they had cut off my intended escape route and effectively forced me to flee across country. Tracking a man is always easier when he is left with few options; his behaviour becomes predictable. It's possible to break the pattern, and I had been rigorously trained to do just that, but the basics of food, water and shelter must come first. Hotels, transport depots, shops and pubs are obvious places to check. It was a small blessing they hadn't started with the convenience store, but I probably had minutes to spare.

Tired as I was, I needed no time to make my next decision. I had to keep moving. I grabbed a plastic shopping basket and hurried round the shop, grabbing a few packets of biscuits, dried fruit, energy bars, a cheese-and-ham sandwich, and four two-litre bottles of water. There was no one ahead of me at the till. The assistant took longer than I would have liked to scan my items, but

I used the seconds to take another look through the window. She placed my purchases into a couple of carrier bags. I handed over some money.

"Is there anywhere around here where I could buy a new fleece?" I inquired. "I'm camping and I stupidly forgot to bring mine."

The shop assistant gave me a sympathetic smile. "There's the Clarks Village outlet just off the High Street," she annunciated in a Somerset accent, taking considerably longer to deliver the vowels than was entirely necessary. "Several outdoor shops down there."

It was a stroke of good news, although her sluggishness in conveying the information might have imperilled me further. "Thanks very much," I said as I accepted my change. I risked another question. "What's the quickest way?"

She pointed. "Take the first left at the roundabout," she told me. "Go past the houses and cut through the car park. It's higgledy-piggledy, but it'll save you a long walk."

"Great," I replied. "Thanks for your help." I grabbed the shopping bags and made for the door.

"You're welcome," the assistant replied.

I paused for a moment before leaving the shop, saw no one suspicious outside, and pushed open the door. I was only sixty yards from the roundabout – the one I'd passed earlier – so I hurried with my head down, one carrier bag in each hand, hoping I looked like a shopper and not an operative.

I rounded the corner and found myself on an attractive residential street. The terraced houses had natural stone walls, cottage gardens and tiled roofs. There was even a red telephone box on the corner, but I dared not stop there. I could see the road was short, so I sprinted ungainly – more a fast waddle, really – to the end while weighed down by the water bottles.

The car park the shop assistant had told me about was gated to vehicles but had pedestrian access, so I slipped through a small gap, bore left and got behind the cover of some trees before I slowed to a walk. I only had eight kilograms of water in the carrier bags, but their awkward position caused my already tired shoulders to ache. I saw another car park nearby and also spotted signs for the factory outlet. It was a large site, so I made my way to the edge, figured out my bearings in relation to the High Street, and proceeded toward the shopping complex.

I wasn't convinced that my inarticulate guide had saved me much walking time, but I was glad that her route had kept me away from the hotel. I hoped the Iranians were wasting time asking after me at the reception desk. I paused to open one of the water bottles, drank a few gulps and stuffed it back into the carrier bag. I needed to eat my sandwich as well, but I didn't want to delay any further, so I ignored my growing hunger.

Having expected to see shops on the scale of warehouses, I was surprised to find mostly small restaurants and boutiques. The site was busy but unhurried, and I attempted to blend with the crowds. Venturing deeper into the factory village, I soon confirmed that it hosted several outdoor shops, including a Jack Wolfskin and a North Face. I didn't need expensive branded items that would stick out like a sore thumb, so I opted instead to enter the Mountain Warehouse store, hoping I'd find some less ostentatious garments.

By now I had accepted that I'd have to shake off my pursuers before I could contact my people. I needed to pass on the information about Farzad Bouzidi and the Iranians who'd killed him, but that depended upon my own survival. It was safe to say I wouldn't be back in London that evening. The prospect of voyaging across the countryside did not intimidate me; I'd experienced far more hostile conditions than this little jaunt in Somerset could throw at me. In fact I was actually looking forward to it in a strange way, for it would restore my adventurous spirit which the capital had done its best to smother during recent months. I refused to underrate my adversaries, but I was confident that the longer this dragged out, the harder it would be for them to find me.

"Can I leave these bags next to the counter while I have a look around?" I said to one of the shop assistants.

He gave me a nod but didn't seem interested. I set the bags down and scanned the shop. I grabbed a cheap medium-sized rucksack from a hook and pulled open the drawcord. I put several items inside it, including a Silva compass, a Petzl headtorch, some thick socks, an aluminium flask, a khaki fleece and a lightweight waterproof jacket. There was nothing wrong with the one I was wearing but Rasul Heyat knew its grey colour. The new one was black.

I carried the items to the till. "Start ringing these up for me, would you? I need a few more bits and pieces." Not waiting for an answer, I walked to the boots rack and looked for a pair of leather boots in my size.

"Don't you want to try them on?" the spotty-faced lad at the desk asked as I dumped them on the counter.

I shook my head, turned away and scanned the shop once more, remembering that all the clothing in the world wouldn't be much help if I didn't know where I was going. I stepped to the map display and picked up a number 141 Ordnance Survey Explorer map because it covered Glastonbury and Street. I turned it over and studied the small-scale panel on the back. Ten seconds later I'd made a decision about my route. I grabbed a number 140 as well, then returned to the till.

The purchases went on the debit card; they'd have burned through a fair portion of my cash. I doubted I'd use the card again. The transaction didn't take long but I needed a couple of minutes to pack the rucksack, starting with the four bottles of water, and I asked the assistant to cut the labels off everything for me. I'd have preferred to swap my damp hiking shoes for the leather boots, but I was already nervous about how much time this shopping trip had cost me. Task completed, I hoisted the rucksack onto my shoulders and walked out of the shop.

There was a road right outside Mountain Warehouse, so I

followed it a short way to a junction and then turned left onto a residential street. The route took me around another of the factory village's car parks. I knew little about where I was going other than my westward heading, but I reckoned it wouldn't take me long to reach the edge of the town. As I had no room for errors, I checked the compass quickly, confirming the mental map etched on my brain.

After three hundred yards I found a cul-de-sac called Wood's Batch. I could hear traffic on a main road ahead but couldn't see it, so I checked it out as the noise didn't match the secluded area. The decision turned out to be fortuitous, for although the road ended at a wall, a footpath and cycle lane split off from it, descending into a perfectly concealed subway that tunnelled under the trunk road. I emerged on the other side among acres of parkland and football pitches.

I carried on past lawns and a children's play area. There were still a lot of houses in the vicinity, but I sensed I was on a green corridor that would lead me away from the town. I stayed on the road for a while to see where it went. I passed an entrance to a cemetery on my left and thought about walking through it, but I could see an expanse of meadows ahead and went there to find out the lie of the land.

The road swung to the left and narrowed. Suddenly the houses were to my back and the fields opened up before me. As tempting as it was to cross the stile and follow the footpath I could now see, I reckoned I'd been steered off course, so I checked my compass once again. Finding that the footpath went north, but I needed to head west, I rejected it in favour of staying on the country lane.

The tree cover was perfect, at least for a short distance, but I soon discovered that the westbound lane encircled the quiet cemetery. It was a large site and I couldn't see anyone in the grounds. I followed the road until I found an entrance gate, pulled the latch mechanism and swung it open. A bench stood just behind the boundary hedge. I swung my rucksack onto it, then sat down and loosened my shoelaces. The sanctuary of the peaceful cemetery was welcome. I knew I couldn't stay there for long, but I had time to eat and put on my new socks and boots.

I consumed the sandwich quickly and followed it with an energy bar. I drank a third of the bottle I'd started earlier, then poured the remainder into my new metal flask. Hunger assuaged, I made adjustments to my attire and repacked the rucksack. I thought about dropping my wet shoes into the nearby waste bin but decided against it. Instead, I placed one shoe in each of the pack's mesh side pockets, hoping that exposure to air and sunlight in this way would achieve what running across fields had not.

Satisfied that my equipment was now arranged correctly, I was ready to plan the next stage of my journey. I unfolded my 141 map, found Street and quickly spotted the cemetery where I was now sitting. A few landmarks caught my eye as I considered the viability of different routes westward, but the other Ordnance Survey sheet covered the greater part of the journey. I opened the second map and laid both down on the grass side by side.

The Polden Hills, rising above the Somerset Levels, would set me on my way to the town of Bridgwater. The gentle terrain would present no difficulty for me, and there were footpaths and hidden farm tracks all over the place. I'd be able to reach my destination without encountering so much as a main road. I folded the maps and placed them inside my rucksack. I got to my feet, hefted the pack onto my shoulders, adjusted the straps and strode back to the cemetery's gate.

19

MURAD ZAM glanced at Samir Davari before returning his attention to the road, slowing for a set of traffic lights on the Street bypass. It was the second time they'd driven the circuit from the hotel. "Seen something?" Zam asked.

Davari turned his head from the passenger window to acknowledge the question from his team leader. "Possibly. Hard to tell. A man with a rucksack. I saw him in the distance, just as we went past those railings."

"But you think it was him?" Zam sped up as the lights went green, flicked on the left-hand indicator and took a residential side road that appeared to curve back in roughly the direction they'd travelled.

Davari shook his head. "He was wearing the same colour trousers that Rasul described. That was all."

"We'll check it out."

They rounded the corner and immediately faced a dustbin lorry that had blocked the road next to a row of parked cars. Refuse collectors manoeuvred wheelie bins to and from the vehicle. Unlubricated hydraulics screeched as the bins were lifted and emptied into the rear section of the lorry. The workers appeared to be in no hurry to clear the road. Zam cursed under his breath and looked in the rear-view mirror. A car was already behind them, preventing them from reversing back to the side road on the bend. Four minutes rolled by slowly until the lorry edged forward and created a gap. Zam steered around the parked cars.

The road followed a gentle incline past detached houses with modest front gardens. Zam impatiently kept his speed to twenty miles per hour, not wishing to draw the attention of the locals, but a white-haired man with a hedge trimmer peered at them for a moment over a four-foot garden fence. As the road dipped, Zam caught sight of large trees and parkland further ahead. They passed a handful of semi-detached houses with steep lawns. Moments later they arrived at a turning area. Zam swung the car round in a slow semi-circle and pulled to a halt.

The MOIS commander made a gesture. "Those railings?"

Davari nodded. He pointed in the opposite direction. "He walked that way, along the pavement by those football pitches."

Zam looked at where Davari was indicating. "How far from here?"

Davari shrugged. "A hundred metres. I only saw him for a fraction of a second."

Zam put the car in gear and pulled forward. Several sweet chestnut trees lined the narrow lane, making Zam wonder how Davari had seen anything at all, but the man had observation skills that were second to none. He drove slowly. There were dozens of kids and adults on the playing fields, making the most of the sunny weather. The road became steeper next to a fenced-off play area. Zam stopped once more, looking carefully at the parents with their young children.

"Want me to get out and ask if they've seen him?" Davari suggested.

Zam shook his head. "Two men of our appearance? They'll think we're child molesters." He drove on again, satisfied their quarry wasn't inside the playground.

The road dipped as they passed the north end of the play area. A driveway appeared on the left, passing through the grounds of a cemetery, but the wrought-iron gate was shut. Zam saw fields ahead and crawled along the narrowing road. He pulled across the lane into the space in front of a farm gate. Zam switched off the ignition and pushed open the driver's door. Davari joined him at the stile next to the gate, looking across the flat countryside. The view went on for miles but there was no sign of a man with a rucksack.

"Reckon he went that way?" Davari questioned.

Zam looked around. "The footpath? I don't think so. The lorry did not hold us up that long. He'd be visible." He made a gesture. "He could've gone down that alleyway behind the houses, through the cemetery or across the playing fields. East, north or west. Wherever he went, he's no longer on the road."

Davari gave his team leader an inquiring look.

"Why would he be?" Zam responded. "He knows we're in a vehicle. And he'd conclude, rightly, that we don't have the equipment to trek across country."

"But *he* does," Davari muttered, not giving much thought to his words. "The rucksack. If it *was* him, he's acquired some gear."

"Exactly," Zam replied, surprising Davari with his certainty. He paused for a couple of seconds. "He had to run from the moment he saw Rasul on Glastonbury Tor. We've controlled him until now."

Davari frowned. "I think it would be more accurate to say we've lost him."

Zam held eye contact. "We don't know where he is right now. There's a difference."

"The man I saw might not have been him."

Zam shrugged. "Perhaps, but what would you do in his position?"

Davari gave the question some thought. "Avoiding the roads is logical."

Zam nodded.

"But it's remote around here. He'd need food and water if he intended to walk any distance."

"And the means to carry them," Zam added.

"Where do you think he's going?"

"I don't know but I have an idea." Zam dug out his phone and opened the map application. "He didn't find that rucksack by chance." The Iranian studied the screen intently for a few minutes.

"Here." He held the phone out so Davari could see the screen. "Several shops selling outdoor gear." He handed the Renault's key card to Davari. "Drop me off at Mountain Warehouse. Their stuff is the cheapest. We'll try that one first."

The men returned to the car. Davari turned around in the lane and headed back past the playing fields. They had to turn left as though heading out of town to rejoin the bypass, but a slip lane on the dual carriageway took them promptly to a set of traffic lights for a right-hand turn into the shopping village's parking areas. They realised the route didn't take them close to Mountain Warehouse, so they returned to the dual carriageway, doubled back and took the Farm Road junction.

They spotted the outlet moments later. Davari parked on the yellow lines in the delivery area behind the building. Zam got out and strode around the corner of the store, looking for the entrance inside the pedestrianised area of the factory village. As he entered the shop he counted nine customers and two members of staff. One, a pretty brunette with long hair in a ponytail, was discussing footwear with a middle-aged man. The other, a sullen-faced lad with ginger hair, leaned on the counter, staring at his colleague's shapely behind.

The female assistant stepped away as her conversation ended, leaving the customer to browse, but Zam spoke to the teenager instead of her. He guessed the lad probably saw shoppers heading toward his attractive colleague instead of him, day in, day out. The young man would, Zam reckoned, be much easier to bluff and manipulate.

Zam walked up to the counter. "Afternoon," he said with a smile.

"Hello," the assistant replied. "Can I help you?"

"I'm sure you can," Zam said cheerily. He lowered his voice as he continued to speak. "I'm with the police proactive squad." He raised his hands in an apologetic gesture. "This is rather embarrassing – I left my warrant card at the station because I was in a hurry. I can come back later if I must, but this is quite urgent."

"What's it about?" the lad asked, a suspicious frown creasing his face.

Zam wondered if the assistant was brighter than he looked, but he persevered with his false account. "We're trying to find a vulnerable missing person," he said. "A male, about my age. We have information that he might have come in here within the last thirty or forty minutes. I really need to check your CCTV."

The lad pursed his lips. "Why would a missing person come in here?"

Zam leaned forward a fraction, closing the gap between them. "He's ex-military. Mental health issues. He camps out when the pressure gets too much. The family is worried he might self-harm. He's done it before. They threw out his gear after the last occasion."

"Oh. That doesn't sound very smart."

"They're just worried, that's all." Zam knew he had the man's interest now.

"Sounds bad."

"Hopefully not – if we can find him quick enough." Zam paused. "The cameras?"

The assistant held his gaze. "I shouldn't leave the shop floor."

"That's fine. I can look through the recordings myself. Just give me the basics on the system."

"It's pretty easy," the lad said. "I'll show you." He led the way to the office and gestured at a computer monitor. "It's not much different from YouTube," he told Zam. "Click on the controls or use the spacebar to play and pause. You can play it through at a faster frame rate by clicking there."

Zam sat down on a chair and wheeled it to the desk. "Thanks. I won't be long."

"No worries. Give me a shout when you're done." The assistant walked from the office.

The Iranian scrolled the recording back an hour and set a brisk playback rate, knowing he'd recognise the man who'd killed his brother as soon as he saw his face. The search didn't take him long; after six minutes of advancing through the footage, he found his target. Zam stepped through to the shop floor and signalled the young man.

"Found him?" the lad inquired as they went back to the office.

"I have." Zam pointed at the screen. "It's definitely him. Can you send me a few still images?"

The assistant shook his head. "I don't think so. I can print them."

"Do that." Zam stood back to allow the man to work. Seconds later the printer buzzed as the first sheet of paper fed through the tray. "It looks like you served him," Zam remarked.

The lad glanced up, concerned that an insinuation was being made about his competence. "He didn't look... Well, you know what I mean."

Zam gave a reassuring smile. "Trust me, I've been with the police long enough to know that most people with mental health problems conceal it well." He pointed at the image on the monitor. "Can you remember anything about him?"

"He knew exactly what he wanted. Bought decent gear but nothing too fancy, you know? In and out in no time. He asked me to cut off the labels, and then he packed the rucksack before he left the shop." The man paused. "Ties in with what you said about him being ex-military," he speculated.

"Good observation," Zam replied, guessing that a little praise would go a long way. "Can you remember what he bought?"

The lad shook his head. "Not really, but I'll print out an itemised till receipt for you." He tapped the screen. "The time's on there. Give me a second to find the transaction."

"Thanks. That's very helpful." Zam waited patiently for the printer to do its work.

"There," the assistant said. "All done. Anything else you need?"

"No, that's it." Zam offered his hand. "I appreciate your help."

"You might want to speak to security," the lad suggested as he rose from the chair. "There are cameras all over the retail village."

Zam nodded. "Thanks again. I'll let you get back to your work." They left the office. "Oh, one more thing," Zam said quietly, nodding toward the female assistant. "I think your colleague likes you." He walked from the shop, imagining the look of surprise on the lad's face.

The Iranian went around the corner of the building and returned to the spot where Davari had parked.

"Anything?"

Zam nodded as he pulled the passenger door shut. "He was there." Showing Davari a printed image, he said, "Good eyes, Samir. It was him." He made a gesture through the windscreen. "Find us somewhere more discreet. I need to read through this."

Davari drove from the delivery area and headed back up Farm Road. He turned left onto the bypass and followed it to a round-about. He went past a McDonald's and continued a short distance before stopping in the car park outside a Lidl store. He killed the engine and looked at Zam who was still scrutinising the till receipt.

"Anything useful?" Davari asked.

Zam handed him the CCTV prints but held onto the itemised bill. "New clothing and new boots," he said, not lifting his head. "He's definitely planning a hike."

"Great," Davari replied cynically. "So we know what he's wearing. How does that help us now?"

Zam made eye contact with him. "We know he went toward that cemetery."

"Yeah. We should have carried on looking up there."

"I'll give you that," Zam replied, "but we wouldn't have found him. Like I said, he was probably already on a footpath somewhere. We weren't equipped to follow."

"What now then? We can buy some decent boots and go after him. Drop me off up there and I'll chase him down."

"We don't have time for that," Zam said. "He's too far ahead."

Davari frowned. "You want to abort?"

Zam shook his head. "Give me a moment." He pulled out his phone and opened a web browser. "Ordnance Survey maps 140 and 141." He handed Davari the paper and tapped it. "We know what direction he's headed. It makes sense." Zam paused. "It's what I would do."

Davari held eye contact, realising they hadn't yet lost their prey.

Zam smiled. "We'll intercept the bastard before he reaches Bridgwater."

20

DETECTIVE SERGEANT PENNY AMBLER turned away from the mephitic coppery smell of spilled blood and walked back to the farm gate. Someone had contacted the farmer and retrieved the key for its padlock; the gate now stood half-open on rusty hinges to allow access for the crime-scene investigators. The on-call police doctor had attended too, although the required formality to confirm death had seemed entirely pointless.

Ambler looked down the lane toward Glastonbury Tor. A marked police car blocked the road; another stood out of view at the north end of Stone Down Lane. Blue and white plastic tape stretched across the road a dozen yards back in both directions to mark the inner cordon in which Ambler now stood. She pulled off her bloodied surgical gloves and dropped them into a contaminated-waste box that the CSI had placed on the ground by the gate.

She stepped across the lane and turned her face to the breeze, grateful for the summery fresh air. The sun was on its slow descent in the southwest, its light refracting through rose and tangerine clouds. There would, Ambler estimated, be another couple of hours' daylight. Plenty of time to remove the brutalised body from the field, but the fingertip search of the crime scene would have to wait until morning. From what she'd observed, Ambler doubted they would find much apart from splashes of the dead man's blood.

Ambler reached into a pocket for her mobile but paused to watch a skein of geese fly across the early evening sky over the Tor, silhouetted against the wispy pink backdrop. The distraction soon passed and Ambler returned her attention to the phone, finding the number for her detective inspector.

DI Jacob Poe answered on the second ring. "How is it down there, Penny?"

Ambler tucked a curl of hair behind her ear. Having reached her forties and noticed traces of grey in her formerly long locks, she'd recently gone for a pixie cut and dyed her hair white. She'd feared the change might have been rather drastic, but everyone had complimented her new look.

"It's a fucking mess," Ambler replied. "Never seen anything like it."

"Foul play?"

"You could say that. The victim was shot at least three times. Judging by the hole in his head and the absence of an exit wound, we're talking about a small-calibre firearm. I'll know more after the pathologist has examined him."

"Deposition site or murder scene?" Poe asked.

"From the amount of blood, I think we can safely conclude he was killed here," Ambler replied. "The spatter appears to be concentrated in one place. The gunshot in the gut put him down and either the one in the chest or the one in the head finished him off."

Poe groaned. "Not a suicidal farmer topping himself with a shotgun then?"

"No way. We're not getting rid of the paperwork that easily, boss. Definitely a murder." Ambler paused. "If I'm right about the type of weapon..."

"Yeah. Did they send a firearms unit?"

"They did, but we had no suspect description, so they stood down."

"No witnesses?" Poe questioned.

"Just the walkers who spotted the body," Ambler replied. "They only noticed him because they trespassed in the field for a decent photo of the Tor. They heard nothing." She hesitated. "Jake, this place has been swarming with tourists all day. The control-room call-takers haven't received a single report of a gunshot. Now, there could be two reasons for that. This is farming country, so shotguns and bird scarers usually get ignored. Or – and remember what I said about the head wound – we could be talking about a silenced handgun."

"I'll ask Gail to review all current firearms intel for the region," Poe said. "Might get a ballistics match if we recover a bullet." He paused. "I'll call the press office and get a media appeal drafted. Anything else you can tell me?"

Ambler grimaced. "I've hardly started."

"Sounds ominous."

"Did I mention the sliced throat?"

"Fuck. You said it was a mess."

"Yeah," Ambler replied. "Jake, this wasn't just a murder, it was an execution. The guy was shot first and then mutilated afterwards. Whoever killed him wanted to make a statement. There was no attempt to conceal the body."

"But he was found behind a hedge," Poe reminded her.

"I don't think that means a lot," she replied. "It gave the murderer some cover for the act itself. Maybe there was some coercion first. A threat, a discussion – who knows? The killer knew the body would be found, but presumably had time to leave the scene unhindered."

"Direction of travel?"

"No idea at this stage. The CSIs will search for blood on the road and in the field near the body." Ambler paused. "I've taken footwear impressions from the witnesses for elimination purposes, but the ground is dry. My guess is the killer walked toward Wellhouse Lane. Probably mingled with tourists. Even if we find some blood on the road, I doubt it will tell us much."

"You'd better give me a description of the victim for the press release," Poe said.

"I can do better than that," Ambler replied. "I can tell you who he is."

"You have an ID?"

"We scanned his fingerprints. Couldn't find any documents on him though. Iranian national by the name of Ismail Khadem."

"Good work. He's on PNC?"

"And our force database. Are you at your computer?"

"Yes."

"I've only got the summary report on my phone, but it looks like he was arrested the night before last in Bristol."

"Let me look him up," Poe said. "Give me that name again."

"Ismail Khadem. Kilo, hotel, alpha, delta, echo, mike."

"Okay." There was a delay as Jacob Poe tapped his computer keyboard. "Right, found him. Oh, that's interesting. He was nicked for GBH. First arrest on PNC."

"Aiming high," Ambler commented. "Unusual for a first timer."

"Give me a moment to look at the custody record," Poe said.

Moments later Ambler heard a chuckle down the phone line. "What is it?" she asked.

"He stabbed Maggot."

"*What?*"

"You must have dealt with Maggot before, Penny. Dwayne Baggot. Smackhead."

"Didn't know we referred to him that way, Jake," Ambler commented with a wry smile.

"Of course not. Wouldn't be so unprofessional," Poe joked. "We got it from one of his addict mates. They all call him that."

"What happened?"

"I guess one of them worked out his surname rhymed with maggot, and it stuck."

Ambler groaned. "That's not what I meant, you twat," she replied. "Tell me about the incident."

"Maggot tried to rob the barber's shop where Khadem worked. Him and Carl Singleton."

"Let me guess – we've got a nickname for Singleton too?"

"They make it too easy, don't they?" Poe replied. "Looks like Carl shat himself and did a runner, but he was identified from the

108

shop's CCTV by the officers and arrested later that night. Dwayne was nicked at the scene for robbery and possession of a bladed article."

"Our dead Iranian acted in self-defence?"

"Looks that way. They released him under investigation from custody, but the interviewing officer was planning to NFA him after speaking to the CPS. The barber's statement made it clear what happened. Dwayne got nothing more than he deserved."

Ambler thought about Poe's information for a few seconds. "Where are Baggot and Singleton now?"

"You're thinking it could've been a revenge killing?" Poe responded right away. "No, that's not it. After being patched up at the hospital, they took Dwayne to the station. He's still there – remanded in custody because of the seriousness of the offence. And Carl had an outstanding fail-to-appear warrant, so he went straight before the magistrates."

"And?"

"They banged him up for a month." Poe paused for a moment. "Whoever killed the Iranian, it wasn't Maggot or Simpleton."

"Their mates?" Ambler questioned.

"I reckon you're giving them too much credit. They're junkies, Penny, not the mafia."

"I can't rule it out."

"Of course not. But push it down the list." Poe thought for a while. "I'm more interested to know how and why Ismail Khadem left Bristol for Glastonbury."

"The thought had crossed my mind," Ambler said. "We need to dig into his background. We're missing something huge." She sighed. "I'll have to start with the barber."

"Harry Beech? He might know something. He gave your victim a job."

"It'll have to wait until tomorrow. I still have to go to the post-mortem. I could be tied up with this all night."

"I'll find someone else to make inquiries with Beech."

"Cheers, Jake," Ambler replied.

"Do you need anything else down there?"

"You could give the control-room inspector a bell for me – I'm going to need quite a few uniformed resources to hold the cordons overnight. The local response sergeant won't be happy about that."

"Not a problem. Look, I'll have to brief the DCI about what you've told me. Then I'll grab a car and drive down there. I know you can handle it, but I'm still required to attend as the inspector-in-charge. It might be a while though."

"That's fine," Ambler replied. "I'm not going anywhere. But I'd appreciate a sandwich."

"Consider it done."

"Park at the north end of Stone Down Lane. We're using a field for the police vehicles."

"Okay," Poe replied. He paused. "Penny, we can expect pressure from the chief constable to solve this job. I'll keep her at arm's length, but we'll be under the microscope. Thought you should know."

"I'd guessed as much," Ambler replied, sighing.

"I'll see you later."

"Will do." Ambler ended the call and put the mobile away.

As she turned around and walked back to the crime scene, Ambler wondered if she'd made an assumption about Khadem's murder when talking to Jacob Poe. That he had died behind the hedgerow was not in doubt, but she'd failed to consider the possibility that someone had abducted him first. Had he been kidnapped in Bristol and conveyed to Glastonbury for his execution? The journey was only about twenty-five miles, but it still seemed a long and inconvenient way to make a point. If the killer had intended the body to be found, why not dump it on the outskirts of Bristol or on farmland nearer the city? Ambler wasn't convinced by her new theory, but scoping for CCTV footage outside the police station in Bristol was a line of inquiry that might help her establish Khadem's movements.

Ambler returned to the farm gate and nodded at the crime-scene investigator who was unpacking a camera from an aluminium case. "I'm going to need pictures from both ends of the lane," she told him. "And from across the field. All potential routes to the scene."

"I'll have to check I have enough film," the CSI joked.

It took Ambler a moment to remember they'd stopped using film cameras at crime scenes years ago. She grinned weakly at him, finally getting the humour. She wasn't really in the mood. Ambler wrinkled her nose. The body seemed to smell even worse now, and it was attracting flies. She hoped it wouldn't be long before the CSIs had finished their work at the murder site; she wanted the corpse at the morgue for the post-mortem with no unnecessary delay.

Ambler stared at the blood-drenched body, endeavouring to smother her revulsion at the sight with professional curiosity, willing the dead man to provide her answers about his fate.

"Who the hell are you, Ismail Khadem?" she murmured under her breath.

21

I STIRRED FROM MY SLUMBER as the dawn chorus rose in melody and intensity. Darkness shrouded me and I wondered if nature's alarm clock had begun too soon. But, as my eyes adjusted to the greyness of the wood, I realised that pale amber light had started to infiltrate the hillside copse. I twisted the lid off one of my water bottles and swallowed a few gulps as my surroundings took shape. I had slept well for a decent number of hours and stayed warm, even though the temperature had dropped during the night.

After a short while I got to my feet and walked to the treeline. A band of phantasmal mist lingered over the low ground beyond my hideout, obscuring my view of the farmland. The landscape's taller features peeped over the diaphanous expanse, like islands in a mysterious sea. But the light increased gently and the shadows slipped away, exposing trees and farm buildings to the south. I returned to my rucksack and ate a small but energy-rich breakfast from my meagre provisions, then drank some more water.

The rest had done me a lot of good. It hadn't been a deep sleep – the nocturnal activities of the wood's denizens predictably prevented the location from falling silent – but I'd rehydrated and banished the headache from the previous day. The fresh air and loamy scent of the earth had restored both my physical and cognitive strengths. With hindsight I realised that the plan I'd sketched out in the cemetery was adequate but not robust, and I hadn't approached it with the clarity of thought it truly needed.

As I'd trekked along lanes and footpaths the previous afternoon, I'd come to the awkward conclusion that my escape strategy was rather more predictable than I'd first believed. And while I'd continued with it as the evening fell, heading west into the Polden

Hills, I knew I had to revise the plan or risk walking straight into a trap. I'd only felt relatively safe about five miles away from Street when I reached a hamlet called Moorlinch. My map had told me that a walking trail across the ridge began there, and I found it easily enough after passing thatched cottages and a rather gorgeous country hostelry which, under other circumstances, I would have enjoyed stopping at for some decent home-cooked food.

I'd originally planned to walk all the way to Bridgwater in one go. The distance was about ten miles as the crow flies; I'd mentally added two more onto that to account for the topography. When I finally figured out that I'd have to cover about a third of the journey in the dark, and it was probably unwise to approach the town wearing a headlamp, I told myself to find a secluded bolt hole in which to rest.

I'd continued as evening fell and found the patch of woodland near a village called Stawell. I'd actually made pretty good progress and wasn't all that far from my destination, but I realised I hadn't even thought about where to go or what to look for in Bridgwater. Wandering around the town without focus at night would have been foolish.

I grabbed my 140 Ordnance Survey map and walked to the other side of the wood, facing the slowly emerging sun as it broke through the fog. It was still too dark to make out the finer details on the map though, so I used the Petzl headlamp for illumination. Something had scratched at my thoughts the previous day, but in my muddled state I'd not had the wits to identify the problem. Now, with the map unfolded before me, the corner I'd boxed myself into became vividly apparent. If I continued on my current trajectory I'd never make it to Bridgwater alive.

The problem was the landscape. Not the hills – they were easy to traverse and barely rose forty metres above sea level – but the wide canal which sliced through this region of the Somerset Levels and blocked my way to the town. I kicked myself for not recognising the same problem that had hindered me between

Glastonbury and Street. This time the waterway – King's Sedge-moor Drain – was a far greater obstacle than before. I couldn't see it from where I stood, but there was a bridge nearby – an easy location for the Iranians to watch. It wasn't the only crossing place, but the next one was over a mile away, and I had no reason to doubt my adversaries would keep an eye on that bridge as well. My decision to sleep in the wood had inadvertently saved my life.

The relief at my good fortune was curtailed by the realisation that I was probably less than half a mile away from an operative of Department 312. They would spot my approach over the flat ground to Parchey Bridge long before I reached the canal. Un-armed as I was, I'd have no chance against even a single enemy. Regretting that I'd neither seen the flaw in my plan nor given credit to the Iranians for predicting my flight to Bridgwater, I accepted all I could do was come up with an alternative strategy.

I flipped the map over to look at the top half of the sheet, knowing I had to divert from Bridgwater and head north. The first feature that caught my eye was another channel – the Huntspill River. I'd have to cross it somewhere, but there were quite a few bridges on the map, connecting various villages across the Somerset Levels. Green dashed lines on the map told me I could take several footpaths and therefore limit the time I'd spend on the local roads. My confidence returned as I realised the Iranians couldn't adequately cover such a large area. The longer this went on, the more likely it was that I'd thwart their attempts to find me. I reluctantly gave them credit for funnelling me toward Bridg-water, but I had belatedly deciphered their tactic. They would soon be forced to abandon the hunt.

That still left me with a couple of problems to solve though. I needed to contact my people to discuss the MOIS team. They hadn't come to England just to find and kill Farzad Bouzidi – of that I was certain. I simply couldn't risk reassembling my phone to make the call – the Iranians would locate me within minutes if they were tracking it. That meant I still needed to find somewhere safe with haste. I couldn't run around the Somerset countryside indefinitely.

I considered my options. I could double back to Street, but a spy never likes to return to a place where his description might have been circulated. Besides, the small town offered little in the way of sanctuary. Nor did it have useful transport links. I had a similar opinion about going back to Glastonbury – which I could reach across country, avoiding Street entirely – because my agency car was probably disabled. My aversion to retracing my steps over hilly ground was compounded by the fact that both towns were on the other map. That silly subliminal detail aside, I knew that a reciprocal journey on foot would further delay my urgent message.

The better choice, I decided, would be to head for Burnham-on-Sea. There were few contour lines on the map between there and the north side of the Polden Hills. Even though a maze of drainage channels – too many to count – filled the sheet, there were plenty of useful paths and lanes I could follow. I didn't plan too far ahead. I still had to make my way down from the ridge and bypass the nearest villages discreetly, but I knew I could head north for a while before turning west toward the coast.

Adding a few more miles to my trek didn't bother me at all; I was refreshed and had enough provisions for a long walk. The seaside town would be bustling at this time of year, affording me cover among the crowds of tourists. The railway from Bridgwater stopped at the town as well; I assumed it could carry me to London via Bristol if I needed public transport. It occurred to me that making my phone call from a train would be assuredly safe, even if the Iranians could pinpoint my location.

For the first time since fleeing Glastonbury, I drafted a contingency plan in case the MOIS cell guessed my strategy and beat me to the railway station. If it came to it, I would use Burnham-on-Sea as a feint because, once there, I could follow the meandering path along the River Parrett back down to Bridgwater. I hoped it wouldn't come to that. I reckoned I had another eight miles to walk across the Somerset Levels to the coastal town; I could ill-afford to lose any more time to this merry jaunt than that.

I folded my map and wound my way through the trees to where I'd left my rucksack. I put on a fresh pair of thick socks and tied the laces on my new boots. I repacked the rucksack quickly but with care, hefted it onto my shoulders and adjusted the straps so the weight transferred comfortably onto my hips. Compared to the military-grade bergens I'd carried in certain inhospitable parts of the world, the load was barely noticeable.

With renewed purpose, I ventured from the copse and headed north through the evaporating mist.

22

ZAM STOOD in a small layby on the A372 and cast his eyes over the rural Somerset landscape. The morning was already warm beneath an unshielded sun. The water of the canal which passed under the nearby road bridge reflected the bright light, glistening like a carpet of white topaz gemstones. Fields and pasture stretched away from Zam's position, but the topography was not uniformly flat.

Zam turned his head to the southeast, gazing upon a forested ridge a mile away. He wondered if his prey had concealed himself there, biding his time before breaking cover. It would have been a great place to hide, Zam knew, but he thought such a tactic was unlikely. The hill stood southwest of Street. Heading for it would have meant a long trek over open ground and innumerable drainage ditches. Furthermore, the benefit of decent concealment was lessened by the hill's remoteness. No, Zam was sure the spy had travelled via the high ground of the Polden Hills.

That deduction hadn't prevented the MOIS commander from watching the bridge just outside the village of Othery, nor its neighbours further north. There was another road bridge near the hamlet of Greylake, plus two footbridges in between. Zam and Davari had spent the night checking every crossing numerous times. They had maintained telephone contact with Rasul Heyat and Orodes Bux in their maroon Vauxhall Crossland SUV. Heyat and Bux had watched three road bridges further along the canal near Stawell, Bawdrip and Knowle.

They'd been stretched thin, Zam admitted to himself, but he hadn't been unduly concerned. The landscape was deceptively difficult to cross at night because of the unpredictable maze of streams. Anyone who endeavoured to make the journey would need a torch to prevent himself from tumbling into an unseen ditch, and the ground which adjoined the larger rivers was so flat that a speck of torchlight would be visible from a mile away. The tracks which led to the footbridges had almost no cover from trees or hedgerows. It *was* possible that their target had slipped through their net, but he thought it unlikely.

However, the man had eluded them one way or another, and Zam's patience was diminishing with every passing minute. The four Iranians had stayed awake all night, and they'd carried on searching through daybreak and the dawn hours. There was only so long they could drag this out. But Zam wasn't ready to accept defeat just yet. If there remained a chance he could slaughter the man who had murdered Ahmad, he would grasp it and savour the moment.

Zam turned around and crossed the road. Samir Davari leaned against the front of the Renault, watching him return, a questioning frown on his face. Zam ignored him, unlocked his mobile phone and thumbed through his contacts. He touched the dial icon next to Rasul Heyat's name.

The call was answered in seconds. "Murad?" Heyat said.

"Give it another hour," Zam instructed, "then head for Bridgwater. Samir and I are going there now."

"Not back to Swindon?"

"I'm not ready to give up the hunt just yet," Zam replied.

"With respect, Murad, I don't believe there is much more we can do out here. If he got past us in the night, we won't find him in the town. The longer we stay visible, the more we risk jeopardising our mission."

"We won't search for him in Bridgwater, but there's one more thing to try." Zam paused. "I am determined to find this man, Rasul."

"I know," Heyat replied.

Zam sensed the man had more to say from the silence that

followed, but he didn't want to get into an argument with his subordinate. "One more attempt to pick up his trail," Zam assured him. "If we are unsuccessful, we'll abort. That's all I ask."

"Fine. Where shall we meet?"

"I'll find somewhere and text you the details. I know we're all tired," he added.

"We're able to endure a few more hours without sleep," Heyat said confidently. He paused. "I did not intend to speak out of turn, Murad."

"You didn't," Zam replied. "You should always discuss your concerns with me. I'm grateful for your counsel and support. If we make no progress, we'll rest and eat and then return to the safe-house."

"Understood."

Zam tapped the screen to end the call but kept the phone in his hand. Making eye contact with Davari he said, "Are you still okay to drive, Samir?"

Davari nodded. "Of course."

"Good. I need to look something up online. Head for Bridg-water."

With the sun behind them, they drove the short distance to Othery. The narrow lane bore right next to an old-fashioned sign-post that showed the route to Bridgwater. The black-and-white sign was tinged with rust and looked like it had been there since the end of the Second World War. The forlorn object surprised Zam; he thought the English cared more for their heritage. A little further on, Davari took a left, following the route marked by a modern sign. The road took them past a village called Middlezoy and then back across open fields with thin lines of trees in the distance.

Davari made a gesture through his side window, inviting Zam to look to the right. They drove alongside what looked like an old concrete runway, but it was overgrown and appeared unusable. Zam guessed it was another relic from World War II, although he'd assumed the majority of the wartime runways were in the southeast of England, and that most had been broken up and returned to farming. The site looked abandoned, but Zam noticed a microlight descending on approach over the nearby fields, informing him that parts of the airfield were still in use.

For a moment Zam wondered if the enemy agent had stolen an aircraft and escaped that way. He soon dismissed the thought. The only workable routes to Westonzoyland – the nearest village to the former military base – were via Greylake Bridge or a footbridge from another remote hamlet. Heyat and Bux would have spotted anyone crossing either during the night. Frankly, Zam reflected, anyone who could traverse the canal unseen and take off unheard from a dilapidated aerodrome deserved victory. He just didn't believe his adversary possessed that amount of luck.

Beyond Westonzoyland they crossed over the M5 motorway and slowed for the sprawling residential streets of Bridgwater. The houses on the outskirts of the town were of simple red-brick construction; they looked like they'd been built in the sixties and seventies. The closer they went to the town centre, the older the houses appeared, standing in terraces which wouldn't have looked out of place in England's northern industrial towns. They crossed a railway line and soon came upon a roundabout which had an exit for the station. Zam made a signal, silently instructing Davari to take the short road to the railway building.

Davari stopped the Renault in a car park which overlooked the platform. Zam got out of the car and looked over the fence. He didn't see the enemy operative next to the tracks, so he had a quick look inside the white-walled station building. It didn't surprise the Iranian that his target was not there, but he would have been a fool not to check. Zam returned to the car and studied the map application on his phone, giving directions to Davari.

Areas of the town centre were pedestrianised, so Davari couldn't park exactly where Zam wanted to go. They found a quiet road with street parking next to a church. Zam told Davari to wait in the car. He got out and checked his phone's map once more, establishing his bearings. He headed off at a brisk walk and, several minutes later, found a mobile phone shop. He purchased a cheap device with a pre-paid SIM and then returned to the Renault.

Pulling the passenger door shut, he told Davari to search online for a Premier Inn or Travelodge where they could rest. Zam unpacked the new phone and inserted the SIM card. The mobile wasn't fully charged, but he only needed to check it worked. He placed it on the dashboard and retrieved the CCTV prints he'd acquired from the Mountain Warehouse store in Street. Zam picked the two clearest images and photographed them with his own mobile. He closed the camera application and flicked through his contact list.

"I wondered when you'd call," Control said through the speaker.

Zam ignored the sarcastic tone. "I need you to do something for me."

"Don't you always? I presume you're not phoning to say you've snared your prey?"

"We're still looking for him."

"Murad, this is taking too long. If you haven't found him..."

"There is one more thing to try. That's why I'm calling," Zam interrupted.

Control sighed. "Alright. This had better be good."

"I need twenty-four hours. If this doesn't work, we'll return to Swindon."

"No," Control said. "You have twelve."

"Fine." Zam paused for a moment. "I'm going to send you the CCTV images from the outdoor shop. Tell the computer people to circulate them on our fake social media accounts. We'll see if the great British public can lead us to our target."

"That's a long shot."

"Perhaps."

"You'll need to invent a cover story."

"I already have one – what I told the kid in the shop. He's a missing person with heart problems and mental-health issues. He left home without his medication. His family is desperately worried about him, and he's thought to be somewhere around Bridgwater or the Somerset Levels." Zam paused as Davari eased out of the parking space and away from the church. The scene reminded Zam of the encounter with the barber in Bristol. "I have a new phone number," he continued, glancing at the packaging he'd just opened. "Put this number on the social media posts. Say it can be called any time of day or night. Emphasise the risk."

"Very well. Give me the number."

Zam read it out and heard Control writing it down.

"There's one detail you've forgotten," Control said.

"What is that?"

"His name."

"I hadn't forgotten. Let's use something the English will remember easily."

"Such as?"

Zam paused in thought for a few seconds. "John Connery. It'll stick in their minds."

"Okay. Anything else?"

"Mention the rucksack and the clothes he's wearing. And say he's nervous and hostile when approached because of his mental state. That should dissuade anyone from talking to him."

"Alright. What name do you want to link to the phone number?"

"I'll be Robert. John's nephew."

"If this doesn't work..."

"I'll do as you instructed," Zam interjected. "The primary mission."

"You realise there's a good chance he's already made contact?" Control said thoughtfully. "They probably know about you by now. He recognised Rasul. The operation could already be imperilled."

Zam shrugged. "Perhaps. But he has no idea about our plan."

"It won't take a genius to work it out," Control snapped.

"It doesn't matter. Everything is in place. We're just waiting for the signal. And trust me, my men and I will not turn away, even if the odds harden against us."

"That's what you're employed for. We expect nothing less."

"And we shall deliver," Zam replied. Keen to end the conversation, he added, "I will send you the images now."

"Do that." Control paused. "Twelve hours, Murad."

Zam ended the call without replying.

23

Penny Ambler tapped Jacob Poe's open door twice with her knuckle. "You wanted to see me?" she said, clutching a mug of tea with her spare hand.

The detective inspector looked up. "Did you get any sleep last night?"

Ambler grinned. "Do I look that rough?"

Poe shook his head. "You had a long day yesterday, and yet you were the first in the office this morning. What time did you finish at the mortuary?"

"Just the wrong side of midnight," Ambler replied as she took a seat and sipped her drink. "Thank goodness for McDonald's breakfasts and hot coffee." She raised her mug. "And lots of tea." Ambler paused. "Should get the formal report from the pathologist today, but it won't add much to what we already know. One shot to the stomach, not fatal. Well, it would've been before long, but the killer left nothing to chance. Two more shots to the chest and one to the head. The slash to the throat was delivered post-mortem, based on the relative lack of blood from the injury." She drank some more tea. "Not that I'd describe it as a clean wound. You saw the body."

Poe nodded grimly. "But a leak rather than a spurt."

Ambler raised her eyebrows. "Interesting description. You're right though."

"Any more thoughts on what happened?" Poe asked.

The detective sergeant put the mug down on the edge of the desk and leaned back in the chair. "Not really," she replied with a shake of her head. "Not if you're asking about motive. But we don't know much about Ismail Khadem, other than his job and the fact he got nicked for GBH."

"Illegal immigrant?"

Ambler held his gaze. "I'm not sure."

"Go on."

"He had a national insurance number."

"But?"

"No immigration record of him entering the UK."

Poe smiled wryly. "Penny, we've had horrendously porous borders since Blair was PM. I've been in the job long enough to remember being forbidden to detain suspected illegals. His government wanted to hide the true numbers from the public."

Ambler gave him a quizzical look. "I thought the police were meant to be detached from ministerial influence?"

Poe smirked and waved his hand to dismiss the train of thought. Instead, he asked her another question. "The lack of immigration data might not mean a lot on its own. Why the doubt over his status?"

"There's no trace of a UK birth certificate," Ambler replied. "We haven't tracked down any family here either. I'm trying to work out how he received an NI number without valid paperwork." Ambler shifted awkwardly in the chair, crossing her legs. "There's something wrong about all of this, Jake."

Poe gestured for her to continue, knowing not to interrupt her on-the-spot deductions.

"The nature of the murder means Ismail Khadem didn't just cut hair," Ambler said. "I think he ran from Bristol. But why? Organised crime? He'd have come up on the radar before if that were the case. No one starts his criminal life at the top level; there'd be history. Low-level drug offences, assaults."

"He was nicked for GBH," Poe mentioned.

"We've established he had lawful justification for what he did," Ambler retorted. "An anomaly. He wasn't a crook."

"Although he probably came into the UK illegally."

Ambler shrugged. "Maybe. Putting the legality of his entry

aside, he apparently wanted to work. Most migrants do." She hesitated for a few seconds. "So, was he a decent citizen who met an extraordinary fate, or a master felon who got what he deserved?"

"Ordinary people don't get executed in Glastonbury," Poe answered.

"Right. But serious villains don't get to the dizzy heights of organised crime without gaining a nefarious reputation beforehand."

"You don't think he was either of those... personality types?"

"I don't," Ambler replied, reaching for the tea. She sipped it but found it had gone cold, so she frowned and put the cup back down on Poe's desk. "He was involved in *something*, Jake. Or he got caught up in something. I don't think he was a criminal, but I do think his murky background is relevant."

"Murky?"

"Opaque. The lack of family bothers me. We released his name. No one's come forward."

"They could be scared."

"Why? We kept most of the gory details out of the press release."

Poe held her gaze. "The family might've known what Ismail was up to. The silence could be deliberate."

"I'm inclined to believe they don't exist," Ambler retorted. "Not in the UK."

"Iran?"

"Was he even Iranian? He said so for the custody record, but that might've been false." Ambler got up and walked to the office window, staring outside for half a minute. Finally she turned around and met Poe's look. "We don't have a clue who he was," she remarked.

"Hold that thought," Poe said. "Any response to the media appeal?"

"Several vague calls about a man running down Glastonbury Tor toward the Chalice Well Gardens," Ambler replied. "I'll follow them up. That's it so far."

Poe raised his eyebrows. "A suspect?"

"Doubt it."

The DI gave her a questioning look.

Ambler smiled at him. "If you were a contract killer and you'd just murdered someone, would you climb the hill and surround yourself with tourists, or would you return to the car you'd parked down some secluded country lane and drive away quietly?"

"Good point," Poe said. "But speak to the witnesses anyway."

"Will do." Ambler paused. "Didn't you want to talk to me about something? Or was it just for an update?"

Poe gestured at the empty chair. "You'd better sit down."

Ambler groaned. "Pressure from the top?" She sat down again.

"No, although I've avoided answering my phone, so I might just be putting off the inevitable." Poe held her gaze for a few seconds. "There's been another murder. I want you to take it on."

Ambler's face scrunched up. "Really? Can't it go to someone else, Jake? I've got my work cut out with the Khadem case."

"It's connected."

Ambler stared. "What?"

"Harry Beech. The barber your victim worked for."

"And when exactly were you going to mention this?" The look on the sergeant's face rapidly morphed into a glare.

Poe held up his hand. "After hearing your perspective on the Glastonbury murder. I think your conclusions are supported by what happened in Bristol. There was a lot more to Ismail Khadem than we've figured out so far."

Ambler relaxed a little. "Tell me."

Poe pushed a stapled bundle of printed A4 sheets across the desk. "That's the command-and-control log. In short, the CID officer in charge of the investigation at Beech's place couldn't contact him by phone. The DC went to the home address and spoke to Beech's mother. She is – *was* – cared for by her son for mobility problems and a catalogue of other illnesses. Mrs Beech confirmed Harry had not returned home. His car was still outside his shop, but the place was locked up. Entry was forced. They found Beech dead."

Ambler stared at her boss but didn't comment.

"He'd been choked to death." The DI paused. "Remember when you asked about Baggot and Singleton?"

"Whether they could have killed Ismail? You said it was unlikely. Are you telling me you've changed your mind?"

"No. If Harry's murder was an isolated incident, I'd have immediately looked at those two scrotes and their shitty mates. It would've been the first line of inquiry."

"But not now?"

Poe shook his head. "What would you say if I told you Harry Beech was killed over twelve hours before Ismail Khadem?"

Ambler wasn't sure what to think. She lowered her gaze and tried to analyse the information. Eventually she looked up. "How long between the robbery at the barber's shop and his murder?"

"A day," Poe replied. "He must've been killed after he closed the shop. Ismail was shot the following morning in Glastonbury."

Ambler closed her eyes and placed her palms against her face. "This is so fucked up."

"Don't give me your emotional reaction," Poe responded. "Think it through."

Ambler inhaled deeply and locked eyes with him. "Two possibilities. Ismail killed Harry and did a runner. Someone caught up with him. I'll need to look into the Bristolian's background. Maybe he was a hard nut and had some dodgy connections."

Poe nodded. "Or?"

"Someone went after Harry in order to get to Ismail."

"Which of those options is more likely?" Poe asked.

"I can't say. I need to stay openminded about both possibilities."

"Fair enough. I'd expect nothing less. But you've already told me you don't believe Ismail Khadem was a criminal." Poe paused for a moment. "Escalating from a self-defence GBH to robbery and murder? That's unlikely."

Ambler picked up on his words. "Robbery?"

"Sort of. The cash was untouched but someone had ripped out the CCTV recorder. There was something else that the medics picked up on – Beech's shoulder was dislocated."

"Fuck." Ambler stared at the senior officer wide-eyed. "They tortured him."

"To get to Khadem. Your instinct about the Iranian was right, Penny." Poe picked up a pen and tapped it idly on his desk. "I've not updated the DCI yet. I wanted to talk to you first."

"Thanks. I think." Ambler sighed. "I'll need some help with this."

"You're the lead investigator but this will be a team effort. I'll speak to everyone later this morning to put them in the picture. I've already asked uniformed officers to scope for CCTV in the streets around Beech's shop. You'll want to supervise their progress."

Ambler nodded. "I'll speak to the council's camera operators as well. There must've been a vehicle, but I have no idea what I'm looking for. I'll run every index number I can trace through ANPR," she added, referring to the UK's automatic numberplate recognition system.

"With luck you'll find one that was in Glastonbury the next day."

Ambler crossed her fingers and held them up. "Anything else, Jake? Please say no."

Poe grinned at her. "Nothing else. But I'll need you to chip in with the team briefing."

"Of course." Ambler stood up and reached for the mug. "I need a refill. Want one?"

"If you don't mind."

"No problem." Ambler scooped up the command-and-control log from the DI's desk and walked out of the office.

24

DEPARTMENT 312 AGENT Haydar Hamidi drove at a gentle twenty miles per hour up the incline of the hedgerow-lined country lane. A sign bearing the National Trust's oak-leaf logo marked the entrance to the car park on White Horse Hill, and Hamidi turned left into it. He found a space under the shade of a tree and stopped there, waiting a few seconds before turning off the Škoda Kamiq's engine.

Hamidi glanced at the passenger. At twenty-seven, Jawad Babolian was eleven years Hamidi's junior, but the younger operative was a veteran of the Islamic Revolutionary Guard Corps Navy. The man's military experience was valuable, Hamidi knew, but it was yet to be seen if Babolian could transfer those skills to espionage work. He'd only been a member of Murad Zam's cell for three months.

"Let's take a walk," Hamidi said, reaching for the compact binoculars in the door's side compartment. He grabbed the door lever and stepped out, feeling the warmth of the midday sunlight as it filtered through the branches overhead.

The two men strode across the grassy hillside behind the car park. A wide path had been mown across the downland toward the nearby landmark of Uffington Castle – a hillfort with steep defensive ditches and a grand view across the landscape to the north of the escarpment. Hamidi knew little about the monument's history, but he'd studied the topography in preparation for the cell's mission. An ancient track known as the Ridgeway lay behind the fort. Once used for trade, it was now one of England's long-distance recreational footpaths.

The path narrowed as the agents headed east. The grass

thinned, exposing the chalky soil of the North Wessex Downs. The hills and ridges were not high – seldom reaching over two hundred and fifty metres above sea level – but the landscape fell away and flattened out into seemingly endless farmland less than a mile distant. The sense of vastness increased beneath the cloudless azure sky, and the horizon faded into a blurry line beyond fields, woods and villages.

The path reached a field boundary and gate roughly a quarter of a mile from the car park. They crossed a narrow lane called Dragon Hill Road and continued along a steeper section of the track, gaining a few metres' height as they approached the celebrated ancient chalk carving of a horse etched upon the hillside. A short distance beyond the landmark stood Dragon Hill itself, which over time had become linked to the Saint George legend. Hamidi did not know how the English had stolen a story from Ancient Turkey and transposed it onto their own green and pleasant land, but he felt the acquisition said a lot about the misplaced confidence and arrogance of the nation.

Hamidi stepped off the footpath and lifted the binoculars. Looking beyond the flat top of Dragon Hill, he scanned the landscape through the lenses. A dense patch of woodland obscured the hamlet of Woolstone from his view, but he wasn't searching for the village. He turned a little to the right and adjusted the focus. The sprawling grounds and manor house of the White Horse Vale Hotel became sharp. Concentrating on the long driveway that led to the elegant mansion, Hamidi noticed several expensive cars parked outside. Security staff stood in the grounds and gardens.

Babolian asked if everything was in order.

Hamidi handed him the binoculars. "Take a look."

The younger man gazed through the field glasses, making a minor change to the focus. "The security is tight," he remarked after a while.

"Of course," Hamidi replied. "Nothing less than we expected. Police roadblocks at both entrances, the Security Service inside the perimeter. Snipers on the roof of the hotel and the outbuildings as well, I imagine, although I couldn't see anything."

Babolian took a moment before speaking again. "I can't tell. The view is obscured."

Hamidi shrugged. "It doesn't matter."

The former navy officer turned round and handed back the binoculars. "Murad and the others should've returned by now. We're almost out of time."

"Do you doubt the word of our cell commander?" Hamidi asked with a frown.

"No, but..."

"Murad will be here soon," Hamidi interrupted. His expression softened. "You were assigned to us only recently. It will take a while for you to find your place. When you do, you'll realise you should trust Murad. He's one of the best."

"I know his reputation," Babolian retorted, "but I also know that Orodes and I are replacements for the men who died under his command."

"One of those men was Murad's brother," Hamidi said sternly. "Casualties occur. This is a dangerous business." He paused. "Perhaps you made a mistake when you asked to join the MOIS."

"I understand the risks," Babolian replied. "I've lost friends in combat." He raised his hands submissively. "Look, I didn't mean to question Murad's leadership. I'm just concerned that two-thirds of the team got diverted from the mission, right before we're due to attack the conference. We should be together, checking our plans."

Hamidi waved his hand toward the landscape north of their position. "What do you think we are doing right now?"

"I meant all of us."

"I know what you meant." Hamidi paused for several seconds before speaking again. "The decision to search for Jerboa was not Murad's, but he did as he was ordered and was successful. The scientist is dead. That's a great victory."

"And yet he stays there, chasing the spy who killed his brother," Babolian replied. "He's distracted. That puts our operation in jeopardy."

Hamidi held the younger man's gaze. "Put yourself in his position, Jawad. If you had the chance to capture an enemy who had hurt your family, would you not be determined to find him?"

"I would, but..."

Hamidi held up his hand. "Now ask yourself this. What if the opportunity were in your grasp but you were denied it? Would that not draw your attention from any other task you'd been given?"

Babolian nodded. "I suppose it would."

"Murad knows exactly when he must come back here. Everything is on schedule. Until then, he will hunt the spy. If he does not find him in time, he will return, lock away his personal feelings, and get on with the primary objective." Hamidi went quiet for a moment. "Murad is not focussed solely on revenge, Jawad. Killing the enemy *there* lessens the risk *here*."

"I understand that," Babolian replied.

"Good," Hamidi said. "I hope I have made myself clear."

"You have."

"It's important that you understand, because if you ever question Murad's decisions again, I will ensure that you are removed from our unit and sent back to Tehran for a disciplinary hearing. They rarely end well for the accused." Hamidi's stare bored into Babolian's eyes. "This discussion will remain between us, but do not give me cause to question your loyalty again."

Babolian nodded. "You have my word. I apologise."

Hamidi's stern expression evaporated. "We're all allowed a moment of doubt, Jawad. But only one." He waved his hand in a wide gesture across the landscape, still clutching the field glasses. "Enjoy the view. Inhale the aroma of the fresh air and the grassy hills. It is important to stay calm and clear-headed." He paused. "You know what Murad would be doing if he were here now?"

Babolian shook his head.

Hamidi lifted the binoculars briefly. "Bird-watching. He's something of an expert. It keeps him relaxed. Perhaps you should take up a hobby to help settle your nerves."

"I find cleaning guns has the desired effect," Babolian commented.

"A little more detachment from your work would be preferable," Hamidi replied. He gestured back along the path. "Seen enough?"

"I think so."

"Good. We'll come back tomorrow. Let's return to the car."

The two men turned around and retraced their steps.

"I enjoyed our little chat, Jawad," Hamidi added with the merest hint of menace.

The younger man met his stare but didn't answer.

25

THE WALK NORTH from my hideout was, despite the circumstances, an invigorating and pleasant trek through attractive farmland. My only regret was not having had the presence of mind to buy myself a hat and shades while at the outdoor shop in Street, for the unshielded summer sun was relentless upon my face and neck. But that was a trivial inconvenience as I walked along seldom used country lanes. A little sunburn was the least of my worries. I realised that footpaths were too scarce to serve me well, so I kept to the hedgerow-lined roads. I needn't have been concerned because, once I passed beyond the hamlet of Chilton Polden, it felt like I had the entire Somerset Levels to myself.

Curiously, there were quite a few secluded lanes in the region, many of which crossed the nearest river. That meant I had several routes open to me and therefore a greater chance of evading my pursuers. Having aborted my original plan to walk to Bridgwater, I wondered if the Iranians had abandoned their pursuit. There was, I believed, very little chance of encountering the operatives as I ventured across the countryside, and while the urgency of my task was not lost on me, I felt I had regained some advantage. But I still wasn't prepared to risk reassembling my phone.

I crossed a stretch of river called South Drain via a bridge whose name, according to my map, was Chilton Moor Bridge. There I encountered a couple of wildlife watchers who had parked their car nearby and were standing on the bank, enjoying the birds and insects which played among the reeds. I was tempted to join them in their observations, for the scenery was delightful. The water was clear enough to see dozens of freshwater fish in the languid canal, darting between bright spots and shade. But I pressed on, leaving the gentle waterway behind me. The lonely lane took me through more farmland, from arable crops to rough pasture.

A while later I encountered a quaint black-and-white signpost which told me I could turn west and reach Bridgwater after nine miles. But I'd already eliminated that destination from my strategy, so I continued on my planned route, putting myself on the north side of the River Brue. It was only after that point that I altered my direction, heading loosely northwest through a handful of tiny villages before the road widened and eventually took me over the M5 motorway. I walked for a further half-mile, passing a large industrial estate, before encountering the bridge which crossed the railway line. At the bottom of the slope I found the access road for Highbridge and Burnham Railway Station.

And it was then that the good fortune of the previous hours evaporated. Not because I watched a northbound train depart the station while I was still thirty yards away, but because I saw a Middle Eastern man standing on the platform after the train was gone. I wasn't close enough to see his face well, but the hair colour and profile were sufficiently clear to cause me a moment's hesitation. He hadn't caught the train, and the fact that he remained there suggested he hadn't disembarked either.

A few passengers walked through the gates in my direction. A slim woman in her late twenties waved at someone who'd parked a car in one of the dozen bays outside the station; a moment later an older man stepped out of the driver's side and gave her a hug. They got in and the car pulled away a few seconds later, following the tight loop of the access road next to the platform. The car passed me on its way to the main road. I realised I hadn't looked closely enough at the three other vehicles in the short row of parking bays. I scanned them quickly but couldn't see much because of the bright sunlight reflecting off the glass.

There was a chance that the man on the platform was entirely innocent, but I couldn't take the gamble. I turned around and headed back along the access road, slipping in front of a group of four teenagers who'd also disembarked the train and were larking around with each other. Quickening my pace, I followed the pavement away from the station. Only when I reached the junction did I glance back. I couldn't see anyone coming after me, but that didn't mean I was out of danger.

I trusted my anti-surveillance skills and survival instinct, but perhaps I'd misread the situation and it was nothing. Maybe I'd got lucky and escaped with my life. Either way, I wasn't prepared to take a risk when I didn't have a weapon and could face an unknown number of foes. That I'd just missed a train and didn't know how soon the next one would be was also a problem. A hunter unit would monitor the train stations, I knew, so if I wanted to escape Somerset by rail, I'd have to be smarter than turning up wearing my rucksack and with my face in full view. I turned left and kept walking.

At least I now knew where the railway station was located. I could return later once I'd ditched the rucksack and altered my appearance. A more wary approach would tell me if surveillants were present. I now had a partial mental picture of the nearby residential streets, and there were several trees and shrubs which could provide a little cover. But I couldn't think about that then; I had to get away from there. I decided to head for the seafront.

I was in a coastal town yet still some distance from the coast. There was little point in looking at my Ordnance Survey map. It was good for footpaths and rivers but less useful for town plans. Besides, studying it when I might have armed men behind me seemed like an incautious move. My sense of direction remained intact, and I could remember several features and their proximity to the train station from the last time I'd looked at my trustworthy chart. I could reach the town's vast beach and esplanade in a blindfold.

At the end of a residential street I found a foot- and cycle-path whose entrance had been blocked to motor vehicles by metal barriers. Following it was both the safest and most direct option, so I walked through the gap and headed across a swathe of parkland. My route brought me to a path which overlooked the River Brue's estuary, and I followed its sinuous line around a holiday park filled with hundreds of chalet bungalows. From the railway station to the southern tip of the esplanade must have been about a mile and a half; the walk took me around forty minutes. I smelled the salt in the air and heard the sonorous cries of the gulls as I headed north along the sea wall.

The enormity of Burnham-on-Sea's beach revealed itself to me then. Whether the tide was coming in or going out I could not tell, but the sands and mudflats stretched before me in a gentle arc, revealing the strange confluence of the rivers which spilled into Bridgwater Bay and the Bristol Channel. The water rippled and shimmered beneath the stern sunlight; the view unbroken except for sailing boats in the distance.

Rather than stay at risk of being seen from the road, I ventured down onto the concrete terrace which bordered the beach beneath the sea wall. It was an ugly construction that continued as far as I could see, but it provided a useful corridor right at the top of the beach. Upon it I could stay invisible from observers on the esplanade above me, and also avoid getting sand in my boots as I walked. I continued for about fifteen minutes, using the time to speculate why an MOIS squad was active in southwest England.

There were, naturally, thousands of sun-worshippers on the three-mile beach, and they were dressed for the occasion. I allowed myself the presumption that a fully clothed Iranian killer would not melt easily into this crowd of mostly white Britons. And while my pursuers might identify my tactic of using the volume of people as cover, knowing where to look along this enormous seafront was an indecipherable problem for them. I'd clawed back some ground after that possible near-miss at the train station.

And yet the swing of that pendulum had not given me the answer to what I should do next. The relative security of the sea wall would be undone if I powered up my mobile phone. If the

Iranians were hunting for my signal, plotting myself to the beach would be disastrous. The irony of being near several thousand mobiles was not lost on me. I dismissed the notion of robbing a tourist because there was no certainty I'd get away from do-gooders alerted to the theft, especially whilst wearing hiking boots and carrying a large backpack. Even if I could scramble up a flight of steps to the esplanade, my description would be noted. I had no idea how many police officers patrolled the seafront at the height of summer.

No, I still had to find a place where I could make a call without drawing attention to myself. I noticed throbbing in my head and realised I'd not drunk for a while. I swung the rucksack off my shoulders and sat down in the shade of the concrete embankment. Sipping from a water bottle, I mulled whether returning to the railway station – more discreetly next time – remained my best option. The problem remained that, despite serving a large town, the station was nearer a country halt in size than the transport hub I'd assumed it would be. It was hardly a place to stay concealed while awaiting the next service.

One thing I knew I could do with relative ease was steal a car. I thought about the large holiday park I'd walked by earlier. I could find an unattended vehicle there, and with several hours before the sun went down, most of the chalets would be unoccupied, lessening the chance of witnesses to my intended criminality. With the ANPR cameras all over the motorway, it would be unwise to use the M5, but there were other options. I pulled out one of my OS maps and flipped it over to remind myself where the principal towns were. Taunton was a short way south of Bridgwater and easily accessible via A-roads. I could drive there while calling in my report.

I desperately needed to eat first though, and I didn't really fancy any more biscuits. I put the map away, drained the bottle and slipped my arms through the rucksack's straps. I got up and carried on walking along the concrete terrace until I found a set of steps which led back up to the promenade. I decided I could afford a quick appearance on the street. Certain that I'd be able to purchase some takeaway chips within a short radius of my position on the seafront, I reached the top of the wall and looked around. Sure enough there was a fish-and-chips shop a hundred yards or so down the road, so I made my way toward it, all the while watching the countless people who surrounded me.

I found myself in a short queue inside the shop, but the service was prompt. My chips were presented in a Styrofoam container. I declined salt because I consider it an unnecessary condiment, and I refused vinegar because Satan's own urine could not taste more foul – not that I verbalised my objection in such words to the charming but overworked lady behind the greasy counter. Keeping the box sealed, I left the shop and crossed the street again toward the sea wall, intending to go back down to the beach and its relative concealment for my reciprocal journey. I would eat as I walked.

A group of young men and women caught my eye. They were sitting on the top of the wall with their legs dangling over the edge. I'd spotted them before entering the shop but hadn't considered them to be a threat. But now they were looking my way – not just in my general direction but *at me*. I glared back, causing a couple of heads to turn around, but others persisted with their curiosity. I noticed several of them fiddling with their smartphones, flicking the screens with quick thumbs. Glances alternated between me and their devices. A furtive discussion took place, and though I was too far away to hear their hushed words, I could guess that my details – a photograph? – had been circulated on social media.

My appetite evaporated, but I opened the box of chips and forced myself to eat half the contents rapidly, all the while keeping watch on the group of friends who had discovered me. I hoped that, by continuing to glower at them, they might leave the area. Sadly they were undeterred or buoyed by strength in numbers. The annoyance I felt at the Iranians increased tenfold, but it did at least prove they hadn't aborted their attempts to hunt me down. I probably had some time in hand before they'd arrive, but I couldn't hang around the seafront. I deposited the chip box in a bin and started walking down one of the residential streets away from the beach.

I took several turns but, on entering the crowded High Street for the second time, I confirmed that some of the youths were following me. By surveillance standards their efforts were worse than useless, but that was hardly the point. They were neither trying to hide themselves nor catch up with me. With patience – which was rapidly running out – I could have evaded them, but I had no time for tricks and subterfuge. The longer this dragged out, the sooner the Iranians would turn up, and that was a danger of considerably greater magnitude.

I spotted a tiny shop with the logo for the Royal National Lifeboat Institution above the door. I darted inside the charity shop, said hello to the elderly volunteer behind the desk, and turned to the displays. Knowing I'd be more likely to find out the information I needed if I made a small purchase, I quickly glanced over the products for something cheap to buy. A sliver of unexpected luck came my way when I saw a small selection of baseball caps. I picked one with washed-look blue fabric. There was a pale blue embroidered RNLI logo on the front but it didn't stand out. I went to the counter and handed over a ten-pound note.

"Keep the change," I said.

"Thank you," the man replied, dropping a two-pound coin into a charity tin.

"Could you tell me if there's a taxi rank nearby?" I asked.

The man leaned round and pointed. "Just at the end of the road," he said. "Turn right at the bottom of the High Street. Far side of the road. You're about thirty seconds away."

"Great," I said. "Thanks for your help."

"You're welcome. Enjoy the rest of the afternoon."

"You too." I left the shop and stood in the doorway, scanning the area for my amateur pursuers.

They were standing outside a Subway food outlet, looking my way. I ignored them and followed the directions I'd received. I found the taxis and went to the one at the front of the line.

"Where to, mate?" the driver said as I walked up to his car.

My first thought was to nominate the holiday park, but I rejected the idea swiftly. It was, of course, within walking distance, which might make it an odd choice. Furthermore, with the hit-team closing in, I needed to get out of Burnham-on-Sea. I recalled the illustration on the back of my map.

"Weston-super-Mare," I improvised as I opened the rear door and pushed my rucksack inside.

"No problem," the man replied as he walked round to the driver's door. "Whereabouts?"

Having never been to the town, I couldn't name a single address. However, like its neighbour, Weston-super-Mare was a famous resort on the coast. I took what I hoped would be a safe guess.

"The tourist information centre," I said, mustering as much confidence as I could.

The man nodded. "No problem," he repeated.

Ten seconds later, we were on the road.

26

MURAD ZAM had returned to Bridgwater Railway Station with Samir Davari after their brief visit to the town centre, intending to conduct discreet surveillance on the ever-diminishing chance that their target would show up there. He'd sent Rasul Heyat and Orodes Bux further north with similar instructions. But, as the afternoon shadows lengthened, Zam knew time was against him. The trail had gone cold, and he would soon have to order the team to return to Swindon.

"I'm going to stretch my legs," Zam told Davari. "The next train isn't due for twenty minutes."

Davari nodded but gave no answer.

Zam pushed open the Renault's door and let himself out. He walked the short distance to the footbridge which crossed the railway lines. His footfalls were unavoidably loud on the metal treads. Within moments he reached the span of the bridge. Stopping halfway across, Zam looked directly north at the nearby station building and its small car park. Terraced houses, allotments and a few business premises stood either side of the tracks. He thought the view was dreary compared to the older buildings of the town centre. He stood there for five minutes, wondering if Heyat and Bux had found their prey. He dismissed the thought – they would have called him.

An electronic melody sounded from one of his pockets. It took a moment for him to recognise the ringtone of the mobile he'd bought earlier. He retrieved the phone and pressed the button to answer the call.

"Hello?" Zam said as he held the device to his ear.

"Er, hi," a male voice responded. "Is this the right number for

Robert?"

"Yes, I'm Robert. I'm sorry, I don't recognise your number."

"My name's Mark," the man said. "I saw something on Facebook about a missing person. I think I saw him."

"He's my uncle, John Connery," Zam replied. "Thanks for calling, Mark. Where did you see him?"

"I can't be a hundred percent sure," Mark said hesitantly. "My friends and I reckon we saw him down by the beach. We weren't all that close, but he looked like the man in the photo you posted. And he did have a rucksack."

"Sounds promising," Zam enthused. "What beach was that?"

The caller gave a short nervous laugh when he realised he hadn't provided all the pertinent information. "Oh, sorry. Burnham-on-Sea. Near the pier."

"How long ago was that?" Zam asked. "Is he still there?"

"No, he left. I think he sussed out we were looking at him. He walked off."

Zam's mood soured at the words. "You don't know where he went from there?"

"Yeah, I do. Well, like, not exactly. He left the seafront and went to the High Street."

"You followed him?"

"Briefly, yeah. He went to the taxi rank and got in a cab. Dunno where he went after that."

Zam forced himself to be patient. The young man on the line needed constant prompting for information, but the lead sounded promising. "When was this?" he asked.

"Ten or fifteen minutes ago. I had another look on Facebook and then called you."

"I'm grateful," Zam said. "I don't suppose you know the name of the taxi company?"

"Seaside Cabs," Mark replied.

"You're certain?"

"Er, yeah. The name was on the door."

"That's great," Zam said. "I'll ring them. I really appreciate your call. We've been anxious about John. He doesn't have his tablets with him."

"Well, I hope you find him soon," the caller said.

"Me too. Thanks again."

"No worries."

Zam lowered the phone and ended the call. He hurried back down the steps to the car park, his feet clanging on the metal boards. He ran to the car, grabbed the driver's door handle, climbed inside and started the engine.

Davari gave him an inquiring glance.

"Just took a call about John Connery," Zam explained as he dabbed the sat-nav controls in the centre console.

"Someone saw him?" Davari asked.

"Yes, but he left in a taxi about fifteen minutes ago. See if you can find Seaside Cabs of Burnham-on-Sea online."

"Will do." Davari fished out his mobile and activated the browser.

Zam took his own phone and plugged it into the slot below the dashboard. He dialled Rasul Heyat's number. Not waiting for an answer, he rolled out of the parking space and drove away from the railway station.

Heyat's voice came through the Renault's speakers. "Murad?"

"Are you still in Burnham-on-Sea?" Zam said.

"Yes. Near the train station."

"There's been a sighting. He took a cab from the High Street."

"Destination?"

"Unknown, but we have the name of the company. He knows they saw him, so he's on the run."

"Do you think he's left the town?" Heyat asked.

"That's my theory," Zam replied. "He's had to react so his options are limited. Stay at the railway station but be ready to move. If he were coming your way he'd have got there by now. I reckon he's gone elsewhere. I'll contact the cab firm and call you

145

back when I've spoken to them."

"Understood."

Zam shut down the call and drove as swiftly as he could, following the route to Burnham-on-Sea that the sat-nav had calculated.

"I have a location for the company's office," Davari said beside him. "Want me to call them?"

Zam frowned as he considered his answer. "Actually, no, I don't think that will work. They're unlikely to give out information over the phone. If we go there in person, I can show them the photograph and prove that it's my number on the social-media circulations."

"It'll take us twenty minutes," Davari muttered as he looked at the sat-nav screen.

"Not if I go via the motorway and put my foot down," Zam replied. "Better than the A-road."

"You don't want to send Rasul the address? He could leave Orodes at the train station."

Zam turned right onto the northbound road through the centre of the town and accelerated. "If he had the pre-paid phone. He doesn't."

"We're losing time. Rasul could gain the information without the mobile."

Zam glanced at Davari. "I'm sure he could, but what do you think would happen if the office suddenly stopped communicating with its drivers? And what about the witness who named the cab firm? No, Samir, we're doing this with good manners and tact."

Davari shrugged. "It was just a thought."

Zam didn't reply, turning his attention back to the road. Soon they were on a two-lane stretch of dual carriageway, passing large industrial units on the way out of Bridgwater. Zam took the last exit off a large roundabout, following signs for the motorway. A minute later they were powering down the slip-road at eighty miles per hour. Zam found a gap as he joined the M5 and made his way over to the fast lane, increasing speed and passing slower vehicles.

It took barely three and a half minutes for Zam to cover the five miles to the next junction. He flew down the exit road and braked hard when he saw the warning chevrons for the sweeping ninety-degree bend. The road quickly led to another roundabout. Zam went straight over, following the sign to Burnham-on-Sea, but he had to match the speed of the other vehicles on the B-road as they passed fields and hedgerows. They crossed a railway line which, Zam concluded, was the same one he'd seen from the footbridge in Bridgwater. Soon they were on the outskirts of the town. From there Zam concentrated more closely on the sat-nav's directions.

It turned out that he didn't need to drive all the way into Burnham-on-Sea for the cab office. He found somewhere to park in a nearby cul-de-sac, told Davari to wait with the car and then walked the short distance to the building he'd spotted moments earlier. He pushed the door open but could see no one inside.

"Hello!" Zam called out, hoping he'd not wasted time.

A fat forty-year-old woman with lank dyed-blonde hair appeared from the narrow hallway behind the desk. "Can I help you?" she said.

"I really hope so," Zam replied. "I'm looking for my uncle. He's gone missing."

"This is a cab firm, darling, not the police," she replied with a frown.

Zam ignored her sarcasm. "Sorry, I wasn't clear. Someone saw him get into one of your cabs at the taxi rank near the High Street." He glanced at the clock on the wall. "About half an hour ago."

The woman's expression softened slightly but the air of suspicion remained. "And?"

"I'd like you to find out where the driver took him."

"I'm not sure I can tell you that."

Zam unfolded one of the CCTV images from the shop in Street and placed it on the counter. "He has mental problems and a heart condition. He hasn't taken his pills. It's urgent that we find him."

The woman peered at the photograph.

Zam continued his story. "We put his photo and description out on social media with my number. I have the phone here," he said, showing her the cheap mobile. "You can give it a ring if you want."

She shook her head. "Nah, that's fine. You're sure it was one of my cars?"

"The man who called me seemed to think so. You do use the rank near the High Street?"

"We do." She picked up the sheet of paper. "We've had a few fares this afternoon. I'll have to call the drivers on the radio."

"Thank you. Oh, he almost certainly had a rucksack with him. He's one of those outdoor types."

The woman nodded. "Give me a minute." She picked up a radio handset, held down the transmit button and asked if anyone had taken a fare from a man with a rucksack from the Pier Street taxi rank. The radio crackled in response but Zam couldn't make out all the words; the combination of radio jargon and West Country accents hindered his understanding.

"Anything?" he asked as the woman gave him back the printed photograph.

"Yeah. Weston-super-Mare. He was dropped outside the Tropicana on Marine Parade about ten minutes ago."

"The Tropicana?"

"Don't know the area?"

"Not very well."

"Building on the seafront. Café and theatre. Laurel and Hardy performed there, back in the day. You won't miss it. Your uncle asked for the tourist information office."

Zam didn't understand the reference to Laurel and Hardy but concluded he had all the information he needed. He folded the paper. "Did the driver say anything else?" he asked.

"Like what? Oh, you mean if your uncle looked ill?"

"Or if he said where he was going afterwards."

She shook her head. "Sorry."

"Never mind. You've been a great help. Thank you."

"No problem, sweetheart." She gave him a wink. "You know where to come if you want a ride."

Zam smiled but found the innuendo distasteful. He turned around without another word and left the building, glad he'd never have to look upon the ill-favoured whore of a woman again.

He was already on the phone to Heyat by the time he got back to the car. "Weston-super-Mare," he said. "Go to the railway station. Same protocol as before. Get up there as fast as you can, Rasul. He was on the seafront ten minutes ago."

"It'll take us twenty minutes," Heyat told him.

"I know. Same for us. But it's a good start. If he intends to catch a train, you'll still be there before him. Samir and I will go to his last known location and work out a radius from there."

"It's a big town, Murad. He might have another means of egress."

"I doubt it. We've forced his hand so far." Zam paused. "This is the best chance we've had."

"Understood. We're on our way."

"I'll call you in half an hour." Zam said, ending the conversation.

27

HAD THE CAB DRIVER not been of the chatty sort, I might have used the journey time to plan my next steps. Instead I found myself distracted and without a strategy outside an unattractive 1930's building on Weston-super-Mare's seafront. It contained a café and some other amenities which appealed to me about as much as a night in a Hamas interrogation cell. But the tourist office did occupy a small alcove a few yards down from the main entrance, so I was in the right place.

Except that the location was entirely the *wrong place* for a man on the run. Someone had spotted me in Burnham-on-Sea, so I knew it would take very little effort for the Iranians to make inquiries with the cab firm – they'd probably already done so. But now I stood on another sweeping promenade with open views and no hiding places. I had to move, but to where? Mindful that any delay would compound my jeopardy, I forced myself to take a few moments to study my surroundings. Failing to plan is planning to fail, and all that.

The broad pavement and its accompanying road were on a north to south orientation, with the sands of Weston Bay stretching west to the Bristol Channel. I'd noticed something curious from the taxi window, so I walked away from the building on the seafront to get a clearer view. Some distance to the south a large headland jutted out from the shore. How far it was from my present position I could not tell with any degree of accuracy, but I reckoned it was at least a mile or two.

When I'd bought my Ordnance Survey maps, I had only planned to head west from Street to Bridgwater, not north to Weston-super-Mare. For that reason the territory where I now found myself was, for my purposes at least, uncharted. I had no way of knowing if the distant headland would provide a safe refuge, or even how accessible it was. There seemed no sense in walking in that direction because the route was so exposed. There wasn't even a sea wall to hide behind.

I noticed an islet to the right of the headland, but it was too far away to see anything more than its shape. Low cloud or sea mist had formed over the water with the onset of the late afternoon, obscuring the horizon and portending showers. I wondered if a change in the conditions could work to my advantage, but at that moment I could not imagine how it might do so, and the weather in the southwest of England rarely performed as expected anyway.

Another road ran parallel to the promenade, overlooked by some rather grand three- and four-storey Victorian townhouses which, I suspected, had latterly been converted to flats. Some residential streets led away from the seafront, running perpendicular to the coast. I decided my safest option was to head that way, but without a decent map I was at risk of wandering around aimlessly. That, however, was a problem I reckoned I could solve with a quick visit to the tourist office.

I put on my recently purchased RNLI baseball cap then crossed the street, away from the leisure building. There was an unoccupied bench set back from the pavement, so I tucked my rucksack beneath it, hoping it would go unnoticed for a few minutes, even though there were a lot of people strolling along the seafront. I didn't want to be seen in the tourist booth with the bag because it was readily identifiable and the obvious item for my pursuers to ask about.

Crossing the road once more, I walked to the tourist office and went inside. It didn't take me long to find a variety of maps. I found a cheap one with a decent street plan. I wasn't interested in tourist attractions, but I scanned the displays of free leaflets in case anything caught my eye that could prove useful. I noticed one with a photograph of the island I'd just seen; the text told me it was named Steep Holm. I slid the leaflet out of the rack and opened it. My eyes flicked over a few paragraphs. I learned that Steep Holm had been fortified against incursions along the Bristol Channel during Queen Victoria's reign. It gave me an idea. I stopped reading and went to the desk.

"Do you have a tide timetable?" I inquired.

"Yep," the assistant said curtly, pointing at a leaflet holder at the end of the counter.

"Thanks. One of those and the map," I said, handing over a banknote.

I stuffed the change into my trouser pocket and walked out. My rucksack was where I'd left it. I slung it onto my back and went up a short flight of steps with the beach behind me. A wide greensward separated the seafront road from the next one where the townhouses stood. I paused there for a few seconds, looking again at the headland to the south. The view was a little better and revealed more of the landscape, affirming my decision to look elsewhere for a hideout. I turned to the north and saw a forested hill beyond the town. It looked like a better option for cover, and although at that moment I wasn't sure how to reach it, I was confident I'd figure it out once I'd fled the seafront. I headed down a side street whose sign identified it as Clevedon Road, passing smaller versions of the grand houses which overlooked the Bristol Channel.

I reached a crossroads and turned left. This street was similarly occupied with attractive stone-built houses. I kept heading north and soon discovered areas of parkland on either side of the road. I found an entrance gate for the one on my right and slipped through it. A children's play area – which reminded me briefly of the one near the cemetery in Street – was in use by several kids under the watchful eyes of their parents. I strode past with my head down and, a minute later, sat on the lawn near the park's northeast corner.

Needing a drink, I pulled one of the plastic bottles from my rucksack and twisted off the cap. I still had about four litres of water left. I ate some biscuits as well, hoping that the sugar would counteract the fatigue that was becoming harder to shake off. I needed better food than my paltry stock, but I wasn't yet at physical risk. I was, however, feeling weary in the psychological sense. I was capable of improvisation but mindful that every time they forced me to adapt my plan, a sliver of doubt crept into my head, no matter how hard I tried to banish the thought.

I reminded myself that, once again, I had evaded my pursuers. My priority was to learn the layout of Weston-super-Mare, so I unfolded the town map and studied it closely, working out where I'd been dropped off on the promenade and my current location. I discovered that I was close to the town's main railway station, but going there would be foolhardy in the extreme. There was a Tesco store nearby which made me think again about food. For some inexplicable reason I had a craving for chocolate cake.

The town's police station was also marked on the map, just a stone's throw from the supermarket. I silently debated the reasons for and against going to the police, starting with the not insignificant point that espionage and crime-fighting are not natural bedfellows. I had no desire to draw attention to myself, although the urgency of my message would undoubtedly quell my superiors' annoyance at finding themselves stuck in a bureaucratic quagmire. I was a covert asset; spending time – for whatever reason – inside a police station was profoundly undesirable.

And, as I mulled over recent events, the more I suspected that Farzad Bouzidi had met his fate because of a rogue agent in the police force. The situation had unravelled from the moment he'd been arrested, so someone must have figured out who he was. I did not know that person's identity or what position he held. He might even have had an office in the very police station I was contemplating visiting. I definitely did not want anyone recognising my face.

Nor did I know why my details had been circulated over social media. Had they named me as a suspect for a crime? The youths' reaction in Burnham-on-Sea suggested that that was a distinct possibility. In other circumstances I might have used the tactic myself to find an adversary. I had no way to know what could happen if I turned up at the police station. The last thing I needed was to be arrested and fingerprinted. That really would create a headache for the people back in London, and it would certainly delay my warning about the MOIS unit.

Even if none of that were true, I had to consider the likelihood that the police station was being watched. The Iranians would realise that I might attempt to contact the authorities. It wouldn't be hard to surveil the building. It was less than a quarter of a mile from the train station, and I was sure they'd have that location under observation already. That realisation forced me to abandon my quest for sandwiches and cake – the Tesco store sat between the two target zones. I'd have to look elsewhere to replenish my food supply.

No, the police station was out of the question. I was going to have to drag this out a while longer. My thoughts returned to the idea which had occurred to me in the visitor centre on the seafront. Could I reach the island? Not with the current state of the tide – it would be several hours before the water covered the sands and flats – but I wouldn't risk it before nightfall anyway. My tide booklet told me that my plan was workable if I tried around ten-thirty p.m. Of course, there was still the small matter of how I might gain a boat.

I realised with some alarm that, despite the great size of the beach at Weston-super-Mare, I hadn't seen a single launch ramp or mooring buoy. At that moment I actually felt a chill. I couldn't believe that sailing from this famous resort town was impossible. I grabbed the map and pored over it once more. It really seemed that Weston Bay was inaccessible. Except...

Knightstone Harbour, right at the top end of the beach. It didn't look like much, from what I could see on the map, but its size meant any boat I found there would be small and easy to handle. The harbour was also at the foot of the wooded hill I'd seen earlier, so I had somewhere to hide until I was ready to put my plan into action. I hoped the pendulum was swinging back in my favour.

There was one more obstacle to get around beforehand. The area where the police and railway stations stood lay directly between me and the forest. Skirting around the centre of town was possible via the beach, but it wasn't a gamble I was prepared to take. The map provided me with a solution. If I double-backed to Clevedon Road, I could continue east and cross the railway tracks before turning north and winding my way through a maze of housing estates. It would take a while – especially if I took measures to avoid being followed – but I'd bypass the danger area and find a way onto Worlebury Hill before it got dark.

Satisfied that I had a plan – or, at least, the sketch of one – I stood up and grabbed my rucksack.

28

MY CIRCUITOUS ROUTE took me to the north end of Weston-super-Mare without incident, but what hadn't been clear from the map booklet was how steep the roads were on the side of Worlebury Hill. I actually enjoyed my exploration of the old town, weaving through narrow lanes that curved this way and that. The randomness reminded me of the Mediterranean coast near the French-Spanish border. There the comparison ended, however, for the buildings were most certainly English in character. The same stone façades I'd seen near the seafront were present on the hillside, and a good number of them were three storeys in height. That meant, despite the elevation, there were only a handful of places from where I could see the small harbour.

I reconnoitred the causeway before concealing myself in the hilltop woodland for a few hours' rest. Thankfully my pursuers had not thought to search for me there. I'd seen eight small boats in the cradling arm of the diminutive harbour, leaning over in the mud as they waited for the tide to lift them. The slowly encroaching water caused the mud to glisten in the evening light. While I wasn't an adept boatman, I'd had training on how to handle a variety of small powered watercraft, and I knew that one of the tiny cabin cruisers would be simple to pilot. A nautical chart would have been useful, but I reckoned that the height of the high tide in the Bristol Channel would permit me to escape from Weston-super-Mare without running aground.

I retreated to the forest and watched the sun dip to the horizon in the southwest in a glorious display of orange and crimson. The sea mist I'd seen earlier must have dispersed or drifted toward the Welsh coast near Cardiff, for the sky remained clear except for wispy brushstrokes of fiery cloud. I'd found a small grocery store on the corner of a nearby street, so I munched through two packets of newly purchased sandwiches and a fresh apple, watching as the sky darkened into an inky afterglow. With the lingering atmospheric light and the electric lights of the town, I knew I wouldn't be operating in true darkness. That, however, was helpful in its own way. Without a chart or instruments to navigate by, I needed to see the silhouette of Steep Holm against the open sky if I were to reach it safely.

Using my headtorch I read the leaflet about Steep Holm, concentrating on the details this time. Although it was now a private nature reserve, traces of its military past remained intact. The Victorians had fortified the island and placed cannon there. The Second World War had seen the installation of gun batteries, searchlight posts and rocket launcher sites. It had also been home to a priory approximately nine hundred years ago. The island rose nearly eighty metres above the water. Much of it was covered in trees and undergrowth. Several buildings and defensive structures still stood there in various states of ruin.

That all sounded very promising – I'd be able to shelter there with no difficulty – but landing a boat there looked problematic. Almost the entire island was surrounded by cliffs. Fortunately there was also a pebble beach on its eastern flank, and I'd approach from that side. The prospect of making shore in the darkness did not enamour me, and I would only discover how the currents swirled about the island when I encountered them. Steep Holm was also roughly five miles from Weston-super-Mare, which implied it was probably out of range of a mobile phone mast. That did not bother me. If my phone were being tracked, I wanted it to ping to the town itself, not the island, but that meant I'd need to make my call while still within sight of Knightstone Harbour.

Feeling restored by the food and eager to turn the tables on the Iranians, I ventured from the shadows of the forest and trekked down the hill as the hues of the twilight sky darkened. Wary about activating my phone, I left it until the last possible minute to put the SIM card back in its slot as I stood beneath a streetlamp near an Italian restaurant, just across the road from the harbour's slipway. I jogged across the street, hoping to remain unnoticed by the diners inside the building. I spotted a lifesaving ring mounted on a board at the top of the ramp and stole it. I descended a flight of concrete steps which took me to the beach. I was then out of view below the promenade.

I put the SIM card into its slot and powered up my phone, shielding the screen as it woke up. Only a fraction of battery power remained – I hadn't thought to charge it before driving to Glastonbury – but it would be enough for one phone call. I wrapped the mobile in two of the plastic bags I'd acquired on my travels and put it inside the zipped section on the top of my rucksack.

With my rucksack in one hand and the rescue aid in the other, I walked to the water's edge and waded in. I put the rucksack on the buoyancy ring and pushed it in front of me. The risk of getting stuck in the mud was not insignificant, but the water wasn't that deep and I'd double-knotted the boots to prevent their loss. As I strode out further, the water reached my waist and then my chest. I felt my feet sinking several inches into the mud, but I dragged my legs up and swam with a frog-kick, using the ring to steady myself.

The water was, as my tide timetable had predicted, deep enough to lift the boats from the suction of the mud. I made it safely to the nearest one about thirty yards from where I'd entered the sea. My rucksack wasn't heavy, so it took little effort to toss it over the side as I trod water. The rescue aid followed, and then I hauled myself up and into the stern of the cabin cruiser. I stayed low, glancing back to shore. I doubted anyone had seen my antics.

The cabin door burst open after I gave it a sharp kick, splintering the wood. I went inside and flicked on my headtorch. It didn't take me long to find a toolbox and a flashlight. The wiring to the starter was, as I'd expected, quite basic. With the tools that the owner had graciously left for me, I had the engine running in less than a minute. Pocketing a decent Leatherman multi-tool from the box, I stepped from the cabin and made my way to the prow where I released the little boat from its mooring. I was soaked to the skin but elated at how easily I'd gained transport.

Soon I was underway, chugging gently from the harbour in my stolen boat. The fuel gauge told me I only had a quarter of a tank of marine diesel, but I did not know the tank's capacity or the boat's range, so I disregarded the problem. I only had to sail five miles. Steep Holm's outline was becoming harder to see, but was obvious enough against the pale blue glow of the horizon, even through the boat's salt-smeared window.

I retrieved my phone from the rucksack. With one hand on the wheel and my eyes to the west, I called Sarah. The one bar of signal would have to do. The call connected and I heard it ringing.

"It's late," Sarah said as she answered.

"Were you asleep?"

"Not yet. The last round of meetings went on a bit. Junior officials trying to impress. I've just got back to my room." She paused. "The signal's crap. Where are you?"

"On a stolen boat," I replied. "We have a big problem."

"No kidding. I don't recall your seamanship being up to much."

"It's worse than that. Sarah, I don't have much time. I'm probably going to lose the signal any second."

"Where are you?" she asked, concern creeping into her voice.

"Bristol Channel. I'm heading for an island named Steep Holm. I need you to arrange an extraction for me."

"Okay, but..."

"Hold on," I interrupted. "There's an active Department 312 cell down here. They're after me. I recognised Rasul Heyat in Glastonbury. They've been tracking me ever since."

"Fuck."

"I'm certain they killed my asset, Farzad Bouzidi."

159

"There was a report of a murder in Glastonbury on the news," Sarah told me. "The victim was named Ismail Khadem."

"Farzad's alias," I replied. "They found him. He called me, sounding paranoid, so I told him to get out of Bristol. They caught him before our rendezvous."

"And now they're coming after you," Sarah said in a low voice that I barely heard.

"Yes, but it's an improvised manhunt. They had no clue I was in England. Heyat and his MOIS friends aren't here for me."

"You think they're planning an assassination?"

"What else could it be?" I paused. "I reckon your conference venue is the target. You need to let the lead agent know, Sarah. You're in danger."

"Shit. The foreign ministers are due to start talks tomorrow." She hesitated. "Do you have any intel about the attack?"

"None. But those diplomats are there to discuss sanctions and counter-measures against Tehran's nuclear programme. They must be targeting the hotel. The Iranians want to make a statement. Slaughtering a dozen enemy politicians would be a propaganda coup."

"Everything about this conference has been kept secret," Sarah countered.

"We both know that means nothing," I responded. "There's always a leak."

"True enough." She paused. "I'll sort things out here. What about you?"

"The Iranians tracked me to Weston-super-Mare but don't know I'm headed to Steep Holm. I'll hide there until you can send someone to pick me up."

"How do you want to do this? A police launch?"

"No," I said, shaking my head. "The Iranians infiltrated the police. That's how they knew about Farzad. It must be our people."

"Fine. Could we put a helicopter down there?"

"I think so. It's about a quarter of a mile wide. I..." The phone beeped in my ear, telling me the battery was on its last legs. "My battery is nearly dead," I told her.

"I'll call London," Sarah said. "They'll have to fly from there. You might have to wait a few hours."

"Doesn't matter. Heyat and the others don't know where I am. Prioritise the hotel's security."

"Will do."

"And, Sarah..."

But the connection dropped out, ending the conversation abruptly. I watched my phone's screen as the device shut itself down. I ought to have removed the SIM card again, but at that moment I had my hands full with the rather more important task of piloting the stolen boat into the treacherous waters of the Bristol Channel. I zipped up the phone in my rucksack and stared through the window. The light was fading badly now, and I was having difficulty keeping track of the island. If I looked away, I needed a while to find it again in the darkness; if I stared at it, the silhouette seemed to dissolve into the horizon.

The boat made slow progress, struggling at an angle against the incoming tide. Ideally I would have attempted to land at slack water, but that was some hours away, and I had my suspicion that it wouldn't have a calming effect on the Bristol Channel anyway. I managed to stay on course as I listened to the strained engine. The island loomed larger and larger before me, its outline clearer now that I was almost upon it, but its features remained indistinguishable. I hoped the beach was in front of me, for I could not see it.

My landing – if it could be so named – was much less graceful and considerably more sudden than I'd hoped. Instead of running onto the pebbles, I collided with rocks some twenty or thirty yards from the shore. The hull of the boat split and groaned, and I was flung against the wall of the cabin as the craft listed suddenly to port. I heard a ferocious bang and the engine stopped. The boat jerked again and tipped over further. Water splashed over the gunwale and poured through the cabin's ruined door.

I probably should have abandoned my rucksack at that moment, but my instinct fought against the decision. I slipped my arms through the straps and fastened the clip on the front. I grabbed the buoyancy ring and clambered outside. Now that I wasn't squinting through the filthy window, I actually had a better view of the stony beach. I turned on my headtorch and eased myself over the side of the boat into the water, glad I didn't have to contend with large waves. My boot touched a submerged rock and immediately slipped, sending me under for a moment. I half-crawled and half-swam for the shore. My hands stung and I realised I'd probably injured myself on barnacles. I persisted, finally reaching the pebbles, and hauled myself out of the water.

I rolled out of the rucksack and lay on the rough beach, trying to fill my lungs with fresh air while expelling salty mucus from my nose and throat. I examined my hands in the light of my headtorch and saw blood issuing from numerous cuts and abrasions. I'd endured worse. There are few activities more tiring than fighting to reach safety from water, and I needed several minutes to get my breath back. Eventually I stood up and looked around, thankful that the Petzl lamp was water resistant and had stayed on.

A steep path was cut into the cliff above the beach. I put the rucksack on again and climbed the steps, passing behind a ruined building whose former purpose I could not decipher. Thick undergrowth scratched at my arms and legs as I went higher and further along the path. I passed another structure on the edge of the cliff. The path turned back on itself and I found myself in a patch of woodland which clung to the slope. Continuing my cautious exploration, I eventually reached the island's summit.

The top of the hill was more scrubland than trees. Several footpaths lay before me, but the light of my torch did not reach far enough to inform me which was the best to take. I just wanted to sit down and get some sleep, even though my sodden clothes would make that improbable. The air was cooler than on the coast and I noticed the breeze picking up. I wasn't about to die of hypothermia – the conditions were mild because of the season – but I needed shelter where I could attempt to dry my clothes and boots.

A few rundown buildings occupied the eastern end of the summit. I was weary by then and didn't spend long deciding which would serve me best. I settled down against an ancient stone wall which, from its evident antiquity, could have been the ruins of the priory that I'd read about earlier. I removed my boots and rummaged through my rucksack. I was heartened to find that the seawater hadn't reached everything, although the remaining fresh food I'd bought was nothing more than mush. My fleece was quite dry, as were my spare socks. I squeezed most of the water from my shirt and then laid it on the stones.

As I made myself as comfortable as I could, I told myself that one more night under the sky would not be a great hardship. I had made contact with Sarah and alerted her to the Iranian operatives. They had no idea where I was, and I'd be picked up by helicopter in a few hours' time. Relief flooded through me.

I prayed I'd won.

29

As he sat alone in the seafront café, his hands around a cup of strong coffee, Murad Zam mulled over his failure to find the spy who'd shot his brother. Keeping someone under surveillance with a four-man team was hard enough, let alone trying to find him in the first place from limited clues. He and the others had worked a rotation of tasks throughout the previous evening and night, ensuring that three of them searched while the other snatched a brief rest. Control had granted an extension to the hunt after the sighting in Burnham-on-Sea and the subsequent information from the cab firm. It infuriated Zam to know he'd been just minutes behind his prey.

The target had fled the promenade at Weston-super-Mare, evidently knowing that the MOIS agents were closing in, but he'd steered clear of the town's three railway stations and several other obvious points of egress. The staff in the tourist information office had been utterly unhelpful, and there had been no more responses to the social media circulations. Zam begrudgingly admitted to himself that the pursuit was over. He finished his breakfast, lined up the cutlery on the plate and stood up. He nodded his thanks to the waitress who'd served him and then walked out.

It was still early but the sun was already bright and the morning was getting hot. Once the others had eaten, he'd order the retreat to the safe-house in Swindon. Zam needed to stretch his legs, so he walked along the promenade toward Weston-super-Mare's pleasure pier. There were already a lot of people on the street, enjoying an early morning perambulation, but the one man Zam wanted to see was not among them. The warm sunlight failed to improve his mood.

His smartphone rang ten minutes later. Expecting the caller to be one of his squad, Zam groaned when he saw Control's number flash on the screen. He touched the icon to accept the call.

"Are you still in Weston-super-Mare?" Control asked.

"Yes," Zam replied. "I'm on the seafront. We've looked for him all night. No luck."

"It was a difficult task."

"We'll leave once the others have had something to eat."

"I can't let you do that," Control replied.

"Excuse me?"

"You forget that I have other resources under my command, Murad, not just you."

"What's that supposed to mean?" Zam questioned, mentally adding, *I'm not under your command.*

"I know where he is."

Zam let the words sink in. "You're sure?"

"Your hunt was actually very productive. You might not have found the spy, but you effectively trapped him. He's still in Weston-super-Mare. Well, that's not quite true. But he's nearby."

"Where?"

"An island named Steep Holm. You can probably see it from where you are."

Zam turned around and looked across the water. "How did you work this out?"

"A boat theft was reported to the police just before dawn. Knightstone Harbour. According to the map, that's at the north end of the beach. My police contact has been keeping track of reports from the town ever since you phoned me yesterday."

"Was he seen?" Zam asked.

"No, but a yachtsman radioed the coastguard twenty minutes ago to report the wreckage of a small cabin cruiser on the east side of the island."

"The stolen boat?"

"Unclear, but that's the obvious conclusion."

Zam thought for a moment. "If he abandoned the boat..."

"Assuming it was intentional," Control interrupted.

"Yes, but if he found a way onto the island, he'll find a way off. He's a resourceful bastard."

"Agreed. That's why you need to locate him before anyone else."

Zam scratched the stubble on his cheek. "Only one problem. I don't have access to a boat."

"Actually, you do. There's a tourist boat leaving in an hour and a half. There were only two seats left, but I've reserved them under fake names through the website. They spend the whole day there, so you won't get back until this evening. Plenty of time to find him."

"With other people there?" Zam questioned.

"It's a big place. Miles of footpaths and ruined buildings. Be discreet. You'll have several hours." Control paused. "You'll have to kill him. We no longer have the means to abduct and interrogate. I want you to bring this to a swift conclusion."

The instruction irked Zam but he understood its logic. "Very well. Two spaces, you said?"

"Yes."

"However much I would like to pull the trigger, I'm not the right person for this job," Zam reluctantly conceded. "I will send Rasul and Orodes. Their army experience make them better suited to hunting on that sort of terrain."

"I don't care who goes," Control stated firmly. "I just want the job done. I'll text you the details of the boat charter. Telephone me when they return." He ended the call, not waiting for a reply.

Zam felt both unsettled and elated by the news. He opened the web browser on his smartphone and searched for information about Steep Holm. From the photographs he found, he realised the place was an overgrown natural fortress, over half a mile long and almost a quarter of a mile wide. Numerous ruined buildings and patches of tree cover provided endless hiding places. Even with ten or twelve hours on the rock, Heyat and Bux would struggle to find one man whose skills were equal to their own.

Digging further into the search results, Zam found a video on YouTube about the island. Tapping the play button, he discovered it had been filmed by a drone-mounted camera, and it showed the island in impressive detail from an aerial perspective. His phone beeped with a text message from Control but he ignored it and returned instead to the browser's search page. He typed in *drone shop Weston-super-Mare* and found several hobby stores and electrical outlets in the town which had a range of recreational drones in stock. The nearest one was close to the town's main railway station – he'd probably driven past it several times during the night.

Zam called Heyat next.

"Murad?" the operative said, sounding groggy.

"I've heard from Control," the cell commander told him. "We know where he is. You're going to kill him for me. For Ahmad."

Heyat sounded much more alert when he spoke again. "Where?"

Zam ignored the question. "Am I right in thinking you know how to fly a drone? The sort videographers use on YouTube?"

"You already know the answer to that."

"I'm going to text you the name and address of a hobby shop. Buy one that you think is suitable. You're going hunting."

30

I WOKE TO A RESPLENDENT MORNING and realised I had slept for more hours than I usually would. The light fabric of my hiking trousers was still damp, but my need for sleep had banished the mild discomfort. The sun was high and hot, bleaching the sky and causing the glassy water of the Bristol Channel to shimmer. However tempting it was to apricate in the glorious warmth, I had work to do.

Sipping water, I stepped out of the ruined building that had been my sanctuary for the night and looked at my surroundings. The island top was rough scrubland mixed with patches of denser tree cover. Remnants of old fortifications were scattered around the edges and on the slopes. There was certainly room for setting down a helicopter, although it would have to land on vegetation several inches deep, for there appeared to be no bare ground.

The abundant greenery and banks of wildflowers released their pollen scents under the heat of the sun, filling the air with a delicate fragrance which blended with the salt from the vast waterway. And although I had the place to myself, it undoubtedly wasn't quiet, for countless seabirds cawed and cried as they launched from their cliff-side perches and circled above the island.

I explored further and discovered a row of intact cottages on the south side of Steep Holm. I guessed they were something to do with the management of the wildlife reserve. They were locked up but appeared perfectly habitable. I assumed there were basic facilities therein, including a means to contact the mainland that didn't rely upon mobile coverage. Footpaths encircled and crossed the higher parts of the island and, from what I could see, ventured outward to some of the ruined observation points and casemates.

Before studying my temporary home in more depth, however, I wanted to check my few possessions and provisions. My rucksack had been partly dunked when I'd suffered the indignity of splashing facedown into the sea, but its sturdy fabric had done its job and kept most of the contents relatively dry. Some water had got in through the top. My Ordnance Survey maps were in a poor state, but I unfolded them and weighed them down with stones so they might dry in the sunlight. I did the same with my fleece and boots. The plastic-wrapped food was fine. I'd flung away the sticky remnants of my extra sandwiches the previous night, leaving them for the birds.

With the sun as hot as it was, I knew everything would dry quickly. I put on my walking shoes and set out on a longer trek at that point, partly to finish drying my underwear and trousers, but also to get a better understanding of Steep Holm's curious topography. I was rather glad that I still had my RNLI baseball cap, for there was nothing else to shield my eyes from the sun. I completed a circuit of the summit on the main path, enjoying the solitude. After an hour I had a good mental map of the island's features. I returned to my camp and ate a couple of energy bars and some dried fruit.

I did not know when the helicopter would arrive to collect me, so I went on another walk and explored the more remote corners of Steep Holm, including the ruined buildings near the beach. The one I'd passed on my way up had, I recalled from my visitor-centre leaflet, once been an inn. I suspected the venue had dealt with illicit goods in centuries past, for the location seemed perfect for the surreptitious antics of smugglers.

Except for the beach, the island seemed fairly consistent in form all the way around. Boulders and rocks encircled Steep Holm at the base of vertical cliffs. Above the precipices the island was more like an ordinary hill, for its sides rose fairly gently thereafter, covered in trees or brambles toward the relatively flat vegetated ground of the summit. However, such a description would not do

169

the impressive island justice, for the various environments blended in places as one would expect of a site left to nature. The eastern flank appeared rather more wooded than elsewhere, presumably because the dominant Atlantic winds gusted from the southwest.

I returned to my shelter. I checked my mobile phone but it had been drenched and appeared to be unsalvageable. My boots were still damp inside but everything else was dry. The boots went into the bottom of the rucksack, followed by the fleece and spare socks. The only water I had left was in the metal flask, and I tucked that into one of the side pouches. I'd eaten everything I'd bought except for some biscuits. The Ordnance Survey maps were battered but still usable, so I stuck them at the top of the pack. I'd probably throw them away once I got back to London, but for now they were little mementos of my Somerset escapade that I was oddly reluctant to part with.

While I trusted Sarah to arrange my evacuation by helicopter – I assumed the aircraft was already on its way from London – I did not know when it would arrive. I was untroubled by the wait because the scenery and fresh air were invigorating and I prefer solitude to company. And while some of the physical stiffness in my limbs lingered – probably not helped by sleeping in damp clothes – the mental tension had all but evaporated. I'd alerted Sarah to the MOIS team and could rely on her to take steps to thwart their attack.

I waited with little else to do apart from watching the seagulls and indulging my curiosity about the ancient gun emplacements. I had rehydrated myself well enough, so, with only a flask of water remaining, I rationed myself to a few infrequent sips as the minutes rolled by. A briar patch supplied me with a handful of ripe blackberries which I enjoyed enormously. It was probably my imagination, but I believed the sugars and vitamins had an instant restorative effect. The wild fruit was undoubtedly an improvement on the biscuits.

The noise of an engine disturbed my seclusion. Not the low-pitched and rapid whump of rotor blades that I expected, but the whine of a fast boat's outboard motor. The sound came from the east. I instinctively grabbed the handle of my rucksack and carried it by my side as I moved location. I hid myself among the thick vegetation on the side of the island above the pebble beach. I spied the boat and discovered it was a rigid-hulled inflatable, with a crew of two and a dozen passengers. As the watercraft slowed and man-oeuvred toward the shore, I read the name of an excursion company emblazoned on the tubes, and realised I was looking at a tourist boat.

The arrival of visitors was inconvenient but not, in itself, alarming. The problem was that I recognised Rasul Heyat among the group, and he was sitting with a younger Iranian man in the boat. With consternation, I drew the rather obvious conclusion that their purpose on Steep Holm was not sightseeing but murder. I flattened myself into the undergrowth and watched as the crew moored the boat. The occupants disembarked via a set of portable metal steps onto the beach. Gradually the tourists made their way up the path cut into the rocks, Heyat and his companion among them. The boat crew stayed on the beach.

I remained in my hiding place for several minutes, waiting for the group to reach the top of the island. I left my rucksack under thick bracken and crawled up the slope, staying some way back from the nearest footpath. As I thought would happen, the visitors broke away from each other into pairs or small groups, each taking their own route. Heyat and the other Iranian stayed on the high ground, walking westward along the island's ridge, away from my position.

It was a small mercy that there were only two of them. I wondered where the rest of the MOIS team was, but they weren't on the island, and that was all that mattered right then. None-theless, two highly skilled operatives were more than a handful, and I knew they would be armed with silenced handguns. The course of events could not continue on this hide-and-seek trajectory; I had to take offensive action. First, though, I needed to decipher their strategy and work out a way to counterattack. Using the thick foliage on the fringe of the island as cover, I kept low and followed them at a distance of roughly two hundred yards.

They walked until encountering the island's triangulation pillar, or trig point, about halfway along the ridge. I had wondered how they expected to find me, given the largeness of the fortress island, but that question was answered when Heyat removed a pair of walkie-talkies and a small drone from his backpack. The younger man walked back in my direction for a few steps, testing the radio. Satisfied their means of communication was functional, Heyat set up the drone and sent it airborne via a small handheld controller.

The tactic had its merits. I assumed the sight of a camera drone was not unusual above Steep Holm. The island was unique and interesting, from its historical buildings to the abundant wildlife – perfect for photographers and filmmakers. With a team of just two and time against them, it was the only realistic way the Iranians could search the half-mile-long island. There was, however, an inherent flaw in their strategy which I intended to exploit.

I observed them for a while to find out which part of the island they were going to check first. Heyat flew the drone above the hillside on the northwest section, guiding it methodically in a neat search pattern. The second agent walked in that direction, and soon I lost sight of him when he went down the slope, but I could tell the overall plan was to work clockwise around the island's edges.

I scuttled back toward the east side but refrained from rounding the corner near the beach – I didn't want to be spotted by the skipper and his friend when I took out my target. Glad that I'd spent some time exploring after I'd woken up, I recalled the features I'd seen earlier. Old gun-battery sites and other stone or concrete features were dotted over the hillside, mostly strewn with bracken and bramble and denser shrubs. I found a location that was close to the path but also beautifully concealed. The hill tumbled away below me before reaching the top of the cliff. I emplaced myself in a hideout that camouflaged me well but also afforded a view of the path, flattening myself on the ground underneath thick leaves and bramble stems.

Half an hour passed before the Iranian operator drew close. I heard the whine of the drone's tiny rotors as the machine passed overhead. While I felt I was almost certainly hidden from Rasul Heyat's lens, I couldn't risk assailing the nearer enemy while the camera was above me. Heyat would sprint the relatively short distance from the trig point to my location if he saw anything amiss, and I'd likely receive a bullet for my troubles. I had to take them out one at a time. The drone moved out toward the cliff edge; I hoped the camera was pointing in the same direction.

The Iranian stepped closer and paused about four yards from where I was hidden. He held his hand inside his jacket, clutching a concealed firearm as he scanned the dense foliage of the slope and the concrete ruins. The weapon was a problem but it occupied his hand, and I was confident I could reach him before he freed it and let off a shot. I had a solid surface beneath my feet which I used as a springboard. Bursting through the undergrowth, I grabbed both his legs and then let gravity take over.

Unbalanced, he fell at once, landing heavily on his spine, but he had the presence of mind to kick out as we both slid down the slope. The blow was awkward and poorly aimed, but it still struck my cheekbone and made my eyes water at the sudden pain. I relinquished my grip on his legs for a second and rapidly crawled a yard back up the slope, pummelling his gut with one fist while I grabbed at his gun arm with the other. He tried to knee-strike me several times but caught me only once with a wincing impact against my ribs.

He pulled the gun free but I held it away, trapping his right arm outstretched against the dirt. I got a knee onto his bicep and then used both hands to punch his face with all the strength I could muster. But he wasn't an adversary to go down easily, and he shoved his left hand into my face, clawing at my eyes. I ground my knee deeper into the muscles of his arm, causing him to lose his grip on the gun. I knocked his left forearm away with my right, hoping to stop his attempts to damage my eyes and throat, but he didn't give up. The man was wiry, younger than me and all muscle. I had to bring this battle to a swift conclusion or I'd be dead.

I backed off, feigning defeat. My adversary glowered at me and pushed himself off the ground with his elbows while finding footholds for his boots, quickly shifting into a crouch. That's when he made his mistake. He lunged at me. I grabbed his arm and used his own momentum against him, flinging him forward. He tripped and turned and I heard a crack as his skull hit concrete. But I was unbalanced too, and I crashed through the vegetation, rolling with all the grace of a sack of potatoes. Something ensnared and ripped my right thigh, stopping my fall but sending a stab of pain into my leg. I knew the wound was bleeding before I looked round. It wasn't bramble that had sliced my leg but a length of rusty barbed wire, and part of it was still hooked into my flesh.

I pulled the wire free as gingerly as I could, wincing against the grating pain. The wound was a three-inch dirty tear that needed attention I could ill afford. My leg throbbed and felt numb, which was not ideal if I wanted to move. I turned around and looked at where the Iranian had landed. He was motionless and I saw a splash of blood leaking from a head wound.

I grabbed the silenced Glock from where it had fallen. I looked skyward but couldn't see the drone. Another noise startled me as I crawled ungainly through the undergrowth, coming from near where the Iranian had landed on the concrete battlement. The radio.

Rasul Heyat's voice, speaking in Farsi, crackled through the cheap walkie-talkie. "Orodes? I've lost sight of you."

There wasn't a twitch from the man I'd wounded or killed. I couldn't tell, but either way his lack of response on the radio meant

Heyat would know something was wrong in seconds.

"Bux? Where the fuck are you?"

The drone whined like a large mosquito and reappeared overhead. I saw light reflecting off its tiny camera lens. I got to my feet and checked the gun, confirming a round was chambered. Standing up sent another wave of pain through my leg and caused my vision to blur. I could wait for Heyat to appear and attempt a shot, but I feared I would come off worse in a one-on-one shooting match. Head thumping, I changed my plan. I hobbled up to the path.

I saw Heyat about two hundred yards away. He dropped his radio and the drone controller, reached for his gun and started sprinting toward me. I fired off a single shot. I missed – I had expected nothing else – but it caused him to dive to the ground, giving me a few more precious seconds.

Banishing the pain, I ran as hard as I could. I ploughed through the undergrowth to where I'd hidden my rucksack and hurled it through the air, hoping it had enough momentum to reach the pebbles below. I trampled through the undergrowth until I reached the path by the ruined inn, hurried down to the beach and aimed the gun at the two unfortunate fellows from the boat. I scurried across the beach to my rucksack and hooked one arm through a strap.

"Give me the fucking keys!" I shouted.

They both stared at me, frozen to the spot. I pointed the gun at the pebbles several yards away from them and fired. The bullet pinged and smashed the stone, sending tiny fragments into the air. That little demonstration banished any lingering doubt from their minds.

"The keys!" I yelled, running across the pebbles toward the boat.

One of the crew held out the keys. I snatched them and waved the gun, ordering them to step back. They did so. At that moment I saw Rasul Heyat high up on the path. Expecting him to chase after me, it caught me by surprise when he concealed his gun and stood there, watching me from above the ruined building. I think I realised what he was doing at that point, but the nuances of the situation eluded me. I clambered into the boat, dumped the rucksack behind me and straddled the bench at the helm. I twisted the key in its slot. The motors fired at once. Thankfully the controls were familiar.

"Unmoor the RIB," I said to the two men on the beach, gesticulating with the Glock.

They obeyed and even gave me a push as I stole their rather splendid vessel. I spun the wheel and engaged the twin propellers. The boat accelerated smoothly, its sleek hull rising from the water as I gained speed.

Seconds later I was heading south at over thirty knots along the gleaming waters of the Bristol Channel.

31

AFTER OBSERVING THE GUNPOINT THEFT of the RIB, Rasul Heyat skulked back up the footpath behind the ruined inn, certain the boat crew hadn't seen him. He shifted his attention to finding Orodes Bux, retracing his steps to roughly the last point he'd seen his fellow operative through the drone's video camera. There was, Heyat surmised, a good chance that Bux had been flung over the edge onto the rocks below. It was with relief that he found the other man leaning against the remains of an overgrown masonry wall, clutching the back of his bleeding head and with swellings all over his face.

Heyat shuffled down the slope. "What happened?" he asked as he reached Bux.

Bux let out a groan through blood-stained teeth. "He ambushed me. Must've seen us arrive."

Heyat shrugged. "Probably. We had no other way to find him."

The younger man looked around for several seconds and cursed. "He took my gun."

"He did. And he stole the boat with it."

Bux held his stare through puffy eyes. "What now? Have you called Murad?"

Heyat shook his head. "No mobile signal out here. I presume the boat crew have an alternative way to contact their people." He paused. "You'd better let me look at your head."

"I'll be fine."

"I'm sure you will, but I'll check anyway."

Bux leaned forward and moved his hand. Heyat made a cursory examination, gently prising apart the matted blood.

"Well?" Bux asked, wincing.

"You probably need a stitch or two, but the wound is clotting. Are you dizzy?"

"A bit. It's wearing off."

"Can you make it back up to the ridge?"

Bux glowered. "I'm not a fucking invalid, Rasul."

"Fine. Follow me and stop complaining." Heyat clambered back up the slope, trampling in the vegetation and pushing branches aside. "You're lucky he didn't kill you," he commented.

Bux followed, unsteady on his feet. "It wasn't a one-sided fight," he countered irritably.

Heyat stopped and turned around. "You were meant to shoot him. Now he's got away."

Bux glared. "You'd have done no better. There should've been at least four of us."

The older man reached the footpath and waited for Bux to catch up. "We can't change that. We need to get your story straight though. You tripped on an unseen lump of concrete and fell. If anyone asks, say you were near the old gun batteries on the north side. Neither of us saw the man who stole the boat."

"I get it. We witnessed nothing."

"Right. I guess the boat crew will contact the police, so we probably can't avoid speaking to them, but they'll let us go if we have nothing to contribute. I assume you can remember your alias and the fake address in your dazed state?"

"Of course."

"Good. Come on, I'll get the water from my backpack and clean the wound."

The two men walked along the path until they reached the place where Heyat had ditched his pack and radio. The drone had returned to its launch point after not receiving commands from the control unit. Heyat dug out his water bottle and splashed some of the contents over the blood on Bux's head. Bux removed his T-shirt and dabbed the cut to dry it.

Heyat handed him the water bottle. "Drink," he said.

Bux nodded and accepted the bottle. The breeze on the summit, laden with the scents of wildflowers and sea salt, helped clear his head. Heyat switched off the drone and put it into the backpack.

"Are you ready?" Heyat asked.

"For what?"

Heyat made a sweeping gesture with his arm. "We'll go down to the cottages on the south side. They'll have a first-aid kit and some antiseptic in the office. Might as well patch you up properly while we wait. And we can find out if the boat captain has contacted the mainland. I have a feeling he'll want to cut this trip short."

They continued toward the west end of the island for a short way before encountering the footpath which cut across the ridge and headed for the south flank. Turning left, they continued over the high ground before descending the hillside. The roofs of the cottages soon came into view, and the path wound its way down through gorse-bedecked heathland.

Bux muttered to himself as they descended the slope, loud enough for Heyat to catch his words. "I'm beginning to see why Murad wants that bastard dead."

32

THE ELATION OF ESCAPING FROM STEEP HOLM with my life intact was tempered by the realisation that my predicament was now worse than during the previous two days. I was the custodian of an instantly identifiable boat whose details would be circulated by the police and coastguard. As the craft powered through the calm waters of Bridgwater Bay with its prow raised, I knew that sailing into any harbour on the English or Welsh coasts would attract immediate and unwanted attention. I'd have to abandon the RIB somewhere discreet, but where? Hiding the boat in a secluded spot would solve one problem but cause me another, namely the difficulty in returning to civilisation by land. I had no idea how I'd make it back to London without getting caught.

If the police had not identified me as a suspect beforehand, they would now. The acquisition of the RIB had been a robbery as English law might define my offence, and an armed one at that. Any endeavour to arrest me would surely be conducted by a fire-arms unit rather than unarmed response officers. And while being a fugitive from the law was tiresome in the extreme, I had no reason to hope my Iranian adversaries would give up the hunt. After what had taken place on the island, I expected nothing less than a redoublement of effort. My one consolation was that I'd told Sarah about their presence.

I'd taken some knocks but no real damage during my fight with Orodes Bux except for the barbed-wire injury. The dirty three-inch wound on my right leg was throbbing, swollen and bloody; I'd have to clean and dress it soon to lessen the risk of infection. That wasn't something I could do while at the helm of the RIB. I dreaded to think how much rust and dirt had found its way into the tear. There wasn't a first-aid box inside the boat. There was, however, a decent pair of marine binoculars on a cord strap, so I put them around my neck. Hardly an alternative to antiseptic but potentially useful in their own right. Circumstances were such that I resolved to steal anything that might aid me.

Beyond that I had no plan; I was back to improvisation; I felt unsettled. I'd eaten, rehydrated and slept well enough, but the gains from my sojourn on the citadel island were fading. The pain in my leg was almost enough to distract me from piloting the boat. I told myself to concentrate, to deal with one obstacle at a time. The priority was to find a place to land. The rest would follow in due course.

I manoeuvred to within half a mile of the coast and continued at speed, keeping the Somerset landscape on my left as I headed south to Burnham-on-Sea, and then west as the geography changed. I saw long beaches, dunes and flat moorland behind them. A few parked cars were visible, but the stretch of coast looked mostly remote and unoccupied. I considered steering the boat to land on that isolated territory but soon rejected the idea. I'd be out of sight but would have miles to walk over open ground, making my discovery by a police patrol more likely.

One feature that stood out further along the coast was the nuclear power plant at Hinkley Point. I recalled seeing the construction marked on one of my Ordnance Survey maps. There was no way I could land at the secure site, of course, but seeing the monstrous building reminded me that the landscape further west was far more undulous and forested than the bare Somerset Levels with which I'd become familiar.

I passed the power station and continued westward, feeling the sun against my neck. The air temperature was now comfortably hot, but being out on the open water – and travelling fast – naturally had a contrary effect, and I was glad of my fleece to ward off the breeze and spray. Beyond Hinkley Point I continued for approximately four miles, looking for somewhere suitable to make shore.

The littoral view changed as I continued on my bearing. Instead of sand I saw beaches strewn with grey boulders. Heavily eroded cliffs rose behind the rocks – not tall or imposing, but enough to block the sight of the land beyond. Layers of different hues revealed the straticulate nature of the cliffs, and I wondered what fossilised leviathans might still be trapped within the ancient rocks. The realisation that these remote beaches were not served by access routes from above surpassed my interest in the geology. I did, however, recall that a long-distance footpath encircled most of the coastline in southwest England. There was a chance I'd encounter a walker when I scrambled up the cliff, but I had seen no one thus far.

Before then I had to work out how to get to shore. The tide was low enough to reveal great cracked pavements of rock which stretched right back to the lower strata of the cliffs. I couldn't tell how far seaward the carpet of rocks extended. I decided I'd just approach the cliffs at a crawl until I ran aground. Well, it wasn't my boat. Nor would I have to complete the manoeuvre in the dark this time, and the RIB's hull was shallower than the cabin cruiser's. I slowed the boat right down and turned toward the beach. Leaving the boat to proceed under its own power, I stuffed the binoculars into my rucksack and then hefted it onto my shoulders.

The boat scraped against rock and came to a halt. I killed the engine and stepped over the buoyancy tube into the shallow water. The rocks were slippery beneath the soles of my hiking shoes, but I could nevertheless proceed with far less trouble than during the similar misadventure of the previous night. I splashed salt water into the cut on my leg, wincing at the acidic sting as I rubbed the wound. Satisfied that I'd cleaned it as best I could, I carried on, wading through the shallows until I eventually made it to dry ground. I didn't want to waste my dwindling supply of drinking water, but I tipped some onto the cut from my flask to wash out the salt.

I sat down on the pebbles and removed my shoes. I had neither the desire to climb up the cliff in wet footwear nor any knowledge of the terrain beyond, so swapping the sodden shoes for my almost dry boots made sense. I slid my arms through the rucksack's shoulder straps once again and then looked for a way up the crumbling cliff. Although the ascent was precarious in places, I managed it well enough while doing my best to ignore the ache in my right leg. The cliff wasn't steep or tall, so it took me just a few minutes to reach the top.

The coastal path was obvious – a grassy track that ran parallel to the cliff edge at a moderately safe distance – but I had no clue where I was. I could see hills and woodland and a few farm buildings, but no distinctive landmarks. This was not an insurmountable problem – I just needed to head inland to the nearest village – but only when I knew my location could I devise a plan. I set off through a field of grazing sheep, aiming for the gate on the far side.

I soon found a footpath which I followed toward a large patch of woodland. Shortly thereafter I noticed an old church with a tower and a large grey-stone manor house. A few attractive houses stood nearby, hidden between trees, and I suspected all the properties might have a connection – historical if not current – to the estate upon whose grounds I now stood. I wandered down a track on the edge of the forest and emerged near a tiny car park. Concerned that someone might spot me as a trespasser, I followed what appeared to be a normal country lane, passing a row of unimaginably quaint cottages and gardens.

There didn't appear to be anyone nearby, although I couldn't dismiss the possibility that someone was watching me from behind a net curtain. I hadn't seen a village signpost, so I still didn't know where I was, but my casual observations were constructing a mental picture. I carried on along the single-lane road, walking past cottages with thatched roofs and low boundary walls. The houses were scattered along the lane, partly concealed from their neighbours, and there were so few of them that I could barely describe the village as a hamlet.

I reached a narrow T-junction and – at last – saw an old-fashioned signpost. It told me that the place I had walked from was called East Quantoxhead. The name was vaguely familiar; I reckoned I must have read it on my OS map. That lifted my mood because I could still use the map if I needed to; I hadn't travelled so far west in the boat to pass beyond the edge of the chart.

The road I'd reached actually had white lines on its surface. Solid ones, as it turned out, reflecting the narrow and hazardous nature of the route. It wasn't a very safe place to walk, thanks to the absence of a pavement and the high roadside hedges, but traffic was almost non-existent. I turned left and walked for about two hundred and fifty yards before finding a field entrance. I stood back in the gap and pulled out my 140 map. It hadn't fared all that well after its soaking, but it was dry now and quite readable.

I found East Quantoxhead and, further east, the nuclear power station at Hinkley Point. The rolling landscape which surrounded me matched the contours on the sheet, and I realised that Somerset's Quantock Hills were only a short distance to the south. But I was nowhere near a town or a railway line, so my options for a route out were curtailed. In different circumstances I might have welcomed being surrounded by hills and rustic villages but, at that moment, the cover of an urban environment would have been preferable for this wanted man.

The ache in my leg reminded me I needed to tend the wound properly before I tackled anything else. My best option, I decided, was to walk to the next village. Kilve was roughly two-thirds of a mile away. It was certainly larger than East Quantoxhead, and the letters PO on my map told me it had a post office. Out in the sticks that probably meant a village store as well. The usefulness of polymer banknotes occurred to me at that moment; my money had survived its salt-water submersion without issue. Less helpfully, there was nothing I could do about my appearance. My bruised face and damaged trousers would get noticed.

I followed the road to Kilve, occasionally having to tuck myself into the hedgerow to avoid being hit by passing cars. Fortunately the walk took me less than a quarter of an hour, even with my leg feeling increasingly numb. I hobbled into the village and soon discovered that the post office did indeed double up as the grocery shop. I'd hoped for a pharmacy but there was none. The pub next door looked incredibly tempting, but I knew I couldn't risk revealing myself to more people than was necessary.

There were only two customers in the shop when I entered, plus an attendant at the till. I grabbed a plastic basket and glanced around the shelves. I selected sandwiches, more energy bars and biscuits. A two-litre bottle of water also went into the basket, and I picked up a couple of small orange juice bottles because I needed a vitamin boost. There was a section of the shop which had limited medical supplies. I grabbed some paracetamol, a tube of antiseptic cream, some gauze bandages and microfibre tape. I selected two cheap toothbrushes – one for the obvious reason and the other to scrub the leg wound. I wasn't looking forward to that. A small but overpriced tube of toothpaste also went into the basket.

"Hurt your leg?" the assistant inquired as I went to pay.

I nodded. "Cut it on some wire on an overgrown footpath," I answered. "Reckon some farmers leave them in that state deliberately."

"True, that," she replied, but didn't make further comment as she put the items into a plastic carrier bag for me. I paid and then left the shop.

Outside I looked at my map once more. Knowing it would be unsafe to stay in the village, I decided to find temporary cover so I could tend to the cut and then figure out my next move. I unfolded my OS map and noticed a green dashed line a short distance south of the village. The footpath would lead me to the edge of the Quantock Hills. From there I could find a copse in which to hide, rest and patch myself up.

I crossed the road and headed down a secluded track called Pardlestone Lane. Soon I was away from the houses and hobbling along a leafy corridor. Gaps in the hedgerows revealed rolling farmland. I kept going, fighting the ache in my leg but buoyed up by distant views of the Quantock Hills.

33

I FOUND MY WAY ONTO THE HILLS easily enough, but the steep footpaths put a strain on my injured leg, so I stopped to swallow a couple of paracetamol tablets. My map told me that several of the smooth hills rose to three hundred metres at their summits. The landscape of the high ground was heath rather than forest, and the views of yellow gorse and purple heather were stunning. But the absence of tree cover was a problem for me. I checked the map once more and realised that, in the northern section of the Quantocks at least, I'd only find concealment in the wooded valleys. The map frequently used the word 'combe' to describe such features.

I didn't have the place to myself. I spied several walkers on the many footpaths which snaked alongside streams and criss-crossed the contours. The distances were, however, too great to be problematic. If I noticed someone heading my way along a ridge, I diverted to another track. Navigation was a straightforward task; my Ordnance Survey map served me well. I headed for one of the combes, hoping to find a sheltered spot where I could clean and bandage the cut.

There was much less tree cover in the vale than I'd expected. I encountered spindly ash and hazel, spaced quite far apart, which was inadequate for my purposes. But I didn't have a choice. After traversing two grid squares of my chart, and taking a slothful hour and a half to do so, I sat down in a pile of leaf litter with a loud groan and hoped that no one would venture through the valley while I had my trousers removed.

I made simple preparations before scrubbing the wound. Using my rucksack as a makeshift table, I cut a large wadding of gauze with the multi-tool and stretched several lengths of the microfibre tape over it. I freed a toothbrush from its packaging and unscrewed the lid from my tube of antiseptic cream. I delayed attacking the cut and peered at it as if to find some reason not to proceed. It had knitted together in places; I needed to sever those sticky connections if I were to clean it properly. The skin was taut and reddened. I splashed some water over the cut, gritted my teeth and scrubbed as furiously as I could bear. I might have yelped a little, but it was the nausea that coursed through my chest and throat which I remembered.

I dropped the toothbrush after a few seconds and squirted an excessive amount of antiseptic onto the raw cut. Next I slapped the improvised bandage in place and taped it down. I wound more of the gauze and tape right around my leg to keep the wound tight and dry. I actually felt much better at that point, partly because I was satisfied that the cut was not infected, and partly because there's something reassuring about a clean dressing. I put my hiking trousers and boots back on and tidied up. There was nothing I could do about the bloodied rip in the material, but I didn't care about that. Being able to walk pain-free was what counted.

One obstacle surmounted. I could now, in relative comfort, think about my predicament. Several hours had passed since I'd woken up on Steep Holm, and I was hungry again. I broke the seal on a packet of sandwiches with my thumb. Nibbling at the food, I unfolded my map and studied the features it illustrated. I made a loose tally of the squares on the chart which roughly covered the Quantock Hills, and concluded that the area was something under a hundred square kilometres, which was about forty square miles. Maybe a quarter of that was woodland. The densest parts lay to the south.

If the police were determined to find me, there was only so long I could hide in the forest and skulk into the neighbouring villages for provisions like a modern-day outlaw. I already knew a photograph was in circulation, so at some point I would be recognised and reported. However charming I found the Somerset landscape, I had no wish to stay while bearing the status of fugitive. I wasn't confident that I'd shaken off the Iranians either – they certainly had some connection to the local police that I'd been unable to decipher. The police wouldn't shoot me unless I threatened them; the Department 312 agents wouldn't be so nuanced.

I had to return to London. My superiors could then resolve any issues with the authorities, presumably after they'd subjected me to a tiresome and pointless debriefing. I've always found those processes are less about getting the facts straight and more to remind operatives about the hierarchy they work under. It's all theatre. But I had to get there first, and transport options were limited and bestowed with risk.

Several car parks were shown on the map. I assumed they would be fairly small clearings in the woods that could accommodate only a handful of vehicles. None were nearby, so I'd have to put in a few more miles on foot. I wasn't exactly armed with tools for car theft, although the binoculars I'd taken from the RIB were probably weighty enough to smash a side window, and I had the multi-tool I'd stolen from the cabin cruiser. My acquisition of a car from a remote spot in the Quantock Hills would probably go unnoticed for at least an hour. Not enough time to avoid the ANPR cameras on the way to London, but probably a sufficient period for a shorter journey.

The area covered by the OS chart showed villages but no towns south of the Quantock Hills, so I looked at the small diagram of southwest England on the cover instead. Taunton wasn't far away, and I remembered the Devonshire town was on the main railway line. Knowing that British police forces were poor at exchanging information, it made sense to head into the next county. I could find transport or arrange an extraction in Taunton without too much trouble. If I identified a threat, I could defy expectations and head further southwest to the city of Exeter. My options would be even broader there.

I sorted out my rucksack and kept the Glock hidden inside it. I'd had no choice when taking the boat, but I hoped to avoid pointing the gun at an innocent driver in order to steal his vehicle. If I needed to observe a car park from behind the trees and wait until all the cars were unattended, I would do exactly that. I couldn't waste much time though; I still had a lot of ground to cover. The police had probably released my description to the media too, and even though my current whereabouts were unknown, they'd figure out I was somewhere in the hills if they found the RIB on the beach below East Quantoxhead.

I got to my feet and gingerly put pressure on my injured leg. It ached but felt much better than before. I'd hardly be setting any speed records, but I knew I could walk for a few miles yet with just a minor limp, even over steep terrain. I slung the rucksack over my shoulders, adjusted my cap to shield my eyes from the sun, and headed south through the wooded valley.

34

PENNY AMBLER glanced up from her computer monitor as Jacob Poe strolled over to her desk, giving the detective inspector a questioning look.

"Do you have a minute?" Poe asked.

She gave him a wry smile. "Do I ever?"

The DI grinned in response. "Did you see the report about the stolen boat?"

Ambler raised her eyebrows. "Sorry, Jake. Too busy working on a murder inquiry. You know the one? Iranian national with no traceable background who was executed in sleepy Glastonbury." She swivelled around on her chair to face him and leaned back, clasping her fingers together across her midriff. "It's not that I'm not interested in boats. I had a nice yacht trip in Turkey when I went there on holiday five years ago. I can give someone in the marine unit a bell if that helps."

Poe chuckled. "They're already involved, actually." He perched against the corner of her desk. "Trust me, you'll want to hear this."

Ambler held eye contact but didn't answer.

"Do you know Steep Holm Island?"

Ambler nodded.

"Someone stole a tourist RIB from there at gunpoint this morning."

The sergeant's eyes widened. "Rogue birdwatcher?"

Poe held back a smile. "Perhaps – in the James Bond sense of the word."

Ambler frowned. "I don't follow."

"Ian Fleming wanted the plainest and dullest name he could find for the protagonist of his book *Casino Royale*. He owned a bird guide written by an ornithologist called James Bond. The name stuck."

"Fascinating." Ambler's tone revealed she thought otherwise.

"I forgot you don't read novels." Poe shrugged. "Your loss. Anyway, whether or not our suspect was a birdwatcher, he had a silenced handgun, according to the witnesses."

Ambler gave her colleague a quizzical stare. "I take it this person wasn't one of the passengers?"

"Correct."

"Help me out here, Jake. I don't have time for a question-and-answer session. Is this connected to my investigation or not?"

Poe stood up, wheeled a chair over from another desk and sat down. "And I was hoping you'd ask how the suspect landed on the island." He paused. "He stole another boat during the night from the quay at Weston. A small cabin cruiser. It was spotted just after dawn today and reported to the coastguard. It was on the rocks at Steep Holm."

"That makes no sense," Ambler remarked. "Why take a boat to get to the island only to steal another to get away?"

"He wrecked it."

Ambler shook her head. "That's incidental. If his motive was escape, why go to Steep Holm in the first place? It's almost inaccessible, especially in the dark. Why not find a harbour further down the coast? Or cross the Bristol Channel to Wales? There had to be a reason to hide on the island."

"You think he was hiding?"

Ambler held Poe's gaze. "I'll consider an alternative if you can offer me one."

"I rather like your fugitive theory. Let me come back to that." Poe tapped his thumb against the plastic arm of the chair. "There's a lot about this incident which feels wrong. Let me summarise what I know. You'll see where I'm going with this."

Ambler waved her hand, inviting him to continue.

"The witnesses to the robbery were the boat crew. They gave a good description of the suspect. They even noticed he'd injured his leg and ripped his trousers. He was carrying a rucksack too. Looked a bit dishevelled but seemed to know how to handle the weapon."

"Who said that?" Ambler asked.

"The boat skipper," Poe explained. "He served with the Royal Navy before civilian life. Knew what he was talking about."

"Okay. What else?"

"A tourist was injured. He claimed he'd slipped on rough ground. I don't believe a word of it."

"You think there was a fight?" Ambler questioned.

"Perhaps. He was there with a friend. They'd made a last-minute booking to get on the trip. Officers took contact details when they were ferried back to the mainland so witness statements could be taken later. The injured fellow and his mate gave monkey details. Neither their addresses nor their phone numbers exist."

"They were involved somehow." Ambler paused in thought. "What do we know about them?"

"Very little. The tour company provided the information that was submitted to their website. It adds nothing useful."

"Shame the officers didn't check their ID," Ambler muttered.

"They had no grounds to," Poe replied. "Those people weren't suspects. They only discovered the problem later when they tried the phone numbers. It wasn't the officers' fault. To be fair, they were more thorough than I'd expect. None of the passengers were near the beach when the boat was stolen. No one but the boat crew saw the man with the rucksack."

"Apart from the beaten-up bloke who claimed otherwise."

"He had a reasonable explanation for his scrapes. It's genuinely precarious up there."

Ambler's forehead creased into a deep frown. "So our two strangers go missing after they return to shore."

"Having booked seats on the boat that very morning," Poe added. "One ends up getting injured a short time before the RIB was stolen at gunpoint."

"It wasn't a theft, Jake. It was an escape."

Poe smiled grimly. "I haven't told you the best part yet."

"There's more?"

"The suspect closely matches the description of a male named John Connery who was circulated on social media as missing. Connery has mental health issues. He also has a military background."

"Great. A nutter with a gun," Ambler replied.

"I don't think so. Call me an untrusting old git, but I think the social media posts were bogus."

"Why?"

"If you were concerned about a missing family member, wouldn't you call the police?"

Ambler stared at Poe for several seconds. "There's no police report?"

Poe shook his head.

"Have you seen the posts?" Ambler asked.

"I have one on my phone." Poe dug his mobile from his pocket and touched the screen. After a few seconds he handed the device to Ambler.

Ambler grabbed her desk phone and keyed in the telephone number for the person listed as Robert. She held Poe's gaze while listening as the call connected.

"Hello, is that Robert?" Ambler said when the phone was answered. "This is Detective Sergeant Ambler. I'm calling about John Connery." Ambler held the phone away from her ear a moment later and looked at Poe. "Cut off," she remarked. She dialled the number again. It didn't even ring. "Dead line," she told Poe as she replaced the handset. "Reckon we can trace it?"

Poe shrugged. "I can authorise a triangulation search, but I think we'd be wasting our time."

"Do it anyway," Ambler urged. "We'll see where it's been, even if we can't follow it now."

Poe took his mobile back and put it in his pocket.

"At least we have a photograph of our likely boat thief," Ambler remarked. "I assume there's been no further sighting?"

"Of him, no. But the RIB was found on the shore at East Quantoxhead. Given what we know so far, it's possible that he's hiding in the hills. Gold command has authorised a search."

Ambler grinned. "Major incident. Best time to commit crime," she remarked.

Poe smiled back. "True. We've pulled officers from their regular areas to help. The firearms tactical adviser is a mate of mine. There are no updates worth mentioning yet."

"Helicopter?"

Poe nodded. "Already deployed. This is a few hours old though, so they don't have a decent search grid. But it can't hurt to try."

Ambler folded her arms. "A fun day in Somerset."

"You could say that."

"But there's something you've not told me."

Poe looked at her askance.

"How is this connected to my murder investigation?"

"Didn't I mention that?" Poe said.

She shook her head.

"You saw Connery's photo?"

"Yep."

"Doesn't he look like the man seen running down Glastonbury Tor?"

Ambler stared for a moment. "Those descriptions were vague."

"The pathologist dug nine-millimetre bullets out of the victim. He was shot with a firearm that no one heard from a few hundred yards away. And now we have someone with a silenced handgun stealing boats. Call your witnesses. See if they recognise the man in the photo."

Ambler shifted in her seat. "I'm uncomfortable with that, Jake. If we're linking him to Ismail Khadem's murder, we ought to run a formal identification procedure at a police station."

"Ways and Means Act, Penny," the detective inspector replied. "At this point we have no evidence he committed the murder. He's not a suspect. We're just following a lead for a missing person inquiry."

"Forget about the boat theft and the injured man?"

"Any link at this stage is speculation. Discrete incidents until we know otherwise." He winked. "I mean, there's always a chance that our Steep Holm visitors might be key players. But as we've lost them, we can only guess, can't we?"

Ambler chuckled. "How the fuck did you get promoted to detective inspector?"

"By lurking in the grey areas of the law," Poe replied. "Plus learning all the buzzwords and diversity crap that promotion boards swoon over. The rest was down to my charm." He got to his feet. "On second thoughts, give that task to someone else. I think you and I should drive down to the Quantock Hills."

Ambler nodded and held his gaze. "Who is he, Jake?"

"I have no idea. But I'd bet my house that John Connery is not his real name." Poe turned around and walked out of the room.

35

MURAD ZAM set the tray down on the table and glanced around the motorway café before taking his seat. The restaurant wasn't busy. He briefly made eye contact with Davari and Heyat but didn't speak. He looked at Bux for a moment longer, noticing that the swelling on the younger man's face had puffed up and caused one eye to partially close. Lesson learned, Zam hoped, as he endeavoured to quell his anger about his subordinate's mistake. Zam frowned as he poked the plate of poor quality and over-priced service-station food with a fork.

He was about to take a mouthful of deflated chicken pie when his phone rang. His fork clattered against the plate.

"Aare?" Zam said quietly after noticing the caller's number. *Yeah?*

"You failed?" Control said, continuing the conversation in Farsi.

Zam clenched his jaw. He'd prioritised their departure from Weston-super-Mare over phoning their London contact, but somehow the man had already learned the truth about the Steep Holm incident.

He drew a breath before speaking again. "He saw the tourist boat and set a trap."

"And?"

"Orodes was injured. The target escaped. He stole the boat."

"Is that all?" Control questioned, his tone implying he thought otherwise.

"What else do you want me to say?" Zam retorted, his irritation growing.

"You didn't mention that Orodes lost his firearm. Is he stupid as well as careless?"

Zam looked at the injured man as he replied. "It was your idea to send just two men to the island."

"Don't twist the truth, Murad. There were only two spaces on the boat. You sent a boy to do a man's job. I'm starting to question your ability as the cell commander. Perhaps Haydar should take over."

"Promote him then," Zam growled. He waited but there was no response. "Ah, but you can't. You don't have the authority. You're a civilian coordinator, not a ranking officer. Why don't you come down here and show your face instead of sitting behind your desk?"

"Are you done with the tantrum?" Control snapped back. "It would be unwise to question the command structure of this operation."

"Is that a threat?"

"A reminder that the hierarchy is in place for a reason. But, rest assured, I won't work with you again after this mission."

"For that we can both be glad," Zam replied. He took another deep breath. "Do you have a reason for calling other than the reproval?"

"Yes. Where are you?"

"A service station on the M5 motorway."

"All of you?"

"After the incident this morning, we needed to get away from Weston-super-Mare."

"Good." Control paused. "From *behind my desk* I have accrued more information. It turns out that Orodes and Rasul's mistake on the island was not a total disaster. There's been a substantial development with the police."

"Your contact?" Zam inquired.

"He's been very helpful. The police have declared a major incident and are searching for your quarry. I'm receiving the pertinent updates from their command-and-control log."

"And?"

"The police found the stolen RIB on the beach near a place called East Quantoxhead. They circulated his description. A shop-keeper in the neighbouring village responded and said he'd bought food and water and basic medical supplies." Control hesitated. "Did Orodes injure him?"

"There was a fight. The outcome was unclear. Orodes was knocked out for a while."

"The witness noticed he was hobbling. Perhaps Orodes slowed him down. That should work to your advantage."

"You still want me to find him?" Zam asked.

"I think that's becoming more and more important, don't you?"

"It will be difficult if the police are involved."

"You're the tactician, Murad. I'm sure you'll find a way."

"That's not what you implied a moment ago," Zam retorted.

"Believe it or not, I do comprehend the limited options you've faced. And I know that you're a skilled tracker. Furthermore, you understand your adversary." Control paused for a moment. "He's somewhere in the Quantock Hills. That's a large territory of heath, moor and woodland. What is he likely to do?"

Zam thought for several seconds before answering. "After the Steep Holm incident, he'll know the police will look for him. He'll take cover, recuperate and then continue to move. The goal will be to find transport."

"He won't hide?"

"Only when resting. Any delay increases the chance of the police capturing him." Zam leaned back in his seat and scanned the restaurant again to check for eavesdroppers – not that he expected anyone in the place to understand his language. "Presumably the police have advised the public to report sightings only?"

"Correct. They've used the photograph from the social media posts we created. He's described as armed and dangerous. The public have been told not to approach him and to call 999 at once."

"Good." Zam hesitated. "The police will try to flush him out. I'll need the command-and-control log updates from your contact."

"Easily done," Control replied.

"You understand there will be a significant risk to us with so many police units on the ground?"

"You'll have to do your best to avoid them. Observe their tactics and respond accordingly."

Zam frowned. "You're giving me operational advice?"

"Merely a suggestion."

"Evading the police might not be as simple as you think. I received a call from a detective sergeant on the burner," Zam said. "She asked about John Connery. I didn't speak to her and I destroyed the phone."

"We made the number public. That's how we cornered him."

"Yes, but we didn't file a missing-person report with the police," Zam replied. "It will add to their suspicion."

"The focus will not be on you."

"I do not share your confidence."

"You should," Control stated. "Look at the local news feed. The police have declared the suspect for the boat robbery as a person of interest in the Ismail Khadem murder inquiry. The update went live just before I called you."

Zam considered the man's words for a few seconds. "That's both good and bad."

"Explain."

"They haven't circulated Rasul's description. We're therefore detached in that respect from the Glastonbury incident. We can also assume they don't know Farzad Bouzidi's real identity."

"Sounds positive," Control commented.

"Right. But they do know that someone was trying to find John Connery. If they've linked him to the murder, they'll deduce that

Bouzidi was a person of significance."

"Perhaps. But by the time they solve it, you and your team will be outside the country."

"I hope so," Zam replied. "We'll study the area and work out a deployment. And I need to know *exactly* what the police tactics are. Every detail."

"I will pass on the information as soon as I receive it."

"Do that." Zam ended the call. He put some food in his mouth and discovered the pie had gone cold, but he persevered with it because he needed to eat. The others had already finished their meals while he'd been on the phone, and they sat in silence, waiting for him to speak.

"So?" Heyat asked finally as Zam pushed the empty plate aside.

"Our target is now a fugitive from the police," Zam told him. "But we're going to find him first."

Heyat nodded. "Perhaps you'll have the chance to avenge your brother after all, Murad."

Zam got to his feet. "May his memory be a blessing." He turned and strode out of the café.

36

A FIERY AMBER LUMINOSITY SMOULDERED over the Quantock Hills as the afternoon softened into a warm evening, bringing ethereal hues to the heather and gorse which had been absent earlier. I stayed on the eastern flank of the landscape, mostly under oak and beech canopies, glad that the woodland was denser the further south I ventured.

But I didn't travel very far. I heard the police helicopter before I first glimpsed it through the gaps in the branches. There was no mistaking the yellow and dark midnight blue livery for anything other than a police aircraft. I was glad I'd made adequate progress but frustrated that once again my plan had been thwarted. I was less than half a mile from one of the heathland car parks.

The helicopter moved away from the area to where I could no longer hear it, but that was not enough to encourage me to proceed. I knew the camera gear installed on law enforcement helicopters was of remarkable technical finesse; it could read a numberplate – or identify a face – from a mile away. There was nothing I could do but maintain my concealment beneath a large oak while the aircraft flew its search pattern over the hills.

Alone in the forest I had plenty of time to reflect on the last few hours. Recalling how I'd been recognised by the youth and his friends in Burnham-on-Sea, I reckoned it was highly probable that the police had gained that photograph and circulated it in connection with my boat theft on Steep Holm. And while the Iranians' tactic and my crime were essentially unrelated, it wouldn't have taken a lot of intellectual adeptness to form a link. I'd been unable to alter my appearance much, and the boat crew would doubtlessly never forget my face.

As the helicopter passed this way and that, occasionally revealing itself to me through the tree canopy, I knew they would not find me by daylight. The forest was simply too great a challenge to breach from the air. I also doubted the police commanders would order their constables to conduct random searches through the wilderness without robust information. I had been seen with a handgun after all, so the likelihood of a routine police response was minimal. If they cornered me, they would send a firearms unit.

In a sense, though, I was trapped, even within the vast hectares of this area of natural beauty. An obvious action by the police would be to assign a patrol car to each car park, so my plan to steal a vehicle was no longer viable – not on the Quantock Hills at least. I could slip away into the farmland east of my current position, but that was a fairly predictable move. I couldn't go west over the open hills and heaths. South remained an option, but would become increasingly hard as time passed. I could go nowhere. Nor did I have any idea where the Iranians were.

And while I knew the police would not find me if I stayed under the oaks by day, that good fortune would be ruinously reversed by night when the helicopter could operate its thermal camera. At that moment, stuck as I was in the woods, I was safe. The entire landscape was radiating heat, so no person or animal would stand out, but I would become a thoroughly identifiable human-shaped white blob on a dark background when the ground cooled. There was only one way to avoid detection at night: find solid cover that would block my body heat from the helicopter's digital optics.

There remained the chance of discovery by a walker or cyclist in the forest. I considered attempting to climb into the branches of a tree, but I did not want to risk splitting open the wound on my leg. The last thing I needed was a sudden jolt of pain that caused me to tumble to the ground. Walking did not stretch the damaged skin and muscle all that much, particularly now that I had dressed the wound. Clambering up an oak with a rucksack on my back would require different effort entirely. And, from what I could see of my surroundings, there weren't exactly many trees with branches low enough for such an exploit anyway.

Hidden in my arboreous sanctuary, it occurred to me that the police helicopter couldn't stay airborne indefinitely – it would need to return to its base to refuel and perhaps swap crews. I had no idea where that airfield might be, but I had a vague recollection that the UK's police helicopter fleet was no longer operated by individual forces but a central agency. Would that factor lengthen the time between searches? I had no way of knowing, but I hoped that a more serious incident, such as a high-speed pursuit of a stolen car, might divert my antagonist.

I unfolded my Ordnance Survey map while I waited for the helicopter to stop its search. Under different circumstances I would have enjoyed lingering in the woods, filling my lungs with the earthy scent and listening to the chirps and chirms of the song-birds, but right then the solitude left me disheartened and irritated. The near misses with the Iranians were taking their toll, and now I had the police to contend with as well. London had never seemed further away than it did right then.

Waiting for the helicopter to depart, I scanned the map. A pursuer might conclude that I would come down from the Quan-tock Hills at some point – at that moment I could envisage no other option – so there would probably be several police units in the vicinity, especially on the east side. The one advantage I did have was the size of the area; I could probably evade the law in the Somerset countryside if I were careful. They couldn't know where I would emerge, and there were patches of woodland and remote churches where I could hide. Contour lines showed the farmland was hilly but not hard to cross. Footpaths were strewn all over the map, giving me alternatives to the narrow country roads which characterised the area. My chances would improve the further I went from the Quantocks.

After an intolerable wait, the helicopter turned for a final time to the south. I gave it another twenty minutes before setting out. The stiffness in my injured leg took a while to dissipate but felt better once I was in motion. My sense of direction was intact, but I checked my intended bearing with my compass because there were no navigation reference points inside the forest, and dusk was encroaching. I swapped the RNLI cap for my Petzl torch but did not turn on the lamp.

I wasn't far from the edge of the wood. I wandered between the trees for a short time before noticing one of the single-track roads which wound across the Quantock Hills. Seeing it confirmed my theory about being close to the clearings used as car parks.

Engine noise caught my attention and I stepped back a few yards to ensure I was hidden. A liveried police 4×4 pickup truck rolled slowly by, towing an equipment trailer containing portable floodlights, closely followed by a regular patrol car. If I had doubted it before, I now had confirmation that the police were taking the manhunt seriously. It made sense that they would set up an operations point in the heart of the hills.

I waited for several minutes after the vehicles had gone by. Neither hearing nor seeing anything else of concern, I ventured through the woods beneath a dusk of soft vermillion and scarlet clouds before breaking cover to descend toward Adscombe. My route took me via steep fields where sheep huddled for the night. I passed a rustic three-storey farmhouse but did not linger there in case someone was peering out through the windows. My concern about leaving footpaths for roads was unfounded. The lanes were barely wide enough for two cyclists abreast, and there was absolutely no one around.

Had I not feared the imminent return of the police helicopter or an encounter with a marked car on the roads, I might have walked through the night. The absence of street lights was a blessing, and my eyes adjusted well as the dusky sky mellowed to indigo. The road signs – of that old-fashioned black-and-white variety – were helpful. But while the thought of achieving distance tempted me, my desire for concealment was greater, and the light would eventually fade into darkness.

The need to stop trekking through the Somerset countryside was emphasised when I scratched my face on a bramble stem that I hadn't seen protruding from the hedgerow. Thankfully the thorns missed my eyes and the cut was minor, but it was enough to hasten my quest for shelter.

It took me just a short time to find a suitable spot. A farmyard revealed itself to me on the corner of a tight bend, and I saw at once that an open barn with a rounded corrugated-metal roof stood close to the entrance. Only stone and tile would have been better, but the modern structure would serve my needs well. There was no way the police helicopter would detect heat radiating beneath the arched roof, although they would spot plenty of cows and sheep nearby. And, even though the barn was open-sided, there were many straw bales stacked inside, providing me with a hiding place and comfort.

Lights were on in the nearby farmhouse but I could see no activity in the yard itself. One last look up and down the lane told me I was alone. Determined to catch a few hours' rest, I stepped into the farm. There wasn't even a gate I needed to climb over. Keeping close to the other side of the hedge, I walked toward the structure and slipped inside. I pulled off the rucksack and sat down on a bale to rest.

My timing was fortunate.

Seven or eight minutes later, I heard the police helicopter overhead.

37

ENGINE NOISE woke me up. I doubted I'd been asleep for more than twenty minutes. Momentary disorientation throbbed inside my head as I forced my eyes to open. The clamour was nearby. My first thought was the police helicopter had returned, hovering right over the barn. But it was the dancing headlight of a quadbike coming down the lane which told me otherwise. I grabbed Bux's handgun and shuffled between the straw bales for a better look.

To my dismay, the small 4×4 swung into the yard and stopped close to the farmhouse. I'd avoided looking at the beam directly to preserve my night vision, and there was still just enough ambient light to observe by. I saw a fifty-something farmer switch off the engine and dismount from the vehicle. He wasn't the problem, even as he unstrapped a broken-open shotgun from a rack over the rear tyres. The problem was the dog who jumped down and immediately stared in my direction, sniffing the air.

The animal started growling and took a few steps forward, then stopped again as it peered toward the barn. A good-natured border collie this was not; I was yards away from a sturdy short-haired mongrel whose entire body was lean and muscular. Thankfully it was tame enough to listen for commands from its owner, although I feared its instinct might overwhelm its obedience at any second. In the barn's darkness I raised the weapon in a two-handed grip, aiming at the dog. I knew I could hit the thing easily enough. Whether the bullets would slow the beast down before it attacked me was another matter entirely.

The farmer noticed the animal's unsettled behaviour. "What you seen, boy?" he mumbled with a strong West Country accent.

The dog's growl rumbled like a steam train from deep inside its body. Even in the half-light I could see the animal was moments away from launching itself in my direction. The farmer slowly lifted the shotgun and went to lock the barrels in place. It was time to put an end to this encounter.

I stepped forward, keeping the handgun pointed at the mongrel. "Stand still," I said, endeavouring to keep my speech peremptory but my voice no louder than it needed to be. I'd drawn enough attention already.

The farmer froze to the spot and glowered in my direction. The shotgun was still cradled in his arms. The dog barked.

"Take hold of the dog," I said.

The farmer reached for the animal's collar with one hand and gripped it. The dog continued to bark, straining against the man's hold. The threat from the shotgun was marginally lessened, but I doubted the farmer could control the dog if this standoff went on for much longer.

"If that animal moves an inch in my direction, I'll kill it and then I'll kill you," I said. "Do you understand?"

The man held my gaze and nodded.

"I don't want to hurt you," I added. I glanced toward the house to make a point. "You have a family?"

The man didn't speak, but his fearful look told me I'd elicited the reaction I'd been aiming for.

"Lay the shotgun on the ground," I said. "And keep hold of that fucking dog."

The farmer crouched awkwardly and set down the shotgun on the cracked concrete of the farmyard. He slowly got to his feet.

"Spare cartridges?" I asked.

"In my jacket pocket," he replied.

"Take them out and drop them."

The man obeyed and tossed five or six shotgun cartridges onto the ground.

"Both hands on the dog's collar," I said next, fearing the growling animal was on the verge of soaring toward my throat.

The farmer did as I instructed. I was tempted to demand the quadbike key but rejected the thought. Driving the vehicle would be noisy and require the use of the headlight, and to get anywhere I'd either have to stay on the roads or waste time with farm gates so I could ride across random fields with no sense of direction. Whatever my next move was, I'd have to do it on foot.

So what should I do? Leave this farm and find another building to hide in? The police would track me down within the hour. The unfortunate fellow before me would telephone 999 as soon as he got inside the house. But I would not murder an innocent farmer and his family just because he'd discovered me hiding in his barn, no matter how much worse he'd unwittingly made my predicament.

I flicked my wrist, waving the silenced handgun. "Take the dog and go inside," I told him. "Lock the doors."

He gave me a worried look that questioned my intentions.

"Move!" I shouted, seeing his hesitation. "I said I wouldn't hurt you. I meant it. Go indoors now. I'm not a threat to you." I could see how that last part might not be entirely convincing when the silenced Glock remained in play.

The farmer didn't need telling again. He backed away, dragging the dog by the collar. It kept trying to turn its head toward me, still growling. Soon both man and animal were at the front door of the farmhouse. I kept the gun pointed at the mongrel, worried it would break loose and assail me as the farmer went for the door key. My concern was unfounded. The door, as I should have guessed, had been left unlocked. The farmer pushed it open, hauled the dog inside and shut it behind him.

A fleeting thought made me question my decision. Yes, I could have held the family hostage and summoned an extraction team by telephone, but I had no desire to terrify anyone, particularly if there were children present. Besides, it might have been too late for that already. Had someone seen me from a darkened upstairs room and already called the police? I had no way to know.

209

I looked at the ground and asked myself if I ought to take the shotgun and cartridges when I fled the farmyard. I rejected the notion at once. Against whom exactly would I use the weapon? I'd have no qualms about killing the MOIS agents if I had the misfortune to encounter them again, but the noise of shotgun blasts would be heard, and there were police firearms officers deployed in the area. I'd have to carry the gun too, which would slow me down, as well as conferring no pragmatic advantage. I decided to leave the gun exactly where it was. I darted into the barn, hooked my arms through the straps of the rucksack, and ran out onto the lane.

I flicked on the Petzl headtorch. I had no choice. If I had to run, I'd need to see where I was going. The close call with the bramble flashed in my memory. The lane was as quiet as the grave, although I could still hear the mongrel barking inside the house. I guessed it would take a while for the agitated dog to calm down.

I could neither hear nor see the police helicopter. I jogged away from the farm along the leafy lane, glancing up at the sky when there were breaks in the tree canopy. No sign of the aircraft's red and green night-flying lights for as far as I could see, although I didn't have an entirely unrestricted view of the sky. Was the helicopter airborne? I had to assume it was, or it would be soon. And there'd probably be an armed response unit hurtling down the country lanes toward the farm sooner than that. I couldn't stay on the roads.

A patrol car I could avoid. There was a risk that a sharp-eyed officer might spot the faint red wash from my headtorch, but the landscape offered plenty of concealment among the hedgerows and contours. A few hundred yards from the road and I'd be out of sight.

But not from the helicopter if it came back and swept the area with its thermal imaging system. My plan to rest in the barn had been well and truly foiled. The predictable move was to find somewhere else to seek shelter – another barn, an outbuilding, a cattle shed – anywhere to hide from the probing electronic eye of the aircraft. But that infuriating predictability was the problem. After receiving the farmer's urgent call, the police would coordinate a precise grid search of every solid-roofed structure within a measured radius. They would find me.

As I continued to jog up the winding road, I realised I was following the reciprocal direction of my earlier route, back toward the Quantocks. Propelled by an instinct to seek familiar terrain or a subconscious rejection of my previous strategy, I did not know, but when I applied some thought to my quandary, a new idea revealed itself to me. I had to reject the obvious choices. Instead of hiding in a remote farm building or garden shed, I would retreat to the hills.

I found the path I'd used at twilight and increased my speed a little, hoping that the ascent would not test my stamina too harshly. I could not know how long it would take for the helicopter to return, but I willed it to concentrate its search on Adscombe and the neighbouring hamlets. I just needed enough time to get back to the dense oak and beech woods. Glancing back at the farm, I saw blue strobe lights flicker as police cars approached. I turned again and continued my hasty trek up the hillside.

The trees, of course, would not shield me from the aircraft's thermal camera. That wasn't the point of my improvised strategy – I had no intention of staying in the forest. As long as I remained a solitary figure on the black canvas of the landscape, I was in jeopardy. I had to place myself near to other people so the helicopter would have no means of distinguishing me from anyone else. And there was only one place where that could happen on the Quantock Hills by night.

The police command post.

38

STANDING NEXT TO the Vauxhall Crossland in the layby at Hawkridge Reservoir, Rasul Heyat watched the flickering white strobes and coloured anti-collision lights on the police helicopter. The lights stood out like beacons against the dark sky, even if the aircraft was too distant to be seen clearly. He could hear the helicopter too, but the engine noise didn't travel well through the air unless the thing was practically overhead.

Heyat and Bux had been observing the helicopter for the last twelve minutes, ever since it had flown in from the south. They'd learned from the anonymous police contact that the Eurocopter was based at Exeter and had a maximum flying time of two hours. That explained the periods during the afternoon and evening when the aircraft had been absent, but it was the helicopter's current position which intrigued Heyat, not its technical specifications.

The helicopter rarely remained hovering in one place as far as the Iranian could tell, but it concentrated its manoeuvres above a relatively small area of farmland east of the Quantock Hills. Heyat couldn't work out exactly where the police were focussing their search because the reservoir was in a dip behind a tree-lined ridge, but the helicopter's flight pattern was perhaps two miles away to the north.

Heyat found his phone and called Zam for a report.

"I can see the police helicopter," Heyat told the cell commander when Zam answered. "We've seen a number of patrol cars too."

"Are you still at the reservoir?" Zam asked.

"We are. Murad, I don't think they're searching the hills. They're over farmland. I've checked the map. Maybe somewhere around the village of Nether Stowey."

"That would be about right. Control passed on an update from his police informant. There was an incident at a farm nearby. The farmer was threatened with a handgun. The description he gave matches our adversary."

The news deflated Heyat. "So we've lost our target then? The police will find him."

Zam chuckled. "It's unlike you to underestimate an opponent, Rasul." He paused. "However much I despise him for what he did to my brother, I concede he is a resourceful man. We've seen that with our own eyes. It will take more than one sighting for the police to track him down."

"What are you saying, Murad?"

"He's not where the police expect him to be."

"Go on," Heyat prompted.

"Perhaps the encounter at the farm was an accident. Perhaps it was sleight of hand. I don't care either way. But I do know he'll be heading in precisely the opposite direction."

Heyat frowned. "You think he went onto the Quantock Hills? What purpose would that serve? The helicopter would spot him on its next pass over the forests. This is not a large area, Murad. It's hardly like the mountain ranges back home."

"You are correct, my friend, and you make my point for me. How long would it take for him to reach the west side while the police busy themselves with a futile search in the east? I thought he would head south initially, but he would've aborted that plan when he saw the helicopter. I reckon he will head for one of the villages between the hills and the border with the next county. He's probably a third of the way across the ridge already."

"That still gives us time to intercept. What do you want us to do?" Heyat asked.

"Is Orodes there with you?"

"He is."

"Put me on speakerphone."

Heyat touched the screen. "Done."

"I'm looking at a map," Zam continued. "There are two tracks he might follow which go from one side of the Quantock Hills to the other. Samir and I will cover the lower route at Triscombe. You and Orodes take the one that leads from the villages you mentioned to a place called Crowcombe. According to my map, there's an ancient earthwork up there called Dead Woman's Ditch."

Bux spoke next. "I know where you mean, Murad. But there's a problem."

Zam sighed. "Explain, Orodes."

"You told us yourself. The police have set up their command post in one of the car parks along that road. It's going to look suspicious if two Middle Eastern men stop nearby. What if we're recognised?"

"You don't really believe that the officer who spoke to you this morning in Weston-super-Mare is likely to still be on duty? Or assigned to a search in a completely unfamiliar area?"

"No, but..."

"Just stay out of their way," Zam interrupted.

"That's easier said than done."

"I've already inquired about the police deployment," Zam continued. "Most of the officers are involved in the search. There are very few at the command site. Does that not seem logical to you?"

Bux directed a glare at Heyat. "I suppose so, Murad."

Heyat spoke again, partly to silence the younger man. "The kill order stands?"

"Yes," Zam replied. "An abduction is out of the question. Whatever happens, we return to Swindon before dawn."

"Understood." Heyat hesitated. "Orodes raises a valid point, Murad, even if he expressed it poorly. The police will check vehicles for the fugitive. We might get stopped."

"Nightjars," Zam said in English after a few seconds' contemplation.

214

"What?"

"You're ornithologists looking for nightjars. That's the English name for a nocturnal bird species. They hunt for insects at dusk and dawn. You have to get there really early to have any chance of seeing or hearing them. Google the name for a picture."

A thin smile formed on Heyat's lips. "Wouldn't it be simpler to say we were watching owls?"

"Too obvious. Nightjars sounds more authentic."

"Do they live there?"

"What does it matter? I expect so. The habitat is favourable. A policeman is hardly likely to know, is he?"

"I guess not." Heyat paused. "And if he does not believe the birdwatching excuse?"

"Kill the officer and get away as fast as you can."

39

THE CLIMB BACK INTO THE FORESTS of the Quantock Hills required moderate effort and thus kept me warm, but I noticed the temperature had dropped markedly and a light mist was forming over the heathland. The damp air cooled my face and was not unpleasant. I stayed in the proximity of the lane that led to the car parks but well out of view among the trees. The terrain was dark beneath the branches and I needed the red light from my Petzl to proceed. Rather than wear it on my head, I held the torch by my thigh and aimed the soft beam at the ground before my feet, reducing the chance of being seen.

Mindful that the police helicopter could abandon the hunt over the villages behind me and traverse the Quantocks at any moment, I pressed on as fast as I could while trying to remain as silent as possible. The easiest route would have been the roadway, naturally, but such a move would have been imprudent on my part. Instead, I waded through undergrowth thick with fern and bracken, catching my feet on unseen roots frequently. Bramble stems did their best to ensnare me, although the scratches were mild compared to the incident with the barbed wire on Steep Holm. My injured leg needed rest but I pushed the limb's protestation from my mind.

At one point I heard a car on the lane and saw its headlights as it climbed the slope. It was unlikely that the driver would spot me, but I crouched down behind a mass of bracken fronds to be sure. I looked down so the sudden brightness of the vehicle's lights would not affect my eyes, and only glanced up when the vehicle passed me. I stepped out behind it and had just enough time to see that it was not a liveried police car. Whether it was an unmarked car or simply a civilian vehicle, I did not know, but it had the shape of a small SUV. The engine noise faded and I continued my walk.

I decided at that point to stay closer to the road. I'd heard the car from some distance away, so reckoned I'd have fair warning of another. The mist was becoming thicker, although whether it would develop into fog which would impel the departure of the helicopter remained to be seen. The forest thinned out in places, to be replaced with heath and scrub where ferns and rough grasses were prolific. And while those patches lacked tree cover, there was more than enough foliage to dive into should the need arise.

The change in scenery told me I was near the parking areas of Dead Woman's Ditch. My guess proved correct when, after emerging from a curved dip in the ground, I saw the glow of floodlights reflecting off the mist in the distance. Visibility was too poor to see the police control point itself, but the diffused light told me it was roughly a quarter of a mile away. The sound of a generator for the lamps reached my ears. I started to believe in the audacity of my plan. I pressed on in earnest, hoping to not only hide right next to the police officers but eavesdrop their conversations and radio messages as well.

A pinprick of light blinked on about thirty yards ahead. I froze. A car's interior light. Was it the same vehicle that had passed me a short time ago? I thumbed the switch on my headtorch to the off position. The car was parked in a scrape or passing place on the side of the road, facing away from me. Giving it a wide berth before continuing to the clearing would have been straightforward, but I felt compelled to get a closer look. I supposed there could be any number of reasons for someone to park in the hills at night, but something about what I'd seen rattled my instinct.

Staying in the dip of a ditch behind the lane's verge, I stepped forward, placing my feet with all the silent caution I could muster. I heard the doors open and saw two figures step out. It is seldom truly dark in the countryside, even without moonlight or starlight, and my eyes were perfectly adjusted to the dim conditions. Perhaps some of the glow from the nearby floodlights assisted my vision, spilling through the damp and diaphanous air. But I was too far away to discern the features of the vehicle's occupants. I went closer still, using the abundant shrubbery as cover.

At twelve yards I was close enough to tell they were both men, but their features remained shadowy. I crouched down, peering through the foliage. One man fished his mobile phone from his pocket and fortuitously – for me at least – turned my way as he dabbed the screen. Faint illumination lit his face.

Rasul Heyat.

Seeing him proved the Iranians had not stopped their chase. I felt a swell of conceit at the discovery – they must have considered me a worthy opponent to expend such effort – and professional respect for their doggedness. Although I was one against two, I knew this time I held the advantage. And while I could have skulked away into the gloomy night, thwarting their search, that option held no appeal at all. I'd been running for days – and nights – and it was time to retaliate.

But not before I'd listened to Heyat's telephone conversation. I stayed low, slid my arms out from my rucksack, and gently pulled out the silenced handgun. I racked the weapon as quietly as I could to smother the noise as the cartridge slotted into place in the barrel. I moved forward, holding the weapon in a double-handed grip, to within ten feet. Neither Heyat nor his associate had a clue I was there.

Heyat started talking in Farsi on the phone. I heard him use the name Murad. It confirmed my suspicion that Murad Zam – the cell leader in France – was in charge of the Iranians' plot in England. The determination of the team to kill me now made complete sense – I'd fatally shot Zam's brother in the throat during my counter-terror operation. There probably weren't many other men who wanted me dead as much as the MOIS commander.

I listened as Heyat told Zam that he and Bux were too close to the police rendezvous point to remain hidden. I hadn't killed the younger man on the island, despite my best attempt in the constrained circumstances, but I'd put that right soon. There was a discussion about the police helicopter flushing me out if it returned, but unless the aircraft made its way back to the hills imminently, they would have to drive away before the police stumbled across their location.

Heyat ended the call after what sounded like a minor disagreement. He dropped the phone into his pocket, turned and made a brief comment to Bux in colloquial Farsi that I couldn't translate.

I stepped forward and fired the suppressed Glock three times, hitting Heyat twice in the chest and once through the left eye. His body swayed for a second and then dropped to the ground.

Bux spun around to face me, instinctively reaching for a gun that wasn't there, forgetting that it was his weapon that I now held in my hands.

"Don't move!" I said gutturally, keeping the barrel aimed squarely at Bux's chest.

The glare on the younger agent's face was visible even in the semi-darkness.

"Drag him into the undergrowth," I said.

Bux tilted his head back for a moment. "See that?" he said in his native tongue, the gesture in the direction of the police floodlights. "That's for you, not us."

I shrugged. "Well, I stole a boat at gunpoint. With *your* gun."

"Not just that," Bux sneered. "Farzad Bouzidi. The traitor. Your asset. Rasul shot him but they want *you* for his murder."

"Kind of you to let me know." I waved the gun for a moment. "Move the body over there."

Bux spat on the ground and glowered. I shot him in the right thigh to encourage compliance. He let out a yelp of pain and fell over, clutching his leg.

"Don't fuck with me, Orodes. That's your name, isn't it? You'd be surprised at how much I know about you. Get up."

Bux somehow rose to his feet, the pain clear on his face. "Or what?"

"You know the answer to that. Move Rasul's body away from the road."

This time the operator complied. He reached down and grabbed Heyat under the arms, then shuffled back, dragging the corpse. Bux nearly fell over again, but I didn't need him to move far. He let go of Heyat when the body was hidden by bracken fronds.

"Keys for the car," I demanded, knowing Bux had got out from the driver's side.

Bux pulled them from his trouser pocket and dropped them into the undergrowth while giving me a look of daggers.

"Why are you here, Orodes?" I asked, not expecting an answer. "It wasn't for Bouzidi and it wasn't for me. I heard Rasul on the phone to Murad." I paused. "What is your mission?"

Bux didn't reply but kept his dark eyes locked with mine.

"Don't worry. I already know. You intend to attack the security conference at the White Horse Vale Hotel."

He didn't speak but his expression altered momentarily before resuming his glare. I had my answer. I squeezed the trigger twice. The bullets penetrated Bux's chest and the man toppled backwards, landing with a thud on the ground. I stood over him and could hear wheezy breaths as he struggled for air. A quick mental calculation confirmed I still had eleven rounds in the weapon. I could afford to lose one more, so I shot Bux between the eyes to put the Iranian bastard out of his misery.

I raked my fingers through the stems and dirt to find the car keys which Bux had discarded. It didn't take long. I think by that point he'd known his fate, hence his half-hearted defiance. I went back to my rucksack and put the Glock inside. The opportunity to gain a phone was now in my hands, but I didn't bother. Leaving the mobiles with their deceased owners was the wiser option, especially if Department 312 monitored and tracked them. It made no sense to steal their car only to have my whereabouts plotted on a map. I then realised that the vehicle – a Vauxhall Crossland – might carry a tracker, but then was not the time to check.

I dumped my rucksack on the passenger seat and started walking to the other side. I now had the means to get away from Somerset and the trouble that had hounded me for the last few days. I resolved to make my way to the North Wessex Downs and contact Sarah once again, now that I was sure the venue was the Iranians' target. But curiosity prevented me from climbing into the car and driving away. It would be a while before Murad Zam realised his associates were dead, so the threat he represented at that moment was minimal. But I remained at the centre of a police manhunt. If there was any advantage that could simplify my escape, I needed to find it.

I started walking along the narrow road toward the police command post.

The floodlights were set up on one side of the clearing, illuminating the parking area and the vehicles within it. I circled around the car park and approached from the back. I was not sure what I expected, but there were few vehicles there. The 4×4 remained attached to its trailer. Three patrol cars, one of which I'd seen earlier with the pickup truck, stood in a line. There was a plain four-wheel-drive, and it too had a trailer. Not a flat one but a solid storage box, which made me speculate that it might have been the equipment rig for a covert firearms team. There were two unmarked cars as well. A trailer-mounted generator stood near the lamps, and there was a small marquee which I presumed was there as a refreshments tent.

A couple of uniformed officers were chatting in a corner of the car park, their hands wrapped around foam cups of tea or coffee. Another officer, wearing a peaked cap, looked to be someone of rank. He was talking into a radio but I couldn't hear what he said, and any replies went into his earpiece, depriving me of information. My hope of learning something about the police operation appeared to be evaporating thanks to the overly noisy generator unit.

I scanned the rest of the clearing and spotted three more people talking on the far side. They all wore civilian clothing. A woman with a grey or white pixie cut looked agitated with the tall man in front of her. He had his back to me so I couldn't see his features, but the other man who stood beside the female officer had a calmer demeanour. I formed the impression that he was a senior officer of some years' service, for he looked imperturbable and unsurprised at the livelier aspects of the conversation.

After a while the discussion ended. All three started walking back across the car park, and I could now see the face of the slim man. The gratification I'd felt at killing Rasul Heyat and Orodes Bux twisted into a wretched knot in my stomach. I crept back from my hiding place behind the floodlights and retraced my circuitous steps to the Iranians' SUV. The man I'd seen was named Alan Rutherford, and I happened to know he was a high-ranking director of MI5. There was only one conclusion I could draw.

It was no longer only the police and the Iranian operatives who hunted me, but British Intelligence as well.

40

ALAN RUTHERFORD entered the small tent, closely followed by Detective Inspector Jacob Poe and Detective Sergeant Penny Ambler. The DI seemed to have grasped what was going on but the sergeant needed more persuasion. He understood her reluctance but had no time for it. Rutherford decided another cup of tea was in order. Not because he enjoyed the taste of whatever vile potion the police had provided, but because Ambler needed to learn patience.

The MI5 director picked up two foam cups and slid one inside the other. He'd learned earlier that a single one was insufficient protection against the scalding water from the urn. He let go of the lever when his cup was two-thirds full; all the remaining volume was for the excess milk that was needed to cool the liquid enough so he wouldn't end up in A&E with burns on his mouth. He fished out the tea bag on its string and tossed it and the wooden stirrer into a bin. Rutherford turned to face the officers.

"Not having a cuppa?" Rutherford asked Poe.

"Are you kidding?" the DI replied with a grin.

"Good point." Rutherford gestured toward the gap in the tent. "Let's go outside."

They walked back across the clearing, out of earshot of the other officers. Rutherford made eye contact with Ambler as though inviting her to speak.

She took the bait. "You're telling me that MI5 can waltz in here and push me out of my investigation?" she said with a glare that somehow looked harsher under the floodlights.

"On a purely semantic point, we're not pushing you out," Rutherford replied. "It's simply a matter of jurisdiction. I'm very grateful for your sterling work, DS Ambler. But I think you know you've stumbled across something rather more noteworthy than a routine police case. It's time for the Security Service to take the lead."

"Let me guess. It's become a national security issue?"

Rutherford held her gaze. "It was one before you ever got involved."

"But you were happy to let me waste all this time running the inquiry? Interviewing witnesses? Trawling through CCTV footage? Didn't it occur to you to mention MI5's interest sooner?"

A thin smile formed on Rutherford's lips. "Not a waste of time, sergeant. And it took a while before the jigsaw pieces formed a coherent picture. Your work has filled in some gaps for us, actually."

"Are you going to tell me how?"

Rutherford shook his head. "Not the whole story, no."

She glowered at him. "What *can* you tell me?"

"This situation is not what you believe it to be."

Ambler huffed. "That clears up everything." She paused. "Try harder." Before Rutherford could reply, Ambler turned to Poe. "Want to help me out here, Jake?"

Poe gave her a thin smile. "Pick your battles, Penny," was all he said.

A look of disgust formed on Ambler's face, although she didn't mean to take out her frustration on her colleague. She quickly diverted her glare and locked eyes with Rutherford, waiting for him to speak.

"Your victim in Glastonbury," Rutherford said, his tone inviting another question.

"What about him?"

"We don't believe he was murdered by the man you know as John Connery."

"Are you telling me that isn't his real name?"

"Khadem or Connery?"

Ambler stared. "Both."

"Connery is an alias. Khadem is probably also a pseudonym, all things considered. I don't know for sure."

"So who killed the Iranian?"

"Some of his fellow countrymen probably. The same ones responsible for Harry Beech's murder in Bristol."

"How do you know about that?"

"I've already read your investigation notes."

"Then you'll know that Beech's death remains unsolved."

Rutherford nodded. "Yes, but I also know you found CCTV footage of a Persian man in the street outside the barber's shop around the time of the murder."

Ambler didn't reply.

"They keep popping up all over the place, don't they?" Rutherford continued.

The detective held eye contact but didn't speak.

"The Steep Holm incident? Unfortunate that you lost your witnesses."

"They weren't *my* witnesses," Ambler snapped. "I didn't make the link until later."

Rutherford raised his spare hand submissively. "Point taken." He risked a sip of his tea. "That really is quite revolting," he said before emptying the cup onto the ground.

Poe spoke next. "What do you need from us?"

"All the material gathered thus far, evidential and undisclosed," Rutherford replied.

"Hang on a minute," Ambler interrupted. "In case you'd forgotten, we're running a manhunt operation here. Your John Connery, or whatever he's called, has threatened three people with a handgun. We have to arrest him."

Rutherford shook his head. "No, you don't."

"He's stolen two boats and terrified members of the public."

"That might be a crime in your world, DS Ambler, but in mine we call that being resourceful."

225

Ambler raised her eyebrows. "Now I get it. He's one of yours."

"Actually, he's not."

"Then why don't you want the police to find him?"

"It's complicated."

"Ah, yes. That national security matter."

Rutherford smiled warmly. "I knew you'd see the bigger picture. Anyway, to answer DI Poe's question, I want you to shut down the search. We all know how terribly expensive it is to fly those helicopters. It would be a shame to waste more taxpayers' money without good reason."

Ambler's glare hardened. "You're fucking kidding me."

"I assure you I'm not." He paused. "And you'll need to put out a press release. A discreet one."

"Saying what?"

"That you've spoken to the man you were looking for in relation to Ismail Khadem's murder. You've eliminated him from your inquiries. The crime now appears to be gang violence over drugs. Don't worry about writing it yourself – one of my officers has already drafted it for you. We'll tell you when to publish it."

"You're asking me to lie to the public?" Ambler said.

Rutherford grinned. "Come on, sergeant. The police regularly manipulate the information they release. You have propaganda units for that very reason."

"*I* bloody well don't. And it's a press office, not a propaganda unit."

"Another semantic point." Rutherford paused for a second. "I suggest you think of it as public reassurance. Calming frayed nerves and all that. Would that make you feel more comfortable?"

Ambler glared. "Gang violence?"

"Public apathy is the goal. They become disinterested when it's villain on villain."

"You're forgetting the boat theft," Ambler muttered.

"Mistaken identity." Rutherford turned to Poe. "John Connery – let's stick with that name, shall we? – needs a corridor. Give him room and he'll get out of Somerset. You'll never hear about him again."

Poe frowned. "I'll need that request to be authorised."

"It wasn't a request, DI Poe, but I understand the protocol. I'll call the chief constable right now to get the wheels in motion." Rutherford glanced at the sky at the sound of the helicopter. Its static and strobe lights pierced the weak layer of mist.

Moments later the helicopter flew right over the rendezvous point, circled back and went a short distance to the east. Suddenly the aircraft's Spectrolab Nightsun searchlight burst into life, throwing a broad beam of intense white light at the ground.

Ambler gave Poe a questioning look. The DI pursed his lips in thought but said nothing. The light, bearing down at an angle of roughly forty-five degrees from the helicopter, was aimed at a spot not more than a quarter of a mile from the control point.

A uniformed inspector walked over to the group, clutching his radio. "You heard this, Jake?"

Poe shook his head. "Mine's in the car. Have they found something?"

"You could say that." The inspector unplugged his earpiece and turned up the volume. "RVP to N-PAS 44. DI Poe is listening. Confirm your last update."

The radio crackled as the police observer in the cockpit responded. "N-PAS 44 to RVP. We've found two bodies in the undergrowth. Caught sight of them on the thermal as we flew over."

Poe took the radio from his colleague. "DI Poe to N-PAS 44. You're sure they're dead?"

"Sir, most people react when we light them up with the Nightsun. And, er, it looks like they've been shot."

Ambler pulled her handset from her coat pocket and remembered she'd turned the volume right down before the conversation with the MI5 spook.

"DS Ambler to N-PAS 44. Confirm you saw them on the

thermal camera?"

"Confirmed, DS Ambler."

"They're *still warm*?"

A pause. "I suppose so, Sarge. Looked like normal heat signatures."

Ambler locked eyes with Poe. "How far exactly from the RVP are you, N-PAS 44?"

"About seven hundred metres, Sarge. The bodies are about halfway between you and us."

"Thanks, N-PAS 44. I know you're due to return to base, but can you keep the light on while we take a look?"

"We can give you ten minutes."

"Understood." Ambler paused. "Is there a vehicle nearby?"

"Negative. And in anticipation of your next question, there was nothing on the track as we approached the RVP."

Ambler shook her head. "Thanks, N-PAS 44. We're on our way."

"Understood. N-PAS 44 out."

Ambler shoved her radio into her fleece and glowered at Rutherford. "Jesus fucking Christ! Are you still convinced John Connery isn't a murderer?"

Rutherford held her gaze. "I don't believe I said that, Sergeant. I think I told you he didn't kill Ismail Khadem in Glastonbury."

Ambler looked at him open-mouthed for several seconds. Finally she spoke, pointing her arm toward the nearby lane. "And who do you think is lying up there?"

Rutherford smiled. "Fancy a little wager? A tenner says they're your missing witnesses from Steep Holm. We believe they are terrorists from the Iranian Ministry of Intelligence and Security."

"Stuff your bet." She glared at him. "You still reckon it's appropriate to shut down the police investigation?"

The MI5 man nodded. "Now more than ever, DS Ambler."

41

I REMAINED ON EDGE as I drove through the hamlets on the east side of the Quantock Hills, expecting to be stopped by a police patrol at any moment. Yet luck appeared to be on my side and I made it to Bridgwater without incident. It was only there that I parked up and studied the Vauxhall's sat-nav. I doubted the police would have identified the vehicle's registration number, but could not assume that was the case. Therefore, in order to avoid the ANPR cameras, I needed to take a rural route to the conference venue.

The motorways were obviously no use to me, nor was the A303. I therefore plotted a course between those two principal routes along quieter roads, starting with the A39 through Street and Glastonbury before working up to Devizes and Avebury. The computer told me I'd drive for roughly one hundred miles before I reached my destination. I couldn't just turn up on the doorstep, of course, for I was not on the authorised personnel list. The hotel would be locked down.

I briefly considered going straight to London. My deduction that the security conference of foreign ministers and assorted officials was the Iranians' target had more or less been confirmed by Orodes Bux before I killed him. I didn't have much more to tell Sarah, apart from the fact that Murad Zam was involved. There was no need for me to be on site to pass on that information, but the antics of the last few days had left me with a strong desire to see the matter through. It wasn't like I'd had no experience with the MOIS operators before. I felt I might be useful.

That did not negate the fact that I was on the run from the police. I knew that obstacle would eventually be smoothed over with a few high-level telephone calls, but getting arrested would have unfortunate consequences, not least the capture of my finger-prints, photograph and DNA on the police databases. The hotel was in the Thames Valley Police area rather than the Avon and Somerset district, but that wouldn't stop them sharing information about an armed fugitive.

I recognised the road in Glastonbury that ran past the Chalice Well Gardens. I wondered if the car I'd used was still in the layby on the corner of the housing estate by the farm gate. Past Glaston-bury, however, the roads were new to me, and I relied on the car's digital navigator to reveal my route. I had plenty of time to think about my next move because a good part of the journey toward the North Wessex Downs was on winding roads. It took me almost three hours, and I found myself squinting at the sunrise.

Knowing I'd be unable to get into the hotel's grounds without agreement from the lead agent made me wonder how the Iranian kill squad was intending to do just that. But that was a problem to work out in the company of fellow security specialists. Before then I had to contact Sarah. Without her help I'd never get beyond the boundary, let alone thwart a terror attack on the assembled dignit-aries.

A bridge took me over the M4 motorway southeast of Swindon, and the sat-nav revealed that I was just half a dozen miles from the Vale of the White Horse. I drove through pretty villages before emerging onto the rolling chalk hills of the Downs. The landscape differed from the Somerset views I had encountered during the last few days, and I realised I was on a broad ridge which descended to farmland on its north side.

I tried to spot a telephone kiosk as I drove, but saw none. I didn't regret leaving Heyat's and Bux's phones in the Quantock Hills; keeping hold of them might have caused me more trouble than I was equipped to handle. The few public houses I passed were closed at that time of morning, so I didn't have the option – short of breaking in – of calling on a landline. I pulled over and took another look at the car's in-built map.

The landmark which gave the area its name stood out. There was a track called White Horse Hill which led to a car park. I thought it probable that some early morning walkers might take advantage of the quiet dawn hours. I noticed the hotel was nearby on the lower ground beyond the chalk carving. Hoping I could acquire a mobile phone – all being well without gesticulating with the handgun – I carried on up the narrow country lane until I saw the turning.

The unsurfaced car park was quite spacious, so I stopped near a footpath which led across the chalkland. A few cars were already there, and I took a moment to surreptitiously check which ones were occupied. Eight or nine people, either sitting in their vehicles or getting out to prepare for their walks, of various ages. After my encounter with the farmer the previous night, I avoided the solitary man with a large Alsatian dog. Nor did I want to approach the two young women who were making their way to the start of the path. They were slight in build and I could have over-powered them easily, but they'd scream like banshees if I tried a robbery.

But, as I looked at an elderly couple who were reading a notice-board, it occurred to me that the simplest option would be a polite request to borrow a mobile. I'd been doing everything the hard way, which was perhaps the reason I thought first of violence. But they appeared to be decent folk who might be predisposed to acts of kindness. I almost laughed aloud when reflecting on how hard it had been to establish comms with Sarah. Yet there I was, willing to use force when a simple request might be enough. Perhaps another appointment with that attractive psychologist might be in order.

I didn't know if my face still looked bruised, but my stubble probably covered the worst of the marks. I put on my RNLI cap to add a little shadow. I hoped the couple would see the logo because the famous lifeboat charity attracted donations from all sorts of English people who never went near the coast. A little subception would do no harm at that juncture. My hiking trousers were dirty, but I hoped they wouldn't notice if I kept talking. I walked over to the noticeboard.

"Good morning!" I said with a broad smile.

"Good morning," they both replied as they turned round.

"Lovely day for it," I commented. "Are you walking far?"

"Dragon Hill first, then down the track to Wayland's Smithy," the woman replied. "Have to keep fit at our age!"

"Then lunch at the pub afterwards?" I asked.

"We brought sandwiches." She glanced at her husband. "Perhaps next time?"

He nodded in agreement but didn't reply.

"I heard the one down the road does great food," I said, hoping they wouldn't press me further about my vague remark. They didn't. "Look, the reason I came over was to ask a small favour. Would you be able to help me? I need to call my friend Sarah, but I stupidly left my mobile at home. She has a job interview and I wanted to wish her luck."

There was a hint of mistrust in the man's eyes, or perhaps it was just surprise at the unusual request.

I reached for my wallet. "I'll happily give you some money. I don't want you to be out of pocket."

"Oh, we couldn't accept that," the woman said. She found her mobile from her coat pocket, keyed in an unlock code and handed me the device.

"You're very kind," I said. "I promise I'll just be a moment."

"No problem, dear. Can you remember her number?"

I grinned. "I'm good with numbers. It's just my memory for dates that lets me down." I tapped in Sarah's number and waited for her to answer.

"Hello?" she said.

"Sarah, it's me," I replied, just loud enough for the elderly couple to hear. I then took a few steps away but kept them in sight.

"The pilot didn't find you."

It took me a moment to remember the evacuation arrangement we'd had in place for Steep Holm.

"No. Trouble with the Iranians," I told her, keeping my voice quiet. "I had to steal a boat."

"I heard. *Another one.* Where are you now?"

"Close. On the hill with the chalk carving. I need you to get me access to the hotel. Murad Zam is running this op. The conference is definitely the target."

"You sure? The security protocols are solid."

"I'm on a borrowed phone so I don't have long," I said. "Can you get me access or not?"

"Yes," Sarah replied. "I'll have to run it by Alan Rutherford. He's the chief MI5 agent."

"Alan Rutherford?"

"You sound surprised."

"He was hunting me in the Quantock Hills last night with the police."

"I thought the Iranians were hunting you."

"Them too." I hesitated for a moment. "I really need to speak to Alan."

"I saw him turn up half an hour ago. I didn't know he'd left the hotel." Sarah paused. "You can't walk in the front gate. I'll send someone to meet you."

"Fine. Where?"

"Walk down the hill to Woolstone. There's a pub in the village. Wait outside."

"Will do." I hesitated. "I don't understand exactly what's going on, Sarah. I don't know if the police tracked the car I stole. I can't walk into a trap."

"You can trust me, you idiot," she retorted. Her tone softened with her next comment. "There have been a few interesting developments. I'll explain when I see you. We were wrong about recent events."

"Go on," I prompted.

"Later." She muffled the phone for a moment. It sounded like she was talking to someone else, but I couldn't make out the words. After a few seconds she spoke to me again. "Right, someone's leaving now. She'll give you a codeword so you know it's not a set up."

"Who?"

"It'll be a surprise."

I groaned. "You can be a pain in the arse sometimes. The code-word?"

"Trafalgar."

"Fine. I'll see you soon." I ended the conversation, cleared the phone's call history and walked back to the lady and her husband. I pressed a ten-pound note into her hand as I returned her mobile. "Thank you."

"I can't accept the money," the woman replied with a look of unease on her face.

"Please take it," I insisted. "Trust me, you've been a lifesaver. Put it toward that pub lunch."

"Well, that's very kind," she said. "How is your friend?"

"She's a character," I replied with a lop-sided grin. "Thanks again. Enjoy your walk."

"You too." She offered her hand and I shook it. "Goodbye."

The husband shook my hand and also wished me a good day. I said goodbye to them both, turned around and went back to the SUV. I grabbed my rucksack and put it on my back. I locked the car and made my way toward the lane. Moments later I was out of sight behind the hedgerows.

42

I HAD PASSED THE HAMLET OF WOOLSTONE on my way to the car park, so I knew I had under a mile to walk. Even though the stolen Vauxhall had not drawn unwanted attention, I was content to abandon it. A distant view of rural Oxfordshire met my eyes as I followed the hawthorn corridor down the hill. The early morning was bright but cooler than I had experienced in Somerset. The fresh aroma of the open countryside was delicate in the air. Chattering birds were the only company I had as I headed for the low ground. Occasional breaks in the hedgerows revealed rolling grassy hills on my right and wheat fields on my left. Patches of fiery pink rosebay willowherb added drama to the landscape's palette.

The lane met a wider but still minor carriageway at a cross-roads. I went straight over, following a signpost to Woolstone. Another steep descent led me into the hamlet. It was a tiny place, hidden from the rest of civilisation, with a mere handful of thatched cottages and mature trees. Were it not for the modern cars and wheelie-bins, I might have felt transported to a bygone era. I took a winding narrow road to the village's only pub which, unsurprisingly, was named the White Horse Inn.

A building of sublime attractiveness and quintessential English character, the hostelry was several centuries old. A small garden, squeezed between the house and the road, had three wooden bench-tables and accompanying parasols. I rounded the corner and saw a parking area for the inn's patrons on the opposite side of the road. I crossed over and stood behind a hedge, waiting for my lift to arrive. I glimpsed movement from within the pub's interior – presumably preparation for the guests' breakfast – but the bar was not open. I saw no other activity, although my view of the nearby cottages was limited.

I heard a car on the road shortly before I saw it. A white Peugeot 508 with French numberplates swung around the corner and pulled into the car park. The driver stopped and turned her head toward me through her open side window. Laure Béraud of the Direction Générale de la Sécurité Extérieure, the French secret service, locked eyes with me. She was an attractive woman with green eyes and dark hair tied in a chignon, but a chill ran down my spine. I stared at the DGSE agent who'd failed to back up my team in Paris, wondering why Sarah – who'd been crippled when the explosion went off – had sent Béraud, of all people, to collect me.

"Get in," she said in English. "Sarah Oren sent me."

I stood my ground. "You were the last person I expected to see."

"I understand. We can talk about that later."

"Codeword?"

Béraud grimaced. "Trafalgar. Sarah thought it would be fucking hilarious."

I couldn't stop a thin smile. There was something oddly charming about hearing an English expletive spoken with a French accent. I opened the rear door and tossed my rucksack inside. I walked around the car and sat down in the front passenger seat. Sarah's choice of codeword was funny, but I'd never forgiven Béraud for abandoning us in France, so my mood took all of a second to sour again.

"She might have lost the use of her legs, but she never lost her sense of humour," I said with venom as I fastened the seatbelt.

Béraud held my stare. "We never talked about what happened," she said calmly. "There was more to the situation than you realised." She put the car in gear and pulled forward hard, driving a rapid circle around the car park that made the tyres squeal.

"I know you let us down," I retorted.

"I won't argue about that," she replied, gripping the steering

236

wheel. She changed the subject as she took the narrow road through Woolstone. "Rutherford granted your access to the hotel. There have been some developments."

"That's what Sarah said."

"We're on the same side here."

"Are we?"

She flicked a glower at me before returning her attention to the road. "More than you know."

"I doubt that," I said, staring through the windscreen.

Béraud sighed. "Perhaps this should wait until we get there."

I didn't answer. The DGSE operator drove on in silence. Mercifully the silent journey took under ten minutes, and we soon arrived at a police checkpoint at the venue's main gate. Two armed police officers, carrying Heckler & Koch G36 assault rifles, stood at the entrance. Half expecting them to aim their weapons at me, I was glad when they waved us through upon recognising Béraud and the Peugeot.

The driveway cut across expansive swards and paddocks. A few large oak and beech trees stood among the lawns in their summer finery. As we neared the mansion, I saw ornamental gardens with smaller trees chosen for the hues of their foliage, elegant walkways with rose-covered arches, and large flowerbeds. But it was the White Horse Vale Hotel itself which dominated the grounds – a grand Georgian mansion with a sculpted balustrade around the roof which looked perfect for sniper emplacement.

Official-looking cars were parked in the sweeping turning circle in front of the hotel's main entrance. Béraud found a gap and reversed the Peugeot into it. She killed the engine and turned to face me.

"You're not really dressed for the occasion," she commented. "You look like you've been crawling through ditches."

I reached for the door handle. "Funny you should say that." I grabbed my rucksack from the back seat. "I'm sure someone can lend me a suit."

Béraud pushed her door shut and locked the car. "Sarah asked me to take you to her room. Rutherford will join us. There's a lot to talk about."

"Such as?" I wondered if I was being overly stubborn, but my reasons for distrusting the DGSE agent had not diminished one iota during the last ten minutes.

She halted in her tracks and spun round. "Oh, I don't know! Maybe your theory that we're about to be attacked by an Iranian kill squad."

I shrugged. "As good a topic as any."

She glanced at the building. "I'll take you in the back entrance. The way you look, the delegates would probably think you're the terrorist."

"It's not a theory," I added as we walked around the side of the mansion.

"Rutherford seems to agree with you," she commented, although she didn't explain what she meant. "The problem is we don't know how it will happen. This is the last day of the conference. All the VIPs are together. But you've seen the security. No one's getting anywhere near the hotel." She paused. "Unless you have new information."

I held her gaze. "I don't. I only know something is going to happen. It's Murad Zam's team," I added, not knowing if Sarah had already told her, but I saw no point in withholding the name of our former adversary.

"I heard," Béraud confirmed. She stepped up to a side door. "Bad news."

"Yeah."

The mansion was impressive inside, even the way we'd come in, but my eyes studied the architecture for its security and surveillance opportunities, not its aesthetics. Béraud led me to a rear staircase with a thick patterned carpet which was held in place with brass rods at the base of each riser. We hurried up the stairs to a small corridor. The Frenchwoman tapped on a door.

"Sarah? It's Laure."

"It's open," Sarah called out.

Béraud twisted the doorknob and we went inside. It was a comfortable room but plainly furnished. I guessed we were in the cheap end of the house – probably the old servants' quarters.

Sarah was sitting in an upholstered tub chair with her laptop open on her knee. Her wheelchair was within arm's reach beside the bed. She frowned at me and opened her arms. I stepped forward and leaned in for a hug.

"You stink," she remarked.

"Good to see you too," I replied with a grin.

"Get in the shower. I'll ask someone to bring up fresh clothes for you. Usual size? I presume you haven't put on weight while touring Somerset."

I raised my eyebrows at her. "You sent Béraud."

Sarah winked. "Thought that would make you smile."

"Hardly."

"We have a lot to talk about."

"She said that," I replied.

Béraud walked across the room and sat down on the bed. "I'm still here."

I looked her way. I was about to make a snide comment but stopped myself. Further rudeness would contribute nothing of value to the discussion, and the fact that Sarah and Laure had obviously formed some sort of alliance left me curious.

"I'll get cleaned up," I said. "Rutherford?"

"I told him I'd call when you arrived," Sarah replied. "Be quick."

"Give me ten minutes," I said.

"There's a spare towel on the rail."

I nodded and then walked toward the bathroom, eager to scrub the accumulated dirt of the last four days and nights from my pores.

43

THE HOT SHOWER eased the knots in my muscles and went some way to banish the fog from my tired mind. I didn't try to calculate how much sleep I'd missed. The wound on my leg was still swollen but showed no sign of infection. With the help of the bandage I'd wrapped around it, the cut had knitted itself together quite well. I'd have a minor scar but wouldn't need stitches. The steaming water revitalised me and helped me focus. In a perfect world I would have shaved as well, but there wasn't time for that. Fresh clothes and a pair of smart leather shoes were waiting for me by the time I'd cleaned up. I emerged from the bathroom to find Alan Rutherford already in the bedroom, sitting in the spare seat.

Rutherford gave me a nod. "You've been busy."

"No comment."

"I presume that was your handiwork on the Quantock Hills?"

I ignored the question and sat down on the edge of the bed next to Laure Béraud. "The threat is real. Murad Zam is involved."

Rutherford held my gaze. "We've had an inkling about this for a while, although we're still short on the details." He paused and glanced at the two women before turning back to me. "Can we all agree we have a common interest here? All information on the table?"

I inferred his remark was solely for my benefit and wasn't really a question. The trio of spies had already collaborated. I couldn't fault their decision but I remained wary.

"What do you want to know?" I replied, holding Rutherford's gaze.

"Let's start with the reason you were in Somerset," the MI5 man said.

"To pick up an Iranian asset who'd fled the regime several months ago – a scientist on their nuclear enrichment programme. He'd been arrested in Bristol and was scared. I arranged to meet him in Glastonbury." I left out the part about the data Farzad Bouzidi had promised which I never gained.

"Ismail Khadem?"

"Not his real name, but yes."

"What happened?"

"Rasul Heyat happened. I assume the MOIS has an informant in the police down there. Rasul killed my man. He saw me. I had to run. I'll save the details for another time, but I moved around and eventually contacted Sarah." I paused. "I surmised the Iranians hadn't entered the country just to find my informant. They had no idea he was in the UK."

"The arrest?"

I nodded. "He'd kept a low profile until then. Heyat and the others must've been sent to kill him when he flagged up, but that wasn't their primary goal. The conference is the logical target."

"Because we're hosting foreign ministers from all over the world to discuss sanctions against Iran and how to suffocate their nuclear ambitions?"

"Right. It takes effort to get a kill team into a country discreetly. They wouldn't do it without an endgame in mind."

"That's the conclusion we reached when Haydar Hamidi came off the ferry at Harwich," Rutherford commented. "Facial recognition pinged him. He'd sailed from Hamburg."

I held Rutherford's gaze. "Hamidi is one of Zam's operators. You tailed him?"

"To a safe-house in Swindon which, as you are no doubt aware, is only a few miles west of here."

I nodded. "You guessed the target?"

"Hardly a guess – I'd say it was a safe bet. But we haven't identified the entire team."

"There would be at least six operatives," Sarah said.

"Zam, Heyat and Hamidi so far then," Rutherford summarised. He looked at me. "Who did we find with Heyat in the woods?"

"Orodes Bux," I replied. "Maybe a replacement for Ahmad Zam." I hesitated for a second. "Alan, what about the police?"

"All sorted, old chap. I choked the police investigation."

"Thanks." I reflected on his earlier comment. "You let things play out?"

Rutherford nodded. "We knew *who*, we knew *where*, we knew *why*. But we didn't know *how*. And that's the puzzle. There's no chance of Zam or Hamidi or the others getting onto the grounds."

I gave him a questioning glance. "How can you be sure?"

"All things considered, it seemed prudent to add another layer of security," Rutherford said with a smile. "We have police dog handlers on constant perimeter patrols and police firearms officers at the gates. There are covert MI5 officers in the building, plus the staff from the other agencies. But more than that, we put the SAS under cover in the grounds. They were in place a week before the talks started. The entire estate is under twenty-four-hour surveillance. Authorised personnel only. We're locked down."

"Sounds like you have everything covered," I remarked. "But there's still an active cell out there. There must be a gap they've identified."

Béraud, who'd said nothing up till that point, spoke up. "You mentioned Orodes Bux."

I nodded.

"The DGSE has a file on him. Former member of the Revolutionary Guards. An explosives specialist."

"Haydar Hamidi has the same background," Sarah commented. I could tell from her eyes that she was thinking about France at that moment. She made eye contact with Rutherford. "Is that the *how*, Alan?"

The MI5 director pursed his lips. "It's their preferred method of attack."

"I found that out the hard way," Sarah said bitterly. "They always want to make it look like terrorism." She paused. "Of course, there's a certain pragmatism in running operations that way. Explosives are easier to move around and conceal than firearms."

"They have considerable skills with both," I said to her. "And I know for a fact they're carrying handguns. One of them is currently in my rucksack." I paused. "But, like Alan said, they can't breach the hotel's perimeter, with or without guns. The SAS would shoot them on sight."

"And there are no explosives in the conference rooms," Sarah added. "They're checked several times a day with sniffer dogs."

I frowned. Something hovered on the periphery of my thoughts but I couldn't pin it down.

Rutherford saw my look of concentration. "There's something we haven't told you." He turned to Béraud. "Laure?"

The DGSE operative nodded. "I believe they have someone on the inside."

I gave her a questioning look but didn't speak.

"Abandoning your team in Paris was not my decision," she continued. "I fought against it. We were ready to help you neutralize Zam and the others."

"But?"

"They ordered me to withdraw." She hesitated. "The instruction came from one of the agency directors, or so I thought. The situation had become too public, especially after you shot Ahmad Zam and left him choking to death on a busy Parisian street. They informed me the DGSE could not be seen to assist an unsanctioned hunt-to-kill mission. They threatened to throw me and my team out of the agency if I did not comply at once."

"We nearly had them," I replied with steel in my voice. "All of them. You jeopardised our pursuit and gave Hamidi time to rig that bomb. They got away because of you."

Sarah snapped at me. "We've discussed this before. The team

carried on. Don't put this all on Laure. We knew the risks and we tried to complete the operation. Hear her out."

I stared at her open-mouthed for a few seconds. I glanced at Béraud. "Sorry. You were saying?"

She sighed. "I knew it was bullshit. I mean, it's not like the DGSE didn't already know your reputation. You people always operate on your own terms."

"Whatever gets the job done," I retorted.

"I share that philosophy," Béraud replied. "In principle, at least. Unfortunately the DGSE is more constrained by bureaucracy. But that's not the point. Afterwards I tried to work out what had really happened. I didn't believe the order came from my superiors. It felt like a cover-up at a higher level." She paused. "I've spent the last year trying to find answers. Quietly, of course. But I figured it out."

"Go on," I prompted.

"Security Minister Julien Lémery," she replied. "The order came from him."

I frowned. "He has oversight of the DGSE. He could give the order."

"Yes, but he didn't do it to avoid a public-relations mess," Béraud said. "He's corrupt. I found evidence that he's been taking bribes."

"From whom?"

"A wealthy Iranian businessman who has extensive portfolios in France."

"Linked to the regime in Iran?"

"He wouldn't be allowed to operate abroad otherwise."

"And the curious thing is," Rutherford interjected, "Monsieur Lémery is in attendance at this conference."

I stared. "The inside man. He's coordinating with Zam and Hamidi."

"That's our theory."

I looked again at Béraud. "That's why you're here, isn't it?"

She nodded. "When I learned the purpose of this conference, I assigned myself to his security detail. I needed proof of his treachery."

"He intends to pass everything discussed here back to Tehran."

"I believe so," Béraud replied.

"But the presence of Zam's unit implies the attack will go ahead as well," Rutherford added. "Laure believes Julien Lémery is due to play a significant role in that regard, and I'm inclined to agree with her."

"There's just one problem with that plan," Sarah said, directing her comment at me. "He'd be in the middle of the attack."

"Making him appear to be one of the targets," I replied. "There'll be a strategy to keep him from getting hurt."

"And yet we're agreed that a strike against the hotel seems improbable," Rutherford said. "Even with a man on the inside."

I stared hard at Rutherford. "Two exit driveways, right?"

He nodded.

"They're going to force an evacuation. They knew they'd never get into the hotel itself. Two men on either side of the estate. IEDs planted somewhere in the road verges – probably three or four hundred yards past the gates so the firearms officers couldn't retaliate. They take out the first vehicle with a bomb to block the road..."

"And then shoot everyone else," Rutherford interrupted. "They'd kill enough people to send a message. But that raises the obvious question."

"How will they force the delegates to leave the building?" Béraud said.

"Call the police with a bomb threat?" Sarah suggested.

Rutherford shook his head. "No. We'd lock down and conduct a search. There's an ordnance disposal soldier from the Royal Logistic Corps on site as a tactical adviser for that very reason."

"So that brings us back to what we agreed they wouldn't do," I said. "They're going to attack the building. They must have a device inside already. Lémery will set it off himself."

"The hotel's been checked a hundred times," Rutherford said with a frown. But I could see he was coming around to my train of thought.

I scanned the faces in the room, hoping for an answer. Then my eyes fell upon Sarah Oren's wheelchair. That nagging thought at the back of my mind suddenly took form.

"Shit," I said. "The device is in the lift." I locked eyes with Sarah. "When we spoke a few days ago, you said the main lift broke."

She nodded. "The manager called out an engineer. It's fixed."

I glanced at Rutherford. "Would an explosives dog be able to detect a small device hidden behind metal walls?"

He held my gaze. "I doubt it. But that would also make it hard to detonate remotely. Wouldn't the panels block the signal?"

"Maybe. I don't know. We need to talk to your RLC man. The Iranians would solve that problem." I turned to Béraud. "How long ago did Lémery know about the conference?"

"Several months," she replied.

"They've had ample time to send someone to stay here overnight. They made a note of the lift maintenance company and figured out how to hack the software."

"Then why do it so recently?" Béraud questioned. "They could've set this up weeks ago."

It was a good point but the answer came to me right away. "They're using a mobile phone as the trigger. The battery would run dry if they left it more than a few days."

Rutherford stood up. "I need to talk to the manager." He looked at me. "Want to help me search for a bomb?"

I grinned. "I do owe you for getting the police off my back."

44

B Y THE TIME RUTHERFORD, BÉRAUD and I had made it down to the ground floor via the rear staircase, we'd posited and agreed that the device had to be small enough to fit discreetly in an engineer's toolbox, probably disassembled and concealed within items of equipment. Having had a unique interest in seeing the main lift functional again, Sarah had seen the workman when he'd arrived and knew he'd been searched. But technical gear was always indecipherable to anyone without the relevant training; a component concealed inside an ohmmeter or even the handle of an electric screwdriver would seldom be found.

Any explosive material and a detonator brought into the hotel would, therefore, be small and easily hidden. But *small* could still mean *deadly*, even if the extent of its blast were confined to a relatively short radius. We debated the notion that it might not actually be a simple explosive. An incendiary device could, even with a tiny amount of fuel, start a catastrophic high-temperature fire in the lift shaft that would spread rapidly. Either way, the attack would force the evacuation protocol.

Rutherford asked one of the MI5 agents to find me a covert radio so I could listen to the security channel. He then went off in search of the hotel's general manager to find out exactly what had happened in response to the lift fault. Béraud and I had a discreet conversation with the corporal from the Royal Logistic Corps. He urged an immediate evacuation when we presented our edited summary of the threat, but we refused because containment and the façade of normality were required, at least until we knew exactly what we were dealing with.

Thankfully the activity in the White Horse Vale Hotel was

mostly inside the dining-room at that hour. Béraud confirmed that the ongoing formal meetings were not scheduled until mid-morning, although several private conversations between the delegates would certainly take place beforehand, albeit not in the main conference suites. It meant I could examine the lift without drawing attention. One of the hotel staff found me some *out of order* signs. I placed one on each floor.

The bomb disposal expert disappeared for a couple of minutes before returning with an assortment of tools and the news that he'd shut down the circuit that powered the lift. Rutherford's man returned soon thereafter with a covert radio for me, and once I'd wired it inside my new suit jacket and inserted the earpiece, I was plugged into the communications network. Rutherford advised the agents on the channel that the lift had broken down again, but gave no indication that anything was otherwise amiss.

Rutherford walked over with a grim expression and met my gaze. "You were right."

I waited for him to continue.

"A staff member reported the fault in the usual manner. The contractor provided a job number and dispatched an engineer. The hotel telephoned the company again to confirm his identity when he arrived. All in order."

"But?"

"I've just called the maintenance firm on my mobile. They had no record of the fault being reported. They didn't send anyone out."

"No record of the engineer?"

Rutherford shook his head. "The company's details are on a sticker inside the lift. Anyone staying here could take a photo."

"They hacked the phone line to intercept calls from the hotel," I said.

"It wouldn't take much to research the lift's specifications," Rutherford added. "They disabled it remotely." He turned to Béraud. "Can you keep Lémery occupied?"

She nodded. "He has a meeting with the Canadian represent-ative after breakfast, but other than that, I think he intends to stay in his suite until lunch."

"Watch him," Rutherford said. "We'll regroup later."

Béraud nodded and walked away across the foyer toward the dining-room.

"We need to know what we have here," Rutherford said to the corporal.

"This won't be a quick job, sir," he replied. "I'll have to take the whole thing apart and check behind every panel."

"Understood." Rutherford paused. "The device was carried into the hotel inside a toolbox. How much damage could it really do?"

The soldier held his gaze. "The lift would probably contain the explosion behind the doors. But the metal sheeting is pretty thin. Sturdy but not reinforced. Anyone inside would be shredded. An incendiary device would have half the building on fire in minutes."

"You'd better get to work."

"Yes, sir." The Army man grabbed an electric screwdriver and stepped into the open lift.

"Do you mind if I ask you questions?" I said to the man in uniform.

"No, sir. If I need you to shut the fuck up, I'll tell you."

I grinned. "We think they'll use a mobile phone trigger. Where would they hide it?"

"Good question," the corporal replied from the lift compart-ment. "Not in the lift itself. The signal could get blocked."

"That's what we thought."

"Don't rely on that. You can often still use a mobile phone inside a lift. But if you were installing a trigger and a detonator, you'd want a reliable method."

"What would you do?"

"I'd place it outside the lift shaft. It needs to be close by because it has to be wired in. And while they probably left the engineer to work on his own, he couldn't spend all day here without looking suspicious."

"He'd know the schematics."

"He would, but rigging a bomb is not a quick job. Simplest is always best."

"Understood."

The button on the small metal plate mounted on the wall next to the lift doors caught my attention. The round button had Braille dots embossed on the plastic and was lightly worn, as if countless thumbs and fingers had rubbed off the gloss over the years. But there was something about the backplate that didn't look right. I ran my fingers over the metal. It felt smooth to the touch, as a piece of stainless steel should, but the edges were not rounded like a properly finished piece of metal ought to be. I rubbed my fingertip along the top edge and detected some tiny imperfections. I pressed the plate gently and it bowed a fraction of an inch under the pressure.

"What about here?" I asked. "I think the call-button panel has been replaced."

The ordnance disposal expert shuffled out of the lift compartment. I pressed the plate again to show him. He met my gaze. "Let me see."

I moved out of the way and stood next to Rutherford as the RLC man quickly removed the four screws. He pulled the plate away and turned it over. The other side clearly wasn't made of metal.

"Balsa wood," Rutherford commented.

"With metallic plastic film stuck on," the corporal added. He shone a pencil light into the hole in the wall and peered inside. A moment later he turned round to face us. "The phone's wedged in the cavity."

"Can you remove it?" I asked.

He shook his head. "Not without knowing exactly how it's rigged." He paused. "You must get everyone out. My team and I will need to take this apart."

"Can't do that," Rutherford said. "Not yet."

"Sir…"

"Can we shield it?" I interrupted.

The Army man held my gaze. "Not unless you can find me the original backplate. And even then, I wouldn't want to rely on it."

"How about a Faraday bag?" Rutherford asked. "Could you fit it around the phone?"

"You have one to hand?"

"Several. All the hotel staff are required to surrender their mobiles at the start of each shift. We don't want them taking photos of our personnel or putting recordings of the meetings on their social media accounts. We've been using Faraday bags so they don't accept incoming calls."

The man nodded. "You want a temporary fix, sir? That's your safest option. But it doesn't come with a cast-iron guarantee. We have no idea if they rigged a backup."

"We shall just have to hope they did not," Rutherford replied. "Give me a minute." He spun around and marched off.

The corporal looked at me and spoke again. "I need to make it clear that everyone should leave the building."

I held his gaze for a moment. "Your advice is noted. But we need to let this play out a while longer. I can't explain why."

"I can guess." He paused. "Mr Rutherford has operational command. But I'm here as the tactical adviser."

"Trust me, he's taking your recommendation seriously."

"But you can't act on it yet?"

"Right." I said nothing else. However much the corporal from the Royal Logistic Corps deserved to know why we were keeping dozens of VIPs and their staff inside the building, he had a designated function, and understanding the broader intelligence picture was not it.

The man nodded but didn't reply. He'd made his point but was disciplined enough not to argue. I had sympathy for his position. The hierarchy he was operating under, and accountable to, was civilian rather than military, despite the historical M in MI5.

Rutherford returned with a handful of black Faraday bags of varying sizes. He handed them to the corporal and reminded him to seal everything up when the phone in the wall was shielded. He and I left the soldier to his work and walked across the grandly furnished lobby.

"I need to contact the SAS captain," Rutherford said quietly.

"Understood."

"I've informed my team leaders. You, Laure and Sarah are obviously already involved. But I'm inclined to keep the circle small."

I got the message. "You want us to watch Lémery?"

Rutherford nodded. "I'll leave that to the three of you. If he breaks his schedule for any reason, I want to know about it."

"He's not likely to act until the final session this evening."

"I agree," Rutherford said. "Have you eaten?"

I'd pushed the hunger from my mind. His comment reminded me I was starving. "Not for a while."

"There's still loads of food in the dining-room. Get yourself some brunch." He paused. "I know you haven't slept. But I don't want to find you curled up in a chair with scrambled egg spilled down that nice new shirt."

I grinned. "Trust me, I'm wide awake. But I need food."

"Work out a surveillance strategy with the others. I'll talk to you again soon."

"Will do." I turned round and wandered off in search of bacon and toast.

45

HAVING SPENT the last four days in a state of alertness comparable to an antelope drinking at a crocodile-infested water hole, I felt a little disoriented at having to wait for hours while nothing happened. We'd taken a gamble by not detaining Security Minister Julien Lémery, but Rutherford had to brief the SAS about the attack scenario we'd envisaged, and they needed time to work out a search-and-neutralize strategy against the MOIS operatives without being observed from outside the hotel's grounds. We also had to agree how to deal with the treacherous Frenchman.

On closer inspection of the mobile in the wall cavity next to the lift, the corporal from the Royal Logistic Corps had spotted a nest of taped wires and a second phone battery. The find had reinforced his view that no attempt should be made to dismantle the device while civilians were in the building, and he'd voiced his objection one last time to Alan Rutherford. The MI5 director stood his ground, so the RLC team had come up with a novel way of further reducing the risk. They'd raided the groundsmen's extensive supply of potting compost, wheeled in the stolen bags on a sack barrow, and stacked them inside the lift compartment to absorb the force of an explosion. I've always been impressed by the improvisation skills of soldiers.

All of this took place under the noses of the delegates and their assistants. The hotel was large enough to shut off certain sections under the pretence of cleaning and preparation for meetings without disrupting the ebb and flow of the diplomatic stratagems. The general manager had, after the call to the lift company, figured out that something was wrong. I think Rutherford persuaded him to keep his mouth shut under threat of consequences that only the Security Service could unleash. It seemed to do the trick.

The delegates and their minions continued their business, oblivious to the intelligence operation that was taking place around them. Security teams and the military were present in most aspects of their professional lives, and they had no inclination to distrust the people who were tasked with their protection. They stayed detached, either because they were too occupied with their diplomatic games, or through straightforward disinterest. That worked in our favour.

Béraud informed the rest of us when Lémery met the Canadian minister. Afterwards, he spent most of the time until lunch in discussions with his attendants, and only surfaced when the meal was announced. Sarah speculated that Murad Zam had told the Frenchman about my presence in Somerset, so I stayed on the periphery of events and used the time to study a map of the district in which the hotel was located. I had my doubts that the cell leader would contact Lémery about anything other than his role in their scheme, but I couldn't reject the possibility out of hand.

The lunchtime break started late and dragged on for two hours, making me wonder if the delegates cared more for the luxuries which their status afforded than the Iranian regime's resolve to develop nuclear weapons. Had it been down to me to ensure the right diplomatic decisions were made and effective sanctions drawn up, I'd have locked them in a room and banged a few heads together until they capitulated. It was probably a good thing that I wasn't involved in politics. I suppose that's the difference between an agent who's seen close up how murderous fanatics ply their deadly trade and a bureaucrat who receives the sanitised briefing document.

The fair afternoon rolled into a cloudy evening without incident; the change in the weather prompting an early switching on of the hotel's lights. As the delegates mingled on the ground floor in anticipation of the final session, Sarah moved between the lobby and the main conference room, ostensibly to coordinate her team's security protocols but actually to watch Julien Lémery like a hawk. Rutherford, Béraud and I waited in an office out of sight, switching our radios to a different channel so we could listen to Sarah's narration.

Twenty minutes, then thirty, ticked by as the representatives from various governments gradually ended conversations and filed into the conference room for the last phase, shepherded by their attendants.

Sarah's voice sounded in my earpiece. "Lémery's just seen the notice by the lift."

I glanced at Rutherford and Béraud. We stayed silent, waiting for Sarah to continue.

"He seems wary," Sarah added. "He's just spoken to one of his staff. Looks like he's excused himself for a moment." She paused. "Yeah, he's stepping away. Laure, what kind of mobile does he own?"

Béraud spoke into the microphone hidden in her collar. "An iPhone. Latest model."

"Well, he's carrying another one. Smaller. He's just pulled it from his jacket. Walking toward the toilets near the dining-room. Looks like he's making a call."

Rutherford spoke next. "Moment of truth. Are you behind cover, Sarah?"

"Confirmed."

The MI5 man spoke to Béraud and me off-comms. "Calling Zam or triggering the device?" Rutherford clenched his jaw. "I want that phone."

I nodded, waiting. I realised I was tensing my muscles in anticipation of the hotel's lift blowing apart. The explosion never came.

"He's out," Sarah told us forty seconds later. "Looks unsure. Nervous. No, he's going toward the conference suite."

Rutherford looked at Béraud and me. "Your move."

We hurried from the office and intercepted Lémery before he reached the conference room's double doors. I'd never seen him in the flesh before, and I took an immediate dislike to him. Not because he was an overweight man with thinning greasy hair and small wire-framed glasses perched on a Gallic nose, but because, as a spy, I'm damn good at reading people, and I knew I was looking at a piece of shit. If Lémery had been alive during the Second World War, he would have been a Nazi collaborator. Everything about his posture and clothing told me this was a man focussed on self-interest above all else.

Béraud placed her hand on Lémery's arm and hurried him away from the doors toward the hotel's main entrance, speaking rapidly in French. My understanding of the language wasn't fluent, but I knew enough to keep up. Besides, I already knew what she'd planned to say. The minister glanced at me, but his concerned expression did not show recognition. It didn't matter either way. He'd already sealed his own fate.

"We have a credible threat against the delegates, Minister Lémery," Béraud said quietly but firmly as she led him through the lobby. "Come with me."

Lémery had no choice. The creases in his sleeve told me Béraud's grip on the man was like a vice. The DGSE operator almost dragged him outside. I followed as she headed toward a row of parked cars.

The Frenchman attempted to glance back at the building. "What about the others?" he protested. "My staff?"

"We'll keep them safe," Béraud replied. "You're my priority." She stopped next to a grey Citroën C5 X; the keyless entry system responding to the fob in her coat. Béraud placed the remote in Lémery's hand. "Go directly to the embassy in London. I'll tell them you're on your way."

Lémery stared, wide-eyed and tense. He tugged at his shirt collar. "What? I need a driver."

Béraud shook her head. "Minister, I cannot spare anyone." She jerked the driver's door open and gave him a firm push. "Go now."

The Frenchman sat down on the seat and pressed the start button. His glower was a mix of fear and incredulity. "You can't expect...?"

Rutherford joined us. Speaking in English, he said, "Minister Lémery, I can assure you there is a genuine risk to your life. Please follow the instruction of your security chief."

"But..." the man stammered.

"We believe the delegates' phones are being tracked. Please hand yours over."

Lémery did as he was told and gave his iPhone to Béraud.

She stared at him for a moment. "The other one as well."

Shock etched itself onto Lémery's face. He fished out a push-button phone and placed it in the DGSE agent's hand. "It was for private use," he said, switching back to his native language. "My family..."

"I don't care about that," Béraud snapped. "You know how to drive an automatic?"

"Of course."

"Good." Béraud stepped back and slammed the door shut. She made a gesture for Lémery to lower the window. Béraud held his gaze before speaking again. "Just one other matter, Julien," she said, deliberately switching to his first name, her tone disdainful. "We know what you did."

Lémery's face fell. "You're setting me up," he said, uttering the words from a suddenly parched mouth. "You fucking bitch."

Béraud smiled. "You should reconsider the company you keep. Now get out of here before I change my mind."

Lémery shoved the gear lever into drive and lifted his foot suddenly from the brake pedal. The wheels flung up gravel as he sped away from the front of the hotel, heading down the drive at forty miles an hour.

Rutherford activated his radio. "Gold command to SAS. Target attempting to escape via the main drive. Grey Citroën SUV. Take him out."

Ten seconds later I heard the distinctive crackle of automatic weapons unleashing deadly volleys into Lémery's car.

A voice buzzed through my earpiece. "Target neutralized, Gold."

"Good job," Rutherford replied. "Move to the next phase."

Béraud turned my way and made eye contact. Her pallor was a little pale. Well, she had just conspired with MI5 to send her traitorous boss to his death. "I told you we're on the same side," she said softly. "Agreed?"

I offered my hand. "Agreed."

46

Murad zam's stomach clenched when he heard the machinegun fire. He glanced at Samir Davari. The man's expression revealed he'd heard the unmistakable sound as well. Not close by, but somewhere across the grounds of the country estate. Coming just a few minutes after the erratic phone call from the French politician, the reports from the weapons confirmed the operation was blown.

Lémery had called in a panic, almost squealing with anxiety. He'd told the MOIS commander that the device behind the lift's control panel had been discovered. The inept idiot hadn't even attempted to ring the concealed phone's number to detonate the explosive. Relying on the security minister had been a profound mistake, he realised, but not the only one. Whether the failure was through Lémery's incompetence or MI5's relentless counter-espionage work, Zam didn't know, but none of that mattered.

More gunfire sounded in the distance. Not police – the British firearms officers used weapons locked to single-shot – but military. And not just ordinary soldiers but – judging by the precise controlled bursts he could hear – special forces. Zam and his men were highly competent fighters themselves, but four men going up against unknown numbers of SAS troopers on home soil was not a battle they could win.

He gripped his assault rifle with both hands and locked eyes with Davari. "We have to abort."

Davari nodded before turning his stare toward the narrow road, peering through the foliage which shielded their observation point. They were covering the road which led to the hotel's second drive-way; Haydar Hamidi and Jawad Babolian were somewhere at the front, tasked with obliterating the main convoy of vehicles that fled the hotel.

That would not happen now.

Zam transmitted on his radio. "Haydar? We're blown. Abort."

No reply.

Zam tried again. "Haydar? Jawad? Respond."

Still nothing.

Davari muttered under his breath. "They're down."

"Fuck!" Zam spat through clenched teeth. He hesitated for just a second. "Back to the car."

Davari nodded and got to his feet.

His last mistake.

A sniper's bullet ripped a gaping wound through the Iranian's chest, shredding his lungs and pulverising his spine before exiting through a massive hole in his back. Davari's body fell against the spindly hawthorn branches before Zam even heard the report from the gun.

Zam inhaled, forcing himself to focus, drawing upon memories of past conflicts. The chaos and disquietude melted into surreal calmness as he switched to survival mode. Keeping hold of his gun, he got on his belly and crawled, determined to remain invisible behind the copious greenery. He slumped into a roadside ditch and shuffled forward as fast as he could, knowing that if the SAS found him, they'd not bother to demand his surrender. Playing Davari's execution over in his mind, Zam speculated his pursuers must be – *might be* – some way behind him if they'd slain his team member with a sniper's bullet.

He dragged himself through the undergrowth with all the effort he could muster, tugging against the thorny stems as they snagged his limbs and the assault rifle, but he didn't even register the minor cuts he endured. Zam made it a hundred yards without taking a bullet to the skull; the minor victory made him hope he hadn't been spotted. He kept going, putting more distance between himself and the killing-zone where they'd planted two IEDs. Another hundred yards. The end of the ditch. Zam crawled out using a bank of ferns as cover.

The black Renault Captur was less than a fifth of a mile away, parked under trees near the entrance to a farmer's field in a scrape at the edge of the lane. Zam's heart thumped when he thought he'd lost the key card, but he'd forgotten he'd moved it to a back pocket when readying his gun. The fob was still there, flat inside the back of his hiking trousers. He stopped moving as the bank of undergrowth thinned. Staying in a low crouch, Zam turned slowly, studying all the angles. He saw nothing in the direction he'd come from, but that didn't mean a lot. He gave it thirty seconds before deciding to move. He couldn't see the car but knew he'd be there in seconds if he ran. Zam filled his lungs with several deep breaths. If this didn't work he'd be dead before he hit the ground.

Zam burst onto the road and sprinted, fuelled by adrenaline and a furious determination to survive. After fifty seconds a familiar bend in the road appeared. Zam lifted the gun, slowing his approach and using rehearsed steps that kept his stance flexible and balanced. He saw no one at the vehicle as he rounded the corner, but pivoted from side to side to check his surroundings. Nothing appeared in his line of fire. Zam lowered the gun and went to the driver's door. He got inside and placed the gun's barrel in the passenger footwell, leaning the stock against the seat.

The engine responded when Zam pushed the start button, purring smoothly. The Iranian gripped the steering wheel for a moment, settling his nerves. Did the security services know about the Renault? Zam couldn't be sure, but the fact he'd found it un-attended had to be a good sign. He took a moment to recall the layout of the roads in the district. Few in number, they'd been easy to remember when he'd planned the mission. The topography of the North Wessex Downs meant there weren't many routes between the nearby villages. His exit route back to Swindon was stamped on his mental map.

Zam released the brake and pulled out. It was getting dark – the twilight hastened by the thickening clouds – but he didn't switch on the car's lights. The safe-houses were, he had to assume, now known to British Intelligence. But it had never been the plan to return there after the operation. They'd left two cars in different supermarket car parks for their egress from the Wiltshire town. Knowing that Oxford and London were obvious destinations which MI5 and the police would check, he'd planned instead to head thirty miles northwest to the city of Gloucester for their extraction.

Zam cursed under his breath as he drove along the lane. No strategy was flawless, he knew, but he'd been sure he'd foreseen and avoided counter-intelligence techniques and surveillance. He thought again about the anonymous voice on the phone who'd irritated him so much during every stage of the operation. Control had screwed up when he'd sent Zam to Bristol to kill Farzad Bouzidi. Zam promised himself there would be payback. But had he committed a fatal error when hunting the spy in Somerset? Had he been so determined to avenge Ahmad's death that he'd jeopardised the attack against the conference delegates? Was it he, not Control, who'd caused his entire team to be wiped out? Or had the operation been doomed from the start, thwarted by MI5?

There would be time for reflection later. And blame. There was always culpability. Zam pushed the thought from his head. Escape was all that mattered. He encountered no traffic as he drove. No farmers' 4×4s, no regular cars owned by the tourists who visited the beauty spot, no delivery vans. It was a quiet area but Zam expected to see *something*, even at night. The answer came when he turned at a junction and saw a marked police car stationary in the road ahead, angled to block both lanes. Zam swore again and kicked himself for not guessing the police would set up roadblocks.

Could he turn around and head in the other direction? Yes, but a three-point turn would look suspicious, and there would prob-ably be another patrol car hindering that route. And, with the lethal Special Air Service on his trail, Zam couldn't afford to tour the English countryside in search of alternative ways out. There was no longer time for subterfuge. He carried on toward the police car. The road was not completely blocked because of the vehicle's angle; the driver had left a small gap at the front and rear so he could manoeuvre out of the spot.

Zam stamped on the accelerator, aiming for the gap at the back of the police car, reckoning he could ram his way through. He glimpsed terror on the seated driver's face as he sped toward the marked vehicle. The Renault smashed into the rear quarter of the patrol car.

And came to a juddering halt.

The Renault's engine cut out as an airbag deployed from the steering-wheel casing, thumping Zam in the face as the inertia rocked him forward. He stabbed the start button with his finger but the engine remained silent. Zam glanced round and saw the police officers attempting to get out of the car. The driver's door appeared to be stuck as a result of the collision, but the policeman gave it a hefty kick and it swung open.

Zam grabbed the assault rifle and jumped out of the SUV. The observer fumbled with his radio and hit the emergency button. The Iranian fired a volley at the officer before he could speak, aiming at the officer's stab vest. Zam spun and squeezed the trigger at the driver before his colleague's body had slumped onto the tarmac. The driver's jaw blew apart as the projectiles smashed into his head and throat. Satisfied the officer was dead, Zam jogged around the car to check the body of the first officer he'd shot, not knowing if the body armour had ballistic protection. It didn't, and it had barely slowed the bullets down.

The SUV was unusable. Zam ran back around the police car, hoping the keys were still in the ignition. But when he'd collided with it, he'd buckled the rear wheel and snapped the axle. His hope of escaping the scene in a stolen police vehicle evaporated, and there was no way the reports from his weapon would go unheard.

The carnage he'd inflicted upon the two police officers was not yet known, but Zam knew that pressing the emergency button on a police radio opened the microphone for at least ten seconds. A dispatcher sitting in a control room would have heard the bullets.

Zam hurled the assault rifle into the verge. The magazine was close to empty and the weight of the weapon would slow him down. Being seen carrying it would ensure a swift and deadly response. If he had to move through the countryside on foot, the darkness might conceal his identity but the gun would not. The Department 312 operator sprinted along the road until he came to a farm gate. He clambered over it and ran as hard as he could across the meadow.

The ground became steeper as he moved through the fields. He reached a hedgerow and stopped, trying to control his breathing and the pounding in his chest. He heard a police siren and saw flashing blue lights somewhere below him. It would not be a regular patrol car that arrived at the scene but a firearms unit, and the SAS were undoubtedly out there too. Zam prayed for a delay before a police helicopter took to the skies. If that happened there would be no escape, but he wasn't out of the game yet.

Zam kept going toward the hill's summit, knowing that fields and footpaths were considerably safer than the handful of roads which wove around the Downs. Orienting himself, he realised he wasn't far from White Horse Hill, the site of the famous chalk carving. A few farm tracks snaked up the hillsides toward the Ridgeway trail, but most of the high ground was inaccessible to vehicles.

It was open ground but remote. Zam had nothing left to lose. If he could make it past the carved horse and find the burial mound known as Wayland's Smithy, he'd get onto the footpath which ran along the high chalk ridge. Seven miles to Swindon. At a steady run, he reckoned he'd get there in under an hour and a half.

Zam drew a breath and scrambled up the hill.

47

RUTHERFORD kicked the diplomats and their staff out of the conference room and confined them to quarters under the watchful eyes of their security personnel, providing only an edited version of events to the officers of the assembled clandestine agencies. Questions were asked but Rutherford kept his information brief. He nominated his second-in-command to act as liaison, thereby allowing himself to concentrate on the Iranians.

We converted the conference suite into an operations room. Sarah and I joined Rutherford and several MI5 officers there, along with Laure Béraud, the captain from the Special Air Service, the corporal from the Royal Logistic Corps, and a counter-terrorism superintendent from the police. A digital map of the hotel and the surrounding district was displayed on a large wall-mounted monitor. As information reached us, the map was updated. The photographs of three dead Iranians occupied a section on the right-hand side of the screen.

"Let's confirm IDs," Rutherford said, pointing. "I know that one's Haydar Hamidi, the bomb maker. Anyone recognise the younger bloke?" No one offered a name. Rutherford turned to one of his team. "Run the picture."

"On it, boss," the agent replied, immediately tapping away on a laptop.

"The other one is Samar Davari," I said. "He was part of Murad Zam's crew in France."

Rutherford nodded and then turned to the map, pointing at the location where the police officers had been gunned down. "I assume that was Zam, but we don't yet know if there were other cell members." He glanced at the superintendent. "Where's that helicopter?"

She shook her head. "Grounded at RAF Benson. Mechanical fault. They're trying to allocate one from another airfield."

"We don't have time to wait," Rutherford snapped.

"My troopers are ready," the SAS captain interjected.

"Sorry, I need you to maintain a perimeter around the hotel. Until we get air support, we can't rule out a second attack by a backup team. I want to know the site is clean before I evacuate the diplomats."

"Understood," the SAS man said with a shrug. "But you still have a suspect out there. You've got the world's best hunter unit ready to go."

Rutherford nodded. "Point taken, but I'm not without an alternative." He glanced at Béraud, Sarah and me. "I believe Murad Zam represents unfinished business for some people in this room." He held my gaze. "You know him better than anyone. What's his plan?"

"He'll retreat to fight another day," I replied. "There'll be an evacuation strategy to get him out of the country. You said you'd identified a safe-house?"

"In Swindon. But there's probably more than one." Rutherford paused. "He'll guess they're blown."

"Yes, but he'll have something in place nearby. He'll head that way."

"You don't think he'll go to ground?"

My recent evasion experience came to mind. "Last resort," I replied. "He has to keep moving. He knows the police, SAS and MI5 are after him."

"He might take a hostage," the police superintendent offered.

I shook my head. "Unlikely," I said to her. "He knows what he's up against." I glanced at the SAS captain. "These boys practise for that very scenario in the Killing House at Hereford. Zam won't trap himself. That only ends one way." I took a moment to think. "MOIS missions replicate the fear and drama of terror attacks, but

266

their agents are highly trained intelligence operatives with military backgrounds, not suicidal zealots. Zam will focus on egress."

Sarah wheeled herself toward the screen. "By road is difficult. Few options." She turned the wheelchair around to face the group. "He had a vehicle but wrecked it. Could he find another?" she mulled out loud. "He already knows we have roadblocks in place. And after he murdered those policemen, he'll assume we've deployed firearms units to replace the unarmed officers."

"You think he'll stay on foot?" Béraud asked.

"He doesn't have much choice," Sarah replied. "It's not ideal." She pointed at the screen. "Hills and fields between here and Swindon. A police helicopter would spot him in the dark."

"But we haven't been able to launch," the superintendent added.

"I'm certain he has an informant in the police," I commented.

She gave me a questioning look. "But not in the National Police Air Service?"

"You want to rule that out?"

The officer didn't answer.

Rutherford's colleague spoke next. "Match on the unknown subject, boss. Jawad Babolian. The Iraqis circulated him as a person of interest. Want me to get the dossier translated?"

The MI5 director shook his head. "That can wait. Call Thames House and run the photos. Let's see if we can find out how they entered the country. I want to know who their friends are in the UK. Something for us to have fun with on a rainy day."

"On it," the officer replied with a grin.

Béraud took another look at the monitor. "Can you bring up a contour map?" she asked.

The agent working the screen switched to an Ordnance Survey chart.

"Thanks," Béraud said. "I don't think he'll stay on the high ground. The Ridgeway trail would lead him to the southwest, away from Swindon. I think he'll drop into this area here," she added, pointing to a broad patch of featureless farmland. "It's the most direct route. He could cross those fields and end up on the east side of the town."

I frowned. "That's what? Twenty square kilometres? I know it's pretty open territory, but it's still quite an area to cover."

The SAS captain stepped up. "The offer stands, Mr Rutherford."

Rutherford looked at him for a moment. "Can you release men without compromising the integrity of your perimeter?"

"I could give you two. Four at a push."

"I'll take two." He glanced at Béraud and me. "They'll make up the numbers." He paused. "Give me a tactical assessment, Captain."

The SAS man pursed his lips in thought. "I should qualify my answer. We're not talking about a battlefield escape-and-evasion strategy. This scenario is different."

"Explain," Rutherford prompted.

"A soldier knows he has to find food, water and shelter while running from hunter teams. There's a balance to be found. Speed is preferable, but it's no good if you're dehydrated and starving to death. The route to safety is rarely direct. None of that applies to Murad Zam. He only has to travel seven miles or thereabouts."

Rutherford took a moment to consider the captain's words. "He'd have studied the terrain and worked out several egress routes. You agree with Ms Béraud?"

The soldier nodded. "It's my best guess, sir." He paused and tapped the screen. "Your hostile killed the police officers here – about fifty-five minutes ago. That suggests to me that he intended to take the A420 west. He can't do that now, but he's unlikely to stray too far from that road."

"Straight past Gablecross Police Station," the superintendent muttered. "Smart. That's Wiltshire's area."

"I'd like to think you're coordinating with the neighbouring force," Rutherford remarked, his tone flat.

She glowered at him. "Had you thought to share the information about the safe-house, perhaps I would have done." She hesitated, evidently embarrassed at sounding unprofessional. "Give me a minute. I'll contact their control room inspector now." The superintendent strode from the conference room.

Rutherford turned back to the SAS captain. "You were saying?"

"He's had time to get onto the chalk ridge. He's probably halfway to Swindon by now." The man paused, checking the monitor. "But that should work to our advantage. The area we need to search is substantially reduced." He pointed at the map. "He needs to end up roughly here. The A420 and this minor road will act as a funnel. It's not a chokepoint, but it gives us a narrower zone to cover."

Rutherford looked my way. "Do you concur?"

I kept my look espionage blank. "It's a starting point," I answered. "We'll need some kit."

"I can spare a couple of C8 carbines," the captain said. "Standard thirty-round magazines."

"Perfect. Night vision gear?"

"Of course."

"Thank you. We'll meet you outside."

The SAS man nodded and walked from the conference room.

I turned back to Rutherford. "I want you and Sarah to stay on comms."

He held my gaze. "Now that our police friend is out of the room, let me say this. I want him dead. But we've never had this conversation. Plausible deniability. If you get killed, I'll declare that you were both rogue agents operating without the sanction of MI5. This is strictly an SAS counter-terrorism operation."

I grinned. "After the last four days, *rogue* is my middle name." I looked at Béraud. "Ready for a manhunt? Let's find Murad Zam."

48

THE TWO SAS TROOPERS assigned to the manhunt left the hotel in a plain blue Iveco panel van that wouldn't have looked out of place in a builder's yard. I hadn't seen the vehicle earlier; I guessed they had parked it discreetly behind an outbuilding in the grounds. Béraud and I took a few minutes to check the weapons and night-vision equipment they had allocated to us, then loaded them into the boot of the white Peugeot 508.

The DGSE operator got into the driver's seat and started the engine. She touched the display screen, bringing up the sat-nav, as I sat down next to her and tugged the passenger door shut.

"Change of plan," I told her.

She gave me a hard look. "Are you kidding?"

I shook my head. "The SAS captain was wrong. Murad won't trek down from the ridge and head for the east side of Swindon."

"I thought you agreed with his assessment? And *mine*, for that matter."

"I don't recall saying that." I paused. "Laure, I know how he thinks. I've spent the last four days and nights running from him. He's bloody good at this. Whether or not he had help, I don't know, but he predicted every move I made. Every time. The only reason I got away was because he didn't have a full team in Somerset."

Béraud held my look with a mistrustful frown but didn't speak.

"He even predicted I'd head west across the Quantock Hills, right past the police command post, while the helicopter was searching another area." I paused. "That's when I got lucky. I stumbled across Heyat and Bux before they found me. The outcome could've been rather different. Not one I'd care to contemplate."

"What's your point?" Béraud questioned.

"I tried to shake him off by being unpredictable. He saw through it." I drew a breath. "He's not just a soldier, Laure. He's a covert operator. Murad thinks like a spy. He does the opposite of what you'd expect. He's a damn good manhunter."

Béraud turned her eyes forward and looked through the windscreen into the darkness. "You don't think he'll go to the low ground?"

I shook my head.

"Even though it's the fastest route to Swindon on foot?"

"Is it? The most direct, perhaps. But he'd have to cross several fields and avoid a couple of villages." I paused. "He'll stay on the Ridgeway trail."

Béraud's lips compressed into a look of doubt. "The footpath turns to the southwest. It never reaches Swindon."

"But it gets close. He'll come off the trail near where it crosses the motorway. That would put him just a mile or two from the south edge of the town."

She stared at me again. "I presumed he'd head for the east side because it's closest."

I nodded. "It's not a large town. We have no intel on his exit strategy. There's some logic to placing a vehicle near the M4. Even if that's not his plan, once he's in an urban environment he'll be harder to track."

"If you're wrong?" Béraud asked.

"Then either the SAS guys get to neutralize a Department 312 commander, or he slips through the net and the police take over and run it as a major incident." A thin smile appeared on my face. "He used a similar tactic against me." I paused. "I don't think I'm wrong. Look at the conditions. Partial cloud cover and moonlight. Wouldn't you prefer to run along a well-maintained national trail – a chalk one – than risk slowing yourself down in cattle fields and water meadows?"

She nodded. "We'd better move. Navigate for me."

I studied the sat-nav as Béraud drove. By the time we reached the police unit at the main gate, I'd worked out a route after finding the point where the Ridgeway met a minor road at a place called Fox Hill. The trail appeared to divert briefly along the road close to the motorway before becoming a footpath once again on the other side.

We only had five miles to drive. The DGSE spy handled the car with practised expertise, rounding the bends with the skill of a rally driver, slowing down only when we reached a police road-block. Rutherford had called ahead though, so the delay took only seconds. We reached a quiet crossroads and flew past a country pub that had been converted into an Indian restaurant. When this was over, I thought I might suggest to Rutherford that we all debrief there over a chicken korma.

The entrance to the Ridgeway trail was just two hundred yards past the restaurant on the right, partly concealed among trees. Béraud made the turn and brought the car to a sliding halt in a small parking area. She flicked off the lights and killed the engine.

"You sure about this?" she asked.

"Sure? No. Confident? Yes. Let's grab those C8s."

Thirty seconds later we were ascending the trail into the gentle chalk hills, wearing the high-grade night-vision kit and carrying the Canadian-made assault rifles we'd borrowed from the Special Air Service. Spindly trees stood on either side of the path, but there wasn't a contiguous hedgerow, and gaps in the foliage frequently revealed the smooth contours of the North Wessex Downs in the soft moonlight. Somewhere unseen to our left, on the low ground north of our position, the SAS soldiers were conducting their own search. I hoped I'd made the right call, and it would be us, not the troopers, who found Murad Zam that night.

The track got steeper and we found an isolated corrugated-metal barn. I signalled to Béraud that we should search the building. Lifting the weapons, we stepped around the walls until we came to an open side. We found only rusting farm machinery. Soon we were back on the path, continuing our hike up the hill. Beyond the barn it was easier to see further across the fields to the north and south, and we kept up steady sweeps with the guns across the landscape as well as the footpath itself.

A long spell of hot summer weather had kept the path dry, and the pale colour of the underlying chalk stood out in the night-vision lenses. Gateless access points to fields were frequent, and I inferred that the tyres of farm vehicles had compressed the path's naturally soft rock. Béraud and I continued up the hill over a ridge-line and eventually found ourselves on level ground. A fox skulked across a field about thirty yards to my left, his muzzle low to the grass, hunting for a scent of rabbit. I silently wished him well, comparing his mission to my own.

In the quietude of that unassuming landscape, it was not a surprise that we heard Murad Zam moments before we saw him. I quickly signalled to Béraud. We stepped off the path – one to each side – and crouched down with our assault rifles pointing toward the sound. There was no way the Iranian could have prevented the crunching of his boots on the chalk trail. The noise indicated strong pace and solid endurance, even though he'd already jogged for several miles. He appeared in the sightline of my weapon. I heard his rhythmical breathing.

"Stop running, Murad," I called out in Farsi as he ran closer.

The Iranian halted abruptly, his boots scuffing the chalk. He leaned forward, placing his hands on his hips as he sucked in deep breaths of air. Despite the exertion, a thin smile formed on his lips.

"Your accent is poor," he replied, staring into the darkness, still unable to see me.

"But you understand me just fine," I said.

He nodded. "Well enough."

I got up from my crouch and took a few paces toward him. I heard Béraud walk a short way behind me and to my side.

"I did not expect to hear my own language out here," Zam said, lifting his arms in a gesture that took in the invisible English landscape which surrounded us.

"No, but you probably weren't expecting to find me in Somerset either."

Zam sneered. "So it's you. My brother's murderer." He hesitated for a moment. "I nearly had you back there."

"I can't deny that. And you got the better of me in Paris, even if I did kill Ahmad. You're a worthy opponent, Murad. For that you have my professional respect."

The smile returned. "It is a real compliment that comes from an enemy."

I recognised the Iranian proverb. "How many others?" I asked him.

Zam shook his head. "Just my team," he replied.

"Six?"

He nodded.

"They're all dead."

"It does not end with us," Zam said softly. "You know this."

"And that's why we are relentless," I told him. "No mercy."

I squeezed the trigger and sent a hail of bullets through Zam's chest, the reports from the assault rifle shattering the night's tranquillity. The Iranian's body shuddered and jerked like a puppet on a string before collapsing onto the ground. I let the gun swing by my side on its strap as Béraud stood beside me. We both tilted the night-vision goggles above our heads and let our eyes adjust to the grey wash of moonlight that illuminated the chalk path.

"It's over," she said, staring at the bullet-riddled corpse.

I nodded grimly. "Until the next time. It never stops, Laure. They want to wipe us off the map."

"But not today."

I smiled at her. "Not today."

49

THE WIPER BLADES swept across the windscreen as I drove through Wanstead, battling with only moderate success against the summer storm that lashed against the glass. The soot-grey clouds suffocated London, trapping afternoon humidity like a blanket and bringing a dour mood to an already drab suburban corner of the city. As the traffic crawled, I turned on the air conditioning, which I rarely did even in hotter climes. I was driving a small Hyundai which was handy for the London streets but lacked the comfort and power of the grey Vauxhall I'd taken to Glastonbury. That car had been recovered and was in the agency garage getting its tyre valves repaired.

I flicked on the indicator and turned left onto Addison Road, looking for somewhere to park. Finding a gap about a minute's walk down the road from the safe-house, I manoeuvred the car into place and turned the ignition key toward me. The street seemed as inactive as I remembered as I let myself out. I pulled the zip of my waterproof jacket all the way to the top, locked the car with the fob, and set off along the pavement with my head down against the raindrops.

I heard a bolt being unlocked as I waited at the front door. Moments later I was inside, glad to be out of the rain but not enthused about the reason for my visit. Yasmin Bouzidi had asked to speak to me. No one had confirmed her brother's death – they'd rightly left that task to me – but I knew she'd seen the edited press reports from the Glastonbury incident and had called Farzad's mobile number to no avail. Her minders' refusal to provide information had doubtlessly been all the confirmation she'd needed.

She caught sight of me from the kitchen as I walked in and

removed my coat.

"I asked to see you days ago," she called out as I put my jacket on a hook in the hallway.

I stepped into the kitchen and found her with her hands around a mug of tea. Her dark eyes locked with mine over the top of the cup for a few seconds. She took a sip and then placed her drink on the counter.

"I know. I've had a lot going on," I replied as I pulled out a stool from under the table and sat opposite her.

"My brother's dead," she said, uttering the words as a statement.

I gave a quick nod. "I'm sorry." I meant what I said, even though I usually remained detached from my assets and considered them to be expendable. That was simply the hard truth about espionage. The opportunity to use Farzad after he'd offered technical information had been too good to miss, but he was just an ordinary well-educated man who was out of his depth. If I thought about it too much, I might admit to myself that the manipulation was cruel. I still hadn't decided if I could have prevented Farzad's murder.

The colour drained from Yasmin's face. She put her head in her hands and rocked slowly on the stool. For a moment I thought she'd wail with grief, but she put her hands in her lap and stared at me with wide eyes. I saw no tears but knew they would come later when she was alone.

"Oh, Farzad!" she said in a soft voice. But then her look hardened. "My brother was scared. He never answered his phone after I spoke to him that one time." A long sigh passed her lips. "What happened?"

I hesitated for a moment before answering. I couldn't tell her everything, but she deserved to know the truth. "I arranged to meet Farzad," I told her. "A team from the Ministry of Intelligence and Security found him before I could bring him to London."

"They said on the news that a Middle Eastern man had been

killed," she said.

I nodded. "In Glastonbury. That was your brother. They didn't know his real name."

Her eyes burrowed into mine. "Were you there?"

"Nearby. They came after me. That's the reason I could not see you sooner."

Yasmin raised her eyebrows. "What happened to you?"

"It doesn't matter. It's over. But I can tell you this: the man who murdered your brother is dead."

"You killed him?"

"I did."

She sighed again. "Do you know the Latin term *lex talionis?*"

I shook my head.

"It refers to the law of retaliation and retribution. A dirty emotion that we would do well to cast aside." She hesitated. "And yet, knowing this, I regret to say I am glad you killed that man."

I wasn't sure how to answer. I hadn't shot Rasul Heyat in revenge for what he'd done to Farzad Bouzidi; I'd killed the operative to survive. That, and to relieve the world of one more homicidal Iranian spy. But I wasn't unfamiliar with the concept Yasmin had just described. I'd inflicted a little *lex talionis* two nights ago on a moonlit hill with a C8 assault rifle.

"Why did you bring me to England?" Yasmin asked while my memory replayed the confrontation with Murad Zam.

I wasn't prepared to answer entirely truthfully. I kept my answer brief. "For Farzad. You were his only family."

Her mouth formed a firm line as she pressed her lips together. "That's not the whole story, is it?"

I held her gaze. "He wanted to be reunited with you. He couldn't contact you in Iran."

She reached for the tea mug. "I think I want to go back."

"You'd be in grave danger."

"What do I have here?" she countered. "I don't know anyone in England."

"We could arrange a new life for you. We'd find you a good job in the National Health Service so you could continue your work. And there are many Iranians living in England. You'd be safe."

"Did you tell that to Farzad?" she asked with an icy stare.

"Sometimes events happen which we cannot predict," I replied.

"Like when he was arrested?"

I nodded. "He did nothing wrong. He was protecting his employer from a criminal. What he did was actually rather brave."

"Thank you for telling me that."

I shrugged. "It's the truth."

"Will you allow me to return to my country?"

"If that is what you want. We cannot hold you against your will. But I would ask you to avoid a decision you might regret. We can't protect you if you return to Tehran."

"I understand." She glanced around the room. "But there's nothing for me here."

"Let my colleagues know what you decide. Take your time." I got up from the stool.

"Not you?"

I frowned. "What do you mean?"

"You said I should speak to your colleagues. Can I not contact you?"

I shook my head. "I've been told to expect another assignment. I don't know where. This is the last time we shall meet."

She hesitated before speaking again. "You didn't ask."

"Ask what?"

"Why I wanted to talk to you."

"I assumed it was to question me about Farzad," I replied.

"That was one reason," Yasmin said. "Not the only one."

I sat back down and opened my hands to invite her to continue.

"I know why your people kidnapped me in Tehran," she said.

"That's a strong word."

"But accurate." She waved the comment away. "That's

irrelevant. Farzad explained when I called him. He said he'd promised you information about my country's nuclear enrichment programme, but he wouldn't give you the data unless you got me out."

"I can't answer that."

"Fine. I know the truth." She paused. "Farzad told me you had kept your word. I was to honour his promise if he could not. I know where he hid the hard drive."

I held her gaze, unsure what to say. This I had not expected. "I thought he took it to Glastonbury," I said finally. "I assumed the man who killed him had retrieved it."

Yasmin shook her head. "He told me he had to leave Bristol urgently. I guess he never had a chance to collect the device." She paused. "The file you're after is still where he hid it."

"And you're willing to tell me?" I asked.

"Willing? I don't know about that. This entire episode – my brother's death – has been about some stupid computer data." She drew a breath. "But I will respect Farzad's request. He said the disk is hidden underneath the counter in the barber's shop."

I slowly got to my feet. "Thank you, Yasmin." For a moment I thought about praising her brother's integrity, but I didn't think I could do so without sounding patronising. I knew honour was not a quality the Iranian woman saw in me. And she wasn't wrong.

"It's a shame I won't see you again," she said as I left the kitchen.

I turned. "It's safer this way."

She gave a shrug. "I could've helped you improve your Farsi."

I gave her a warm smile. "My Farsi's just fine. Look after yourself, Yasmin." I held her gaze for one last time and then walked out.

50

THE DIRECTIONS they had given me were straightforward. I walked from the exit at Golders Green Underground, turned left to skirt around the stands and lanes of the neighbouring bus station, and then joined the pavement outside the old Hippodrome Theatre on North End Road. Soon I was walking up a moderate slope past large semi-detached houses and older three-storey terraces. Pollarded London plane trees stood at intervals on the pavement, their resplendent crowns adding colour to the street.

The road became steeper but I enjoyed the walk. It put just enough strain on my bandaged leg to tell me the wound was healing well. The rain of recent days had vanished and cloudless skies had returned to London, bringing back the dry heat that was uncomfortable in the grimy heart of the city but less oppressive in the leafy streets near Hampstead Heath. After several minutes I found the pedestrian crossing by Golders Hill Park. I crossed the road and went through the park gates.

The spell of wet weather hadn't restored the parched lawns, but they drew the crowds anyway, and the café next to the main path was busy. I took a quieter footpath to the left, heading for the woods near an old-fashioned bandstand, and followed a route through the trees for about two hundred yards until I emerged near a rectangular ornamental pond. A few people sat on the brittle grass or peered at the fish, but I formed the impression that this secluded area at the top of Hampstead Heath was relatively unknown.

I saw the location they had instructed me to visit behind a dense wall of shrubs. I strode past the pond and stepped into a building of stone and brick construction. Part folly, part garden pergola, the

Edwardian structure was an intriguing place in which to find myself. I went up a flight of stone steps to the top level and emerged on an elegant walkway. Ancient timber beams formed a lattice above my head, supported by rows of neoclassical columns. Ivy stems as thick as my arm were entwined around the pillars and balusters, and shrubs of innumerable hues poked their slender leaves through the gaps.

The aerial photo I'd found online had told me the structure was an irregular W shape, approximately three hundred yards from end to end, but the picture had failed to do justice to the setting. Surrounded by woodland, the pergola had a uniquely charming aspect, and its peculiar architecture seemed lost in time.

I walked along the worn flagstones between lichen-covered balustrades to a circular shelter built of stone. The feature had a domed roof of copper which had turned azure blue with age. The walkway continued through the round building and became a bridge over a footpath. Below me was an attractive garden, full of exotic plants and enclosed by iron railings. I looked across the garden at the next wing of the pergola and saw the man I'd come to meet. He was not alone but his minders were keeping a discreet distance.

He turned to face me as I approached, offering a warm smile that added more creases to an already lined face. His grey hair was neatly brushed, and he wore a tailored suit and waistcoat which would have been too hot for me but didn't appear to give him discomfort. He transferred a black walking cane from his right hand to his left as I stepped up to him so he could shake my hand. His grip was strong, belying his age. A charming man if you were on his good side, Reuven Bronstein also happened to be one of the most calculating and dangerous operators I knew. I suppose that's why the Mossad had assigned him to their most senior position in London.

"You've had a busy week," he said in Hebrew, a deep timbre in his voice.

"Eventful," I agreed. "And I was meant to be on administrative duties."

Bronstein moved back to the stone balustrade, his shuffle hindered by a slight limp, and returned his gaze to the garden below. He made a gesture. "Had you come here before?"

I shook my head. "It's pleasant. Calming."

"I like it, even though I was shot here once," Bronstein commented.

"Unfortunate."

The director shrugged. "The man who pulled the trigger has departed," he said, using a familiar Mossad euphemism. "So, you finally caught Murad Zam?"

"He was unfinished business."

Bronstein made eye contact. "You did well. The Mossad never forgets."

"I didn't even know he was in England until they killed my asset."

"No, but you improvised and fought back. That is what counts." He paused for a few seconds. "So much for administrative leave, eh?"

I chuckled. "I'd rather be operational. Dealing with the Iranians reminded me of that."

"The situation was temporary. Tel Aviv always wanted you back. Your flight is booked."

"The psychologist cleared me?"

Bronstein smiled. "There was never any doubt. We just needed things to quieten down after the incident in Paris. That's why you were brought to England. And it was fortuitous that you ended up with some time on your hands. You were the right person to handle Farzad Bouzidi after he contacted the embassy."

"He died."

"People do."

I didn't answer that. I reached inside my blazer pocket, pulled out the hard disk that I'd found in Harry Beech's shop, and proffered it to Bronstein. "Here it is."

The Mossad chief didn't touch it but signalled for one of his minders to take it from me. The man concealed the device in his suit before stepping away.

"The information should prove useful," Bronstein commented.

"If it's as good as Farzad promised."

"We'll pass it on to Unit 8200," Bronstein said, referring to the technical branch of the Israeli Intelligence Corps. "After our own people have looked at it, of course." He smiled again. "I hear the conference was actually a success, despite the interruption."

"According to Sarah Oren," I replied with a nod. "The diplomats were motivated to get back in the room and agree new sanctions against Iran."

Bronstein shrugged, his face impassive. "The politicians can do whatever they want – our own representatives included. Nothing that comes out of those meetings affects the Mossad."

"Because we always take the fight to the enemy."

He nodded. "Enjoy your flight to Tel Aviv."

I shook his hand again. "Goodbye, Director Bronstein."

The warm smile returned to the Mossad chief's face as he gripped my hand. "Shalom."

I turned away and retraced my steps along the flagstones.

AUTHOR'S NOTE

THANK YOU so much for reading THE FILE. Please write a review if you enjoyed the book. I've wanted to craft a manhunt thriller ever since I started writing novels, so I'm delighted to have completed one at last. If this story entertained you, I reckon you might enjoy my earlier work, so visit my website to find out more.

STATION HELIX SERIES

Station Helix
The Elzevir Collective
Torus
Short Fuse

RYAN KERREK SERIES

Sinister Betrayal
Deadly Acquisition
Black Scarab
Hunting Caracal

FOR MORE ONLINE

Website: www.ashgreenslade.net
Twitter: @AshThrillers

Printed in Great Britain
by Amazon